D0210185

ADELE ASHWORTH

Duke of Sin

An Avon Romantic Treasure

AVON BOOKS
An Imprint of HarperCollinsPublishers

This is a work of fiction. Names, characters, places, and incidents are products of the author's imagination or are used fictitiously and are not to be construed as real. Any resemblance to actual events, locales, organizations, or persons, living or dead, is entirely coincidental.

AVON BOOKS
An Imprint of HarperCollins*Publishers*
10 East 53rd Street
New York, New York 10022-5299

Copyright © 2004 by Adele Budnick
ISBN: 0-06-052840-0
www.avonromance.com

First Avon Books paperback printing: November 2004

Avon Trademark Reg. U.S. Pat. Off. and in Other Countries, Marca Registrada, Hecho en U.S.A.
HarperCollins® is a registered trademark of HarperCollins Publishers Inc.

Printed in the U.S.A.

10 9 8 7 6 5 4 3

He is called the
"DUKE OF SIN . . ."

———⟨⟨9♥9⟩⟩———

. . . a notorious rogue and recluse whose reputation is as black as the Cornish night. They speak of his conquests, his past, and his mysteries in breathless whispers. And now lovely and desperate Vivian Rael-Lamont has no choice but to enter William Raleigh's lair.

Vivian prayed that the scandal that drove her from London would never be revealed—but now she will be exposed to the world . . . unless William can protect her. She has heard the rumors about the infamous Duke of Sin, yet she is unprepared for the man's raw, sensuous power . . . or for the traitorous response of her own body. Surrender, however, could prove most dangerous indeed—for both of them. For while the duke is intrigued by the guarded, intoxicating lady who has invaded his solitude—and fully intends to discern her every secret through sweet, unhurried seduction—it is his own heart that will be imperiled when passion takes them further than he ever intended.

For my darling Edmund

Acknowledgments

I'd like to thank many good friends, for without their encouragement and support I fear I never would have finished this book.

In St. Louis: Jill Abinante, Julie Beard, Carol Carson, Eileen Dryer, Elizabeth Grayson, and Shirl Henke.

In Flower Mound: Cara Arnould, Angela and Lucien Carignan, Brianna Gherardi, Ed Gherardi, Sharon and Kevin Goldman, Tori Major, and Ward Smith.

And my greatest writer friends: Anna Adams, Michele Albert, Elizabeth Boyle, Wendy Etherington, Susan Grant, Leann Harris, Lisa Kleypas, Julia Quinn, Theresa Ragan, Kathryn Smith, and especially the marvelous Avon Ladies.

Much love and thanks to you all.

Chapter 1

Southern Cornwall
July 1856

Vivian stared at the handwritten note: *His grace desires . . .*

Smiling wryly, she decided she rather wished he did. But then she'd only seen him from a distance and entertaining such a thought was *beyond* scandalous.

She folded the note without further ridiculous considerations and shoved it into the large pocket of her work smock. The orchids—her prize among the flowers she maintained—would be ready for him day after tomorrow, as his butler requested. This would be work for hire, or rather expertise for hire, nothing more than it was each year at this time.

1

Again, she would fill the standard and formal order for fresh flowers from the reclusive Duke of Trent, displayed to beautify the rooms of his coastal estate that stretched for miles on the western slope overlooking the Lizard Peninsula. And again this year, she would do her best to get a peek of the enigmatic man who'd managed to escape the noose for the murder of his wife.

"Mrs. Rael-Lamont?"

Vivian started at the interruption and turned swiftly toward the doorway between her house and garden, where her housekeeper stood with a totally unreadable look on her aging, sun-weathered face, seemingly not at all concerned that her mistress had been daydreaming instead of potting.

"Yes, Harriet, what is it?" she replied forthrightly.

The older woman hesitated, wiping her hands on her apron. "There's a ... *person* here to see you. A man. The ... um ... stage actor from the Shakespearean Company that's been playing at Cosgroves for the summer."

Vivian caught herself from gaping. "An *actor* is here?"

Harriet lowered her voice. "Gilbert Montague, he said his name is. He didn't have a card, and of course I didn't admit him, but he's choosing to wait just the same. Said his business with you is urgent."

Mildly intrigued, Vivian moved toward her housekeeper, stepping into the shade created by vines that wove through the trellis-covered porch, and reached for a hand towel on the garden bench. "Did he say what he wanted?" She couldn't begin to imagine

2

what business an actor might have with her, personally or professionally.

Harriet stepped out onto the cobblestone, her plump figure erect and her expression firmly set in a line of disapproval. "He didn't offer a reason for his visit, no," she replied succinctly. "He only said he wanted a few minutes of your time, and would you oblige him. I told him I'd see if you were at home."

Vivian smiled inwardly. She was obviously at home, but adhering to social protocol, Harriet had to check. And of course one would never allow someone so common into one's private residence.

She smoothed her hair away from her face; the midday heat never failed to add an annoying bounce to loose curls that framed her cheeks and forehead, preventing her from keeping it tidy. She no doubt looked a fright, spending the last two hours working with soil in the sun and humid air, but then it hardly mattered, she decided. Mr. Montague, being a person of the stage, had certainly seen far worse in his line of work or on the street.

"Very well, I'll receive him," she informed her housekeeper, reaching behind her to untie her dirt-stained work smock. As Harriet's eyes opened a fraction in surprise, she added, "But don't bring him through the house; inform him that he'll find me 'round back and through the gate."

Harriet nodded once, her disapproving expression giving way to one of solid relief at such wisdom. "Yes, ma'am. I'll send him on momentarily."

Once again standing alone in the afternoon shade in her secluded patio, Vivian tossed her smock on the bench and shook out her brown muslin skirt. As one of her three work gowns, she'd chosen this one in particular this hot morning because of its looseness through the bustline and waist, but it didn't do a thing to flatter her figure. As much as she adored the theater, she'd never in her life greeted an actor—or anyone of so lowly a station—in her home, so how she looked to this one probably didn't matter in the slightest.

Stepping back into the sunlight, she poured herself half a glass of lukewarm water from a pitcher on the nearby potting table. As she drank thirstily, she heard the creak of the thick wooden gate as it gave way to intrusion on the westernmost side of the house.

Quickly, she patted her mouth with the bottom of her smock and turned to face the approaching sound of heavy footsteps on the cobblestone walkway. Standing with as much formal bearing as the circumstances allowed, her hands clasped behind her back, she faced the small, tufted palm tree that jutted out from the corner of the property until she saw his legs appear, then his body in full form.

Vivian backed up a step as the man approached her. She'd expected him to be large, as she'd twice seen him perform rather magnificently on stage. Still, she wasn't prepared for the wide-shouldered, long-limbed person of supercilious elegance now standing directly in front of her, between two rare species of prized orchids, blocking the sun with his head as he gazed down at her face.

His appearance, however surprisingly fashionable, couldn't hide the coarseness of his stoic features as he focused on her quite intently, perhaps expecting her to glance away with uncertainty or discomfiture. She couldn't, however, allow herself to cower. Instant uneasiness deep inside quickly alerted her, sharpening her senses, warning her to keep her mind focused and her stance one of indifference, even arrogance. She refused to be intimidated by his sheer size. Surprisingly, though, she wasn't afraid.

"Mrs. Rael-Lamont," he acknowledged with a slight nod, his tone a deep drawl, his diction perfect.

She tipped her head toward him once in reply. "Mr. Montague, I presume. What may I help you with today?"

He almost smiled as he studied her, though he didn't move any closer.

"Lovely garden you've grown here, madam."

He hadn't really looked at the flowers at all, she noted, but she didn't argue that point. He seemed to be highly interested in her—or perhaps just her reaction to him. "It is lovely," she replied good-naturedly, "though in fact this is not a garden but a nursery."

A half corner of his mouth twitched up. "I stand corrected."

Vivian didn't know whether he wanted her to like him or not, although he did seem pleasant enough.

"What can I do for you, Mr. Montague?" she asked once more, directly. The midday heat was beginning to make her head pound.

After seconds of eyeing her levelly, he took two

5

steps closer. "I've noticed you once or twice at the theater." He scratched his dark and rugged side whiskers very slowly with long fingers, as if considering a very serious question. "I think you attended last Saturday's production of *Twelfth Night*."

That surprised her greatly. She'd seen the production, and perhaps one or two others earlier in the summer, but she certainly hadn't been obtrusive as part of the large, local audience. A very strange circumstance, and Vivian tried hard not to show how uncomfortable she suddenly felt. "I did, indeed," she returned without elucidation. Crossing her arms in front of her defensively, she pressed, "But that's hardly why you're here. What may I help you with today, Mr. Montague? I'm very busy."

"Ah. But help *is* the word, is it not, Mrs. Rael-Lamont?"

Her brows shot up. "*Help*, Mr. Montague?"

He stepped closer, looking down to his side and fingering the leaf of a bright pink orchid. She reigned in her annoyance at that. Her abruptness clearly hadn't intimidated him.

Slowly, he asked, "What has become of Mr. Rael-Lamont?"

For a slim moment of unreality, flashes of another life, a whirlwind of indescribable emotions she'd fought hard to suppress rushed to the surface, shooting through her veins to scorch her memory like wildfire. Vivian felt her throat constrict, the blood rush to her face as her entire body began to burn hot beyond what was normal for the midday, southern coastal sun.

6

"I beg your pardon?" she whispered after a period, her voice suddenly husky and raw.

Smiling, he placed one large hand on his shirtfront, over his heart. "I see I've startled you."

The trepidation within overpowered her good manners. "Please leave, Mr. Montague," she ordered, lowering her arms to her sides, her mouth set grimly.

He nodded politely in her direction, his wide, odious mouth upturned in a widening grin of satisfaction. "Of course, dear lady."

He made no move to depart.

"However," he added, "before I take my leave, there is a . . . situation I believe we should discuss."

Standing in her backyard nursery, Vivian still, oddly enough, didn't feel afraid of the man. Not physically, anyway. Harriet remained inside and would alert the neighbors should she cry out. But the actor clearly knew that. No, his reason for calling on her took on a far more sinister meaning. She believed that instinctively.

Bracing herself for the shock she knew would follow, she asked, "What do you want, Mr. Montague? Get to your point."

"Indeed."

He fingered the orchid petals openly, infuriating her intentionally.

"I wonder," he continued thoughtfully, "how you'd respond to the knowledge that I have proof you're not who you say you are."

Her anger at his purposeful assault on her expensive, fragile flower evaporated. She blinked quickly

7

twice, fighting the urge to take a step away from him. "I would say you are mistaken," she returned defensively.

He tipped his head to the side and glanced shrewdly at her face again. "Am I?"

The standoff between them after that broad, vague question left her clammy and chilled in spite of the midday heat. And the fact that he hinted at her deepest secret, made her nearly bubble over with fear.

He apparently expected her silence. With a sudden ruthlessness coloring his deep voice, he added in a whisper, "Perhaps you'll be interested to know I'm fully aware that you're not a widow." He paused. "Are you, Mrs. Rael-Lamont?"

Her mouth went dry; she began to shake from an inner, overwhelming cold. She refused to let him see her consternation.

In a calm, icy voice, she replied, "Get off my property or I shall have you arrested for trespassing."

"Of course," was his quick response. And yet instead of turning and leaving as ordered, he stepped closer to her, his shoes making crunching sounds on the patio stone.

"I think perhaps you should hear me out first," he added, his full lips curled up in a tight smirk, his eyes roving over her figure from bosom to hips.

Vivian cringed from the look he gave her, one of menace coupled with blatant lust. Outwardly, she stood stiffly straight, a warning fear of being exposed preventing her from screaming for help. Her greatest concern was knowing the man in front of her understood this and used her anxiety against her.

"This is the problem as I see it, Mrs. Rael-Lamont." Suddenly he picked the orchid by the stem and lifted it to his nose.

That enraged her. "How dare you—"

"I know about your husband," he whispered, his tone dripping with malice he no longer contained. "I know many of the truths of your so-called marriage, where your *living* husband is now, and of course why you're hiding in Cornwall."

Hiding.

He chuckled, then crushed the orchid in his palm, dropping it to the ground where he stepped on it. "For a price," he added pleasantly, "I'll keep your secret."

Seconds—or perhaps minutes—ticked by in slow motion, in a nightmare of unqualified depth.

Vivian couldn't breathe, couldn't move or respond.

He stepped so close to her now she was sure she could smell him: a smell of utter foulness that seeped from the core of him to raid her senses, revolting her.

"What do you want?" she whispered hoarsely at last, lips trembling.

"Ah. We get to the reason of my visit. I need your kind help."

He was mad, a figure of pure insanity. And no one believed a madman, she tried to reassure herself.

"Call it a bit of blackmail," he clarified congenially.

"You're insane," she spat in return.

He laughed again, this time genuinely as he tossed his head back. "Hardly that, madam. I assure you I am very sane, and prepared. I'm simply in need of monetary substance. Acting doesn't pay all that well."

She glared at him, her eyes focusing on his finely tailored morning suit of dove gray, his silk shirt and expertly trimmed hair. For an actor of limited means, he didn't want for luxury. That thought worried her as much as anything else. He'd likely done this before to some other unsuspecting soul and had succeeded.

For the first time since he'd arrived in her garden alcove, Vivian felt not only fear and loathing, but betrayal and a terrible sadness settle deep inside her. But it didn't matter. Her good senses returning, she refused to be a victim. He certainly couldn't know *everything*.

Standing straighter, she offered him a purely false smile.

"I'm sorry, Mr. Montague. I refuse to help you in whatever scheme you've concocted. In point of fact, I find it difficult to believe you're actually here, on *my* property, suggesting I would be so insecure and afraid as to bow down to your disgusting requests." Her upper lip twitched as she lowered her voice to add, "Leave now or I shall scream and you will surely find yourself acting within the walls of prison."

Undaunted, he nodded once. "As you wish, madam. However, before I do so, I think you should see this."

Vivian watched as he reached into his breast pocket and pulled out a folded sheet of paper. Opening it, he read from the top line.

"Dear Mr. Hathaway, I have read the provisions in the separation agreement, and I shall adhere to them immediately . . ."

Vivian grabbed a post at her side as her body began to shake.

"... *My husband has agreed to the terms and has made his plans to retire to France posthaste*—"

"Stop it. *Stop!*"

He ignored her.

"*My gravest concern is, naturally, that this legal matter remain our secret. I will be moving to Cornwall in the coming months, there to live quietly on the settlement funds provided at my marriage. I know that as my solicitor you'll keep this matter confidential. My family cannot be harmed socially by the knowledge of my*—"

Vivian reached out and snatched the note from his fingers, crumpling it in her trembling hands.

He crossed his arms over his chest. "Of course that's just a copy. The original is in very safekeeping."

In safekeeping. As she'd always thought of the legal documents.

She swallowed, staring at his stomach. "How ... How did you get this?" She jerked her head up, her eyes piercing his with loathing. "How much did this cost you, Mr. Montague?"

His lids narrowed. "Not nearly what it will cost you should you not comply with my wishes."

Comply with his *wishes*? She positively could not speak to that. Never had she been more appalled.

The man must have sensed her hesitation, the heat of her disgust. With one final glance down her person, he turned away from her and began a casual stroll between the flowering plants, toward the side gate where he'd made his entrance, his large hands

11

clasped behind his back. From this angle, Vivian thought he looked deceptively like a gentleman.

He's an actor.

"To be able to keep this . . . standard of living, shall we say, you will acquire something for me," he informed her, his voice now brusque and to the point.

Her mouth opened slightly in disbelief, not only at his demand of conspiracy, but at the idea that should she fail, her life as she knew it would end.

"It is a pristine, original sonnet, written and signed by the great one himself."

That left her thoroughly confused.

"This manuscript," he continued, his back to her as he eyed fine yellow roses to his left, "is in the possession of the Duke of Trent."

Vivian sucked in a sharp breath, which he undoubtedly heard, even from where he stood.

"I'm sure a woman of your age and experience won't have trouble calling on the secluded man for something." He glanced back to her. "He'll have it locked away, so you cannot steal it. You must use . . . other means to actually get him to let you see it, acquire it."

"I won't do it," she managed to breathe, her tone chilled and raspy.

He turned to face her fully again, his hands still clasped behind his back. "Of course you will, madam. It shouldn't take you long. Send a note to me at the theater when you've finished your task and I'll quickly be in touch."

Again, he moved toward the gated entrance, then

stopped abruptly, caressing his tapered beard. Over his shoulder, he said matter-of-factly, "I should take care of the matter soon, as well. I'll only be in Penzance for another fortnight after which I will be traveling to London. I wouldn't want there to be any confusion regarding what society at large might or might not know of your separation decree. And I shouldn't have to tell you not to mention my name, my involvement, or this meeting between us."

Vivian could see the side of his mouth lift into a twisted smile.

"Good afternoon, Mrs. Rael-Lamont."

With that, he took his leave, closing the gate behind him most meticulously.

Vivian stared at the spot where he last stood, forever, it seemed, realizing that since he had walked into her presence she hadn't moved her feet.

Slowly her eyes dropped to the wilted, crushed orchid on the cobblestone path, and a burst of absurd laughter threatened to escape her suddenly. How very odd that with such drama, such *flair*, in a matter of ten little minutes, her secure world and future, which she'd so perfectly constructed for herself, had been stolen.

Chapter 2

~~~⟡~~~

His full name was William Raleigh, Duke of Trent, Earl of Shreveport and Kayes, Baron Chesterfield, and husband of Elizabeth, the wife he'd been rumored to have murdered. Of course Vivian didn't exactly believe that . . . exactly.

Standing now at his front gate not far from the cliff's edge near Mouschole, she paused to take in the elegance of his stately home, simply called Morning House, as noted on the engraved plaque at the entrance. The look of the rectangular, light brown brick building, with its dark gray shutters and fifteen-foot-high, massive black front doors suggested more of a home in *mourning* than an example of the beautiful countryside around it. But then that

14

was a play of words that likely didn't occur to the duke himself.

Vivian had come here several times by coach to deliver floral arrangements but had chosen to walk the distance from the village to the duke's house on this day since she carried nothing but a reticule to match her pale plum-colored day gown. It had been raining at dawn, and though still cloudy this early afternoon, a fine mist lingered in the air, and the cool breeze off the ocean made the skin on her face and neck tingle. It was a feeling she adored.

It was rumored that although the duke spent as many as eleven months of the year here, he owned very little of the land, presumably only the immediate area surrounding the home itself. The view was certainly incredible, though. From where she stood now, Vivian could see not only the house and grasslands, but the sea beyond—cold, gray and ominous today, as it dropped to the horizon behind the building proper.

Drawing a full, deep breath, Vivian pushed the heavy gate open to enter the small, beautifully landscaped yard and centered her thoughts on the business ahead. And it would be business, she'd decided before she'd stepped foot from her cottage this morning. She would offer the duke a business proposition. She was, after all, a businesswoman.

Vivian didn't see any footmen upon her stroll up the walkway. She climbed the stone steps with a swift lift of her skirts, and after straightening her bonnet and smoothing her stays, she rapped twice with the heavy brass knocker.

A level of anxiety coursed through her as she waited a good three or four minutes for an answer. One would think a duke of immense means could afford efficient help. But then the Duke of Trent was known for being as mysterious as he was wealthy, in every measure.

At last she heard the bolt slide back from the other side of the door, and after a few seconds of patient waiting, it slowly opened to reveal an older gray-haired man she assumed to be the butler given his impeccable dress and flat, formal demeanor.

"Good afternoon, Mrs. Rael-Lamont," he said with a curt nod.

Vivian's mouth dropped open a fraction at his presumptuousness. Of course he knew who she was because she'd brought flowers to the servants' entrance before, but this day it seemed as if he expected her as a guest. She hadn't even had a chance to hand him her card.

"I would request a moment with his grace," she said, recovering herself. "If he is at home."

The butler nodded once. "Do come in, madam."

He pulled the door open fully and moved to the right to allow her entrance. She stepped into the foyer, withholding a gasp of surprise. Far from the look outside, the inside stood out brightly, cheerful and inviting, revealing white marble floors, a fringed chair or two in white satin, a large crystal chandelier hanging from a rounded, pale ceiling, all pointing attention toward the gold-leafed table at the center, on top of which sat an enormous crystal vase filled to overflowing with daisies, pink roses, and wild buttercups. For a second—only a second—Vivian felt offended that the duke obviously purchased flowers elsewhere from time to time.

"This way, if you please," the butler coaxed, gesturing to his left. "His grace will receive you in his library."

Vivian held her tongue from asking where these particular flowers had come from, when it suddenly occurred to her that rarely anyone but the duke and his staff ever saw them. True, even a socially shunned duke occasionally would need to entertain business associates, but Vivian had serious doubts that much business would be conducted in so remote a place as south Cornwall. How unfortunate to own such a grand and beautiful home, adorned so tastefully, with the knowledge that no one could appreciate it but oneself.

She followed the butler down a long hallway, her shoes making a rather noisy clacking sound on the hard marble floor, her eyes drifting to the long bay windows on her left, thick cream-colored curtains pulled back with gold tassels allowing an unhindered view of the cresting ocean beyond.

Seconds later they stopped at the double doors that led to the library. The butler opened them without knocking then stepped aside for her to enter. Of course at first glance it looked just as a library should, although the Duke of Trent appeared to have exquisite taste of the most expensive kind.

The room was quite large, taking up perhaps a third of the entire southeast wing, smelling faintly of tobacco and leather. Both the walls and high ceiling

17

were papered with dark brown and navy stripes in a style that matched fringed floral lamps and the brown leather furniture that surrounded an ornately carved tea table sitting directly on an oblong, inlaid Oriental carpet at the center of the dark wooden floor. A small conservatory of sorts extending out from the far wall displayed a variety of greenery before huge arched windows that no doubt featured a spectacular view of the sandy beach coastline and ocean beyond.

The glass-enclosed bookcases were only six feet in height or so, lined across the westernmost wall to her right, and stuffed top to bottom with reading material. Above them hung portraits and painted landscapes in gilded frames. An enormous, dark oak secretary stood against the northern wall, likely where the duke worked when handling estate matters, as it neatly seated two, side by side, in black leather rockers. On the easternmost wall, and displayed as the focal point of the room, was the overlarge fireplace, trimmed in brown marble and ornately carved wood, now cold and swept perfectly clean of ashes.

Despite the fact that the library had been decorated in a purely masculine flavor, as befit a library, this one was simply gorgeous.

"Please make yourself comfortable, madam," the butler chimed in at her side. "His grace will be here shortly. My name is Wilson, and Bitsy will serve you while you wait."

She turned her attention to him once more. "Thank you, Wilson."

Giving her a slight bow, he took his leave, closing the doors behind him. Only seconds later, as Vivian began to remove her gloves, in walked a parlor maid carrying a large silver tray. Pretty and tidy and all of about sixteen, she curtsied once, then strode toward the center tea table.

"Would you care for coffee or tea, Mrs. Rael-Lamont?" the girl asked in a soft, flat tone.

"Tea would be fine," she replied with a formal smile, though inwardly intrigued by the manner in which she'd been treated in this home thus far—not as a woman from the village who sells flowers for a living, but as an honored guest, whom everybody seemed to know by name. Very odd, indeed.

While the parlor maid poured tea into a white china cup from a silver pot, Vivian sat unobtrusively in a leather chair across from the large, high-backed sofa of the same quality material. As soon as she'd arranged her skirts, the girl placed her full cup and saucer on a short round table to her right.

"Is there anything else, ma'am?"

The fragrant, steaming tea smelled heavenly. "No, this is quite . . . lovely."

The maid curtsied once more, then quickly took her leave, closing the large doors behind her, her footsteps echoing down the hallway as she departed in relative haste.

Vivian swiftly untied her bonnet and removed it, smoothing the hair at her forehead back into place. She'd plaited the length of it, winding the braid and pinning it at her nape, but loose strands had detached themselves as they always did. Funny how she rather cared about her appearance this morning, wanting to make an impression on the Duke of Trent. How she managed to be here now, alone in this exquisite room, served immediately her choice of fine tea *or* coffee, left her suddenly amused and squelching a laugh of pure absurdity. For just a second, she had to wonder if perhaps the duke had inherited his obviously substantial income from the death of his wife. Such wealth represented in this room alone could be motive for murder, she supposed.

Vivian lifted her cup with surprisingly calm hands and sampled the tea, a wonderfully strong Lapsang Souchong. Somewhat unconventional for standard fare, especially when serving to a guest of the lower class. But it certainly brought back memories.

For nearly ten minutes she heard nothing aside from waves crashing against the shoreline through the open conservatory windows. It irked her a bit that he'd kept her waiting for so long, but then she wasn't altogether ignorant of the well-bred and their plays of command, if that's what this would prove to be. And of course the time alone allowed her to grow more nervous with each passing minute, though he couldn't possibly know that.

The sudden click of the latch on the double wooden doors made her start. She immediately turned her face to the entrance of the library, then shifted her bottom on the chair uncomfortably when she found him looking at her, his dark, probing eyes piercing hers with cold intensity.

Vivian nearly dropped her tea. If she'd thought Gilbert Montague seemed tall and intimidating, it did nothing to prepare her for the magnificently . . . sturdy physique of the noble Duke of Trent. Flustered, she placed her cup and saucer back on the small table and slowly rose to face the man for the first time.

He stood just inside the doorway with an air of grand, even forceful, sophistication. Though dressed somewhat unobtrusively for an individual of his prestige, he nevertheless wore an expensive silk morning suit of deep brown, tailored to fit his large form to perfection as it detailed the strength he exuded from his broad shoulders to his long, muscular legs. His cream-colored shirt, certainly made of silk as well, pressed against his chest, subtly revealing brawn he didn't attempt to hide. He wore no waistcoat, and his necktie, light brown and knotted loosely, only worked to focus more attention on his marvelous facial features—his clear, dark complexion, strong jaw, wide mouth, straight, sharply defined nose, and even his forehead, where attractive lines of middle age were only beginning to appear.

But it was his rich, hazel eyes that arrested her, increasing her nervousness by the second. Serious of expression as he was now, he pierced her with a gaze that left her feeling quite enveloped by his power. What kind of power that was, she couldn't be sure, though she was somehow instinctively aware that he knew exactly what she was thinking. It made her waver on her feet. One thing was certain: Being this close to him for the first time, Vivian was quite sure she'd never been made so speechless by the mere appearance of a man.

Moments passed in silence as they more or less just stared at each other. Her mouth went dry and she licked her lips.

Slowly, he began to walk toward her. "Mrs. Rael-Lamont," he drawled with the slightest tip of his forehead, his deep voice both smooth and coaxing. "A pleasure."

"Your grace," she replied with a gentle curtsy, sounding—thank God—less anxious than she felt.

"Please, sit down," he fairly ordered, moving closer to her.

She paused, unsure whether to remain standing and extend her hand due to the serious tone of the meeting about to take place, or sit and chat as if they were good friends. Awkwardness made her mumble simply, "As you wish."

His dark brows lifted minutely. "Indeed."

Vivian felt her cheeks grow hot as he continued to assess her. With graceful distinction, she seated herself once more in her chair, arranging her skirts while trying to avoid watching him as best she could, relieved now that she hadn't applied rouge to her skin before leaving her home this morning. She certainly didn't need any.

At last he stopped, his impressive form only two feet or so from her, hands behind his back, candidly eyeing her, or at least she felt his gaze on her face. She could smell his subtle cologne—woodsy, with a touch of spice—

"It's lovely to finally meet you, madam."

She jerked her head up, to find no flattery in his expression, not even a trace of humor. It wasn't as if he seemed at all suspicious, but she knew he had to be. Nobody ever came to call on the duke who'd killed his wife. Or so it had been rumored.

"Please join me, your grace."

That inappropriate insistence surprised him as thoroughly as it did her after the words were out of her mouth. He pulled back, and for just a small, significant second, Vivian noticed a flash of amusement cross his features. She wanted to shrink into the fine leather chair.

"As you wish," he answered very slowly, his voice lowered.

Vivian knew he'd purposely repeated what she'd said to him only moments ago. She just wished she knew if he were teasing, or mocking her in his arrogance.

"Indeed," she returned, lifting her chin—and brows—a fraction, knowing he could toss her out of his house for such audacity. Instinctively, though, she knew, just *knew*, he wouldn't.

He stared down at her, assessing, making her hot all over from his probing stare. Then moments later one side of his mouth began to curl up. Suddenly their word play seemed rather like a game, and much of her nervousness vanished. Odd that it didn't at all feel to her like they'd only just met.

He broke the connection first, turning and striding around the tea table to sit comfortably on his leather sofa. Studying him, Vivian couldn't help but be in awe at his presence. Strange, that she'd never felt so unusual around a man before, even her husband.

"What can I do for you today, Mrs. Rael-Lamont?" he began formally as he returned to the point of her visit, helping himself to steaming coffee.

She forced herself to breathe deeply. Gazing directly into alert, hazel eyes, she replied, "How is it that your household knew of me the moment I arrived, your grace? I didn't even need to leave a card."

If her turn of phrase surprised him again, he didn't let it show, though his forehead did crease in frown while he poured cream into his cup.

She waited.

Finally, sliding his spoon across the rim and laying it on the saucer, he admitted, "My staff are aware of you, madam." He looked into her eyes once more. "And so am I, naturally."

That answer, however vague, gave her an instant, almost wicked sense of elation.

She smiled triumphantly. "Naturally."

He took a sip of his coffee.

"You do frequently buy flowers from my nursery, after all."

"Yes."

When he added nothing to that, she lifted her cup of tea and held it in front of her. "The arrangement in your foyer is lovely, although not mine."

She thought for a second that his lips pinched in amusement once more.

"Professional rivalry, Mrs. Rael-Lamont?"

She straightened and lifted her cup to her lips. "Not at all." She sipped, then placed it back on the saucer gingerly. "Only an observation."

He nodded once. "I see."

He probably did, since her cheeks were undoubtedly pink again. She ignored that. "May I ask from whom you purchased the arrangement?"

"I've no idea," he replied, taking another drink of his own morning brew. "Wilson, or my housekeeper Glenda, purchases them. I'm not privy to their choices for the temporary decoration of my home."

Of course he wasn't. She felt ridiculous in asking.

"But from this day forward, I shall order my employees to buy only those you grow and supply, Mrs. Rael-Lamont," he added quite casually.

She blinked, astonished. "Oh, no, your grace, I didn't mean—"

"I know you didn't," he cut in. For a second or two, a droll smile crossed his mouth. "That's irrelevant, really. When it comes to personal items, I buy what I like."

She laughed lightly, enjoying his mood. "Flowers as personal items, your grace?"

"They can be, don't you think?"

"Like shoes or pocket watches?"

"I suppose so," he maintained.

She shrugged. "And yet a moment ago you didn't care about household decorations," she said mildly, challenging him. "And household decorations can hardly be compared to the fit of a shoe or the expense of a pocket watch."

"True enough." His grin widened a fraction and he lowered his voice minutely. "But you have changed my mind for me, madam. I imagine a flower arrangement is a display of creativity, or can be, and is therefore a reflection of the artist, the one who grows the flowers and then displays them." He cocked his head a bit and assessed her, face and figure. "As in all artistic displays, from painting to sculpture, I buy what I like."

I buy what I like. He'd said that twice, specifically, and Vivian didn't know exactly how to interpret his point, if indeed he had one. Deep inside, though, she felt a stirring of something warm and intimate, as if he'd touched a part of her she seldom revealed to anyone. An odd feeling, to be sure. Yet on the surface she was thrilled that he seemed to single her out among many, first with his knowledge of who she was, and then with his spontaneous decision to buy only from her. But it was his low, silky-deep voice that threatened to melt her into submitting to his every wish.

Silence reigned for a moment, awkward in one manner, remarkably friendly in another, as they both took refreshment. At last, after finishing his coffee, he placed his cup and saucer on the tea table and relaxed against soft leather to regard her speculatively.

"I don't suppose you came calling on me today to discuss the floral arrangements in my home, did you Mrs. Rael-Lamont?"

A rather polite way of asking her to state exactly what she wanted with him, she supposed, though his return to the reason for her visit unsettled her momentarily after the lightness of the time they'd only just shared.

"No, actually." She cleared her throat and placed her teacup and saucer back on the small table at her side. Smoothing her skirts then folding her hands in her lap, she faced him directly, giving him a polite—and hopefully charming—smile. "It's interesting that we should be discussing art endeavors, your grace, as I've come with a personal proposition for you. From one collector to another."

"I see," he acknowledged. "You're an art collector, then."

She couldn't read his suddenly insipid expression.

"I hope that my unexpected calling is not at an inconvenient time," she said quite properly.

He frowned then, his eyes narrowing. "I'm not inconvenienced," he said stiffly, his tone subdued. "I don't receive many visitors, so having you here is a refreshing change."

It had bothered him that she'd returned to strict formality. She knew that instinctively. Perhaps it was only the words he'd used, perhaps the distant sound of the ocean beyond, but Vivian felt a tinge of the loneliness he likely experienced every day at being an accused murderer and forced to live outside the grace of polite society. She certainly understood that well enough. Then again, she really knew nothing about this uniquely handsome man sitting across from her. It was just as likely he enjoyed a self-imposed solitude.

But it would do her no good to speculate on his troubles. She pushed her thoughts away to concentrate on the reason for her visit, as ugly as it was.

"Your grace," she began, trying not to squeeze her hands together too tightly, "I've been given some news lately which I feel obligated to explore to its fullest."

His dark brows shot up a fraction. "News?"

She carried on; the faster she reached the object of her quest, the less time she had for panic to settle in and expose her.

"It's come to my attention, sir, that you are in possession of a rare Shakespearean document—a sonnet, I believe. I would be most interested in acquiring it."

For the longest minute he didn't move or respond in any way, only watched her with a fierce concentration. Then his lips twitched, just once. She tried to ignore what immediately felt like a negative reaction and continued before he dismissed her outright.

"I know this is rather . . . sudden, but I would like to suggest that perhaps we can come to some sort of satisfactory agreement for which you might be willing to sell me such a valuable piece of history." She hesitated, looking quickly to her hands then back to his face again. "I'm very interested in the work and believe I can manage the expense, whatever that might be."

She knew at once how ludicrous that must sound coming from a woman who worked more or less for her own self-maintenance, and directed to a duke of unquestionable wealth. But he didn't mention that. Instead, he remained quiet and still, studying her so intently now she grew cold beneath her stays and petticoats, even with the warm, moist summer air drifting through the room from the open windows beyond. Vivian wasn't sure how to continue until she received some verbal response from him.

She waited. So did he, apparently. Moments later, she murmured, "Your grace?"

"Would you tell me how you became aware of such a treasure, Mrs. Rael-Lamont?"

His tone had cooled, and she realized he suspected less than honest reasons for her request. She attempted a smile to convey confidence.

"Actually, I came across the news quite by accident."

"By accident. Really . . ." he replied, now leaning on his right elbow, finally shifting his large frame so that he could relax into the sofa. But he never took his probing gaze from hers.

"Yes, indeed," she continued, attempting to sound pleasant and congenial despite the solidifying dread at the center of her stomach. "But of course, as a buyer of fine art from time to time, I wouldn't want to reveal where I get my good information." She raised her brows in an air of sly, almost teasing defiance. "I'm sure you understand."

"Certainly, I do," he said, tipping his head to her once. "But a manuscript isn't exactly art, is it?"

Vivian drew a deep breath and exhaled quickly. "Not exactly, no. But it can be a collectable piece of history." She leaned toward him and added, "I'm also an admirer of the theater. A piece like this one would satisfy my desires on more than one level. I would take very good care of it, your grace, of that you can be most assured."

For several long, tense moments, she candidly held his gaze, noting that sunshine from the windows cast a light upon his irises that made them appear deeper in hue, almost forest green. So striking, and if it were any other time she might think—

"How old are you, Mrs. Rael-Lamont?" he asked very quietly, gently rubbing his chin with his fingertips.

Her mouth dropped open a fraction as her shoulders shot back. "I—I beg your pardon?"

He leaned all the way forward with that, resting his elbows on his knees, clasping his hands in front of him. "How old are you?" he asked again without pretense.

"I'm middle-aged, as I suspect you are."

"Ah." He grinned. "Not a proper question to ask a lady, am I right?"

She fidgeted, crossing and then recrossing her ankles beneath her skirts. "You know that, sir," she said in reply, trying to sound a bit more playful in her response, hoping he didn't see through the sham. Her cheeks were hot again as she grew ever more uncomfortable in this home, in his presence, and God willing, he would consider her rise in color part of her embarrassment, not fear of exposure.

"In your thirties?" he pressed.

Oh, what did it matter? She sighed. "I will be thirty-five years of age in November, your grace," she revealed with only a hint of annoyance.

He continued to stare at her, nodding vaguely as if piecing together a puzzle.

She needed to get back to the point of her visit. "And how old are you, sir?" Vivian closed her eyes briefly as soon as the words were out of her mouth.

30

She absolutely could not believe she asked him that. What the devil was wrong with her?

His head shot back a bit in obvious surprise. "We have so very much in common, Mrs. Rael-Lamont," he drawled. "I've been thirty-five for well nigh two months now."

So much in common? She ignored that. "Your grace—"

"And what of your husband?"

"I—" She blinked, feeling a sharp, stabbing shock. Twice in one week the man she'd married had come up in conversation, and this time it made her shiver to her toes. "My husband?" she murmured thickly.

Much of the humor left the duke's expression as his eyes roved over her face.

"What happened to him, madam," he clarified, his voice calm and controlled.

She squirmed in her chair. "He died."

His brows rose fractionally again. "Yes, I would imagine so if you are a widow."

"I am a widow, your grace." Flustered, Vivian added, "I'm not sure how my personal affairs have anything to do with the reason for my visit, however."

"I'm not sure, either. But I find you fascinating."

Vivian's lips parted with a shallow gasp. Her heartbeat suddenly thudded against her chest as her eyes opened wide. He simply watched her, certainly noting her reaction of shock to such a personal disclosure. Or maybe it wasn't the actual words but the manner in which he expressed them that made her mind and body feel charged with energy. It had been years since a gentleman had been so very forward with her, and she couldn't, for the life of her, recall a proper thing to say.

He sat up again, leaning casually against the sofa back. "Would you like to see it?"

She swallowed. "Your grace?"

The right corner of his mouth lifted wryly. "The manuscript, madam. Would you care to see it?"

She shook herself. "Right here? Now?"

He shrugged minutely. "Of course. I imagine you're curious, and where else would one keep a document of such value but in one's library?"

Her first reaction was to reply a safe. But instead, she attempted a smile again, regaining her composure. "Where else, indeed?"

Immediately he stood, towering over her as he offered his hand to help her rise.

The thought of touching his physical person, even for something as innocuous as this, filled her with a most peculiar dread. She decided to ignore the feeling as she gently placed her palm in his.

His skin felt rough and warm, his hand large and solid, and just as she raised herself to stand beside him, she grew acutely aware of the heat radiating from his body, even though his fingers only faintly brushed hers. She pulled away at once, realizing he felt all too human and real—not at all like a murderer should feel.

The side of his mouth lifted with a hint of a smirk, as if he'd read her thoughts and dared her to comment. Then suddenly, he bowed his head slightly and gestured to his left.

Vivian nearly had to brush up against him. She avoided that as much as possible, even as he seemed to expect it, though she did catch another delicate whiff of his cologne.

Nerves rattled now, Vivian clutched her reticule to her waist and allowed him to lead her as he walked with swift, purposeful strides toward the glass-covered bookshelf at the northwest corner of the library, the farthest from the open windows, she noted, as sea air was undoubtedly bad for the preservation of books, especially valuable and very old copies.

As they approached, Vivian noticed that one side of the bookcase was locked; presumably this particular side of shelves held the priceless work she sought. Not exactly a safe, but adequate protection, she supposed.

The duke reached into his jacket pocket and pulled out a key. He inserted it, turned the lock, and opened the glass door.

The shelf was replete with books, including an old family bible, which the Duke of Trent reached for without hesitation. With careful hands, he pulled the large, black, leather-bound copy from the shelf and balanced it against his outstretched arm.

Apprehension, coupled, oddly enough, with a surge of excitement, overwhelmed her as he opened the hard cover, its fragile, worn pages crinkling as he turned toward the middle. She stepped closer so that her skirts couldn't help but brush his legs. She regretted that, but she wanted to be near enough to get a good look at the piece of history that could ultimately—if fears became realized—bring her social degradation.

"There is no place safer than this, Mrs. Rael-Lamont," the duke maintained, his voice low and grim. "This book in itself is more than one hundred years old."

"Remarkable," she replied, glancing up to his face, now only inches from hers. "A family treasure, is it not?"

His gaze shot briefly to her lips. "Indeed."

A piece of stray, dark hair now hung low across his brow, his eyes narrowed and surprisingly intense as he worked to find the manuscript between fragile pages.

At last he stopped at what appeared to be a piece of sheer cloth. Gently, he unwrapped it until the work she sought lay exposed.

Vivian stared at it. Written in scrawled handwriting, she could barely make out the words of the short sonnet. Time had taken its toll on the fragmented parchment, but the signature was undoubtedly written by the hand of William Shakespeare.

"Incredible . . ." she whispered.

"Yes," he replied, his breath touching her ear and cheek.

She shivered, despite the warmth of the room.

"May I ask you something, madam?"

She crossed her arms over her breasts, eyeing the sonnet because she found herself unable to look at him. "Of course."

"Why are you really here?"

Her gaze shot up to his face. Staring into probing eyes of dark hazel, her first thought, absurdly enough, was how very polite he was in asking a question that implied nothing but the knowledge of deception on her part. It also caught her completely off guard, and for a moment, rendered her dumbstruck.

He carried on as if he expected no immediate answer from her. With a light chuckle and a shake of his head, he said, "Forgive me for being blunt, but I have such trouble believing you're a collector of rare documents, that you have the means by which to purchase this should I want to sell it, and that, in the end, you learned of this particular priceless sonnet by accident." Huskily, he revealed, "Only ten or twelve people in all of Great Brittan know it still exists in original form, and of those, only five or six know I own it." He watched her intently. "So you can understand my curiosity as to how a middle-aged widow who sells flowers in Penzance became aware of something so unique."

Vivian didn't know whether to laugh or scream, but her insides felt like crumbling, admitting all and to the devil with propriety and a future of relative ease and contentment. And yet somewhere deep within her she couldn't let go of her dignity. She had made a good life for herself, tucked away in the safety of Cornwall, and nobody, least of all a thieving, lowly actor, would take it from her without a fight.

But she couldn't fight the Duke of Trent. She knew that instinctively. She could, however, play his game.

Standing rigidly, she lifted her chin slightly to the side and smiled at him coyly, hoping he didn't take note of the boiling fear within her.

"It happened exactly as I said, your grace, though

I now understand why you don't need a safe," she intimated, trying to keep her tone warm and teasing. "And yet, under the circumstances, I find it odd that you showed this to me anyway without reservation. Why?"

He blinked, clearly taken aback by her audaciousness, if not her subtle evasion. Then he slowly grinned, mesmerizing her with the simple lifting of his marvelous mouth.

"Because, Mrs. Rael-Lamont," he murmured softly, his gaze burning into hers, "you have a quick wit and smell like flowers. I like that."

Vivian drew a sharp intake of breath, felt blood rush to her face, no doubt pinkening her cheeks to expose the heat she felt from such an intimate . . . confession? She had no idea what to say. Once again, he'd managed to stun her into silence. And God, how many times had he made her blush this day?

He saved her from further embarrassment, though, as he abruptly turned his attention back to the manuscript, recovering the parchment and then closing the bible, tucking it safely back into the bookcase with a shutting of the door and a click of the lock.

He turned to face her fully, hands behind his back. "I shall consider the reasons for your visit today, madam. Now if you'll excuse me, I've got estate matters to which I must attend. Wilson will show you out." He nodded once. "Good day, Mrs. Rael-Lamont."

She'd never been dismissed more abruptly in her life. Still standing only a foot away from his distinguished form, her skirts still resting against his long, sturdy legs—though he didn't appear to notice that—Vivian could do nothing but excuse herself.

Curtsying once, she pulled her reticule against her stomach. "As you wish, your grace."

His brows rose fractionally at that, but he didn't respond.

Turning, she walked to the door. "Thank you for your time, sir," she mumbled as she reached it.

He nodded curtly. "Until we meet again, madam."

Another shiver coiled up within her, and as Vivian quickly made her exit from the property, she couldn't help but feel the Duke of Trent's clever eyes on her back, ever watching.

Chapter 3

Vivian stood in her dining room. She placed her hands on her hips and surveyed the arrangement on her polished pine table—a red rose and white orchid pattern in a blue glass vase that she'd just completed for the Finley wedding that evening. After forty-five minutes of work, she'd finally attained perfection to her standards, as this arrangement would be on display beside the church altar, in front of some of Cornwall's best families. This one had turned out lovely, if she did say so herself.

She only faintly noticed the rapping of the knocker on her front door, so caught up in as she was with her project, but seconds later, the great stirring of her small staff brought her out of her concentration when one of her two maids dashed past the dining room door toward the kitchen, her skirts rustling with the quickness of her step.

A commotion had begun in the entryway, muffled voices carrying little distinction, though clearly both male and female.

Vivian started to call for Harriet, then thought better of it. Instead, she smoothed her auburn, lace-trimmed skirt and ran a palm over her pinned, plaited hair before walking with confidence toward the front of her house. As she turned the corner into the entryway, she stopped so quickly her gown swung out in front of her, forcing whalebone to smack against his knees. *His* knees.

Dear God.

Her mouth dropped open—in either shock that he'd ventured to the village in person, horror that he actually stood in her cluttered house, or maybe just that he looked so fabulously handsome despite his too-casual attire of a white silk shirt and unassuming brown pants. At this moment, he looked so *un*-like any nobleman she'd ever known. More like a person of the middle class ready to take a stroll in his small, private garden.

And what was he *doing* here? It had only been yesterday that she'd ventured to his estate with her proposal. Her heart began to race with possibilities.

"I see I've left you speechless once again, Mrs. Rael-Lamont," he drawled.

That pronouncement from him jolted her from her thoughts and her mouth snapped shut. "Undoubtedly," she agreed without argument, smiling flatly. "I don't often entertain gentlemen of your . . . prestige, your grace."

She regretted that statement as soon as she said it.

Slowly, without hint of implication, he replied, "That's so very good to know, madam."

Color burned in her cheeks. Then with the clearing of a throat, Vivian remembered Harriet still stood behind her and to her left, waiting for direction, hearing everything.

Reigning in her dignity, she turned toward her housekeeper.

"His Grace, the Duke of Trent and I will be discussing business in the parlor, Harriet. Please serve us refreshments there at once."

Unable to hide her continued astonishment, a wide-eyed Harriet curtsied as required to the duke first, then her employer, then backed out of the entryway to do as ordered.

Turning again to her unexpected guest, Vivian drew in a slow breath and clasped her hands in front of her. "Well, then. This way if you please, sir."

She brushed by him before he could comment, chin high, her stride expressing a self-assurance she didn't feel at all, escorting him into her small parlor, the only room in her home decorated appropriately for the little entertaining she did.

"You do like your flowers, do you not?"

She couldn't tell if he meant that with wit or sarcasm, though she did know he hadn't asked it as a question requiring answer, and she didn't feel the need to offer one. But her parlor was the one room where she shared with others her own vision of beauty, being rather conspicuously adorned with every imaginable display of sun-dried flowers. The plain, pink-papered walls and dark cherry wood furniture were covered with arrangements of assorted cultured roses, orchids, and carnations, as well as wild poppies, daisies, and sea lavender, in every shade that could possibly grow in southern climes. Dried roses framed the large, oblong mirror over the mantel, filled large crystal vases on the oriental rug and tea table, placed directly between a brocade settee in pale pink, and two matching chairs that faced it. Her parlor was a room she was quite proud of, and where she seated prospective buyers when they came to her for business.

"Flowers are more than a hobby of mine, your grace," she explained after a moment or two of watching him gaze about the room. "They are my means of support."

"Indeed." He stopped in front of the large vase at the center of the tea table. "How do you get them to do that? Don't they wilt?"

Vivian withheld a smile of satisfaction when she realized he genuinely wanted to know how one dried flowers without the flowers curling over when they died.

"We hang them upside down while still fresh. Depending on the weather, I usually hang mine from a line in my nursery, in the sun. But they can be hung from almost anywhere as long as they remain untouched and dry for several days."

He nodded. "I see. Very distinctive." He glanced

41

up to her face again and folded his arms across his chest. "I'm sure this is why we employ your services."

Vivian felt a stab of embarrassment for giving more of an explanation than he likely wanted. For an awkward moment, they looked at each other from across the tea table, saying nothing. Then he gestured with an open palm to the settee.

"May I?"

"Of course. Please," she replied, gracefully seating herself as he did in a facing wing chair despite the fact that the gown she wore today, while fitted in the bodice, had very wide hoops that got caught between the legs of the tea table and the chair. She tried to make adjustments to no avail. Finally she ignored her predicament, deciding not to move the chair so that she could fit, instead sitting rigidly, her hands folded in her lap.

At that moment her housekeeper entered the parlor carrying a white china tray with tea and accompaniments, cups and saucers, which she placed on the table in front of Vivian.

"I'll serve us, Harriet. You may leave."

"Yes, ma'am," she murmured, curtsying again, her eyes on the man in front of them.

As soon as her housekeeper's retreating footsteps faded, Vivian reached for the teapot, pouring with calm hands despite her suddenly clenched stomach. He could only be here for one thing.

"I've considered your offer for the manuscript, madam," he said matter-of-factly, as if reading her thoughts, fingering the fine velvet at the end of one

42

soft cushion, his brows drawn together in a slight frown.

Vivian placed his cup on the tea table a bit too harshly, ignoring the slight catch in her throat as she quickly replied, "In less than a day, your grace?"

The Duke of Trent stretched his long legs out and under the table, resting one strong arm across the back of the settee. "I'm very fast when something interests me. And very thorough."

Vivian blinked, unsure how he wanted her to decipher that bit of babble. "Are you?" she replied with a forced little smile, replacing the teapot on the tray and reaching for sugar.

She added two teaspoons and began to stir gently. His cup remained untouched, and she could—without looking straight at him—positively *feel* his eyes burning a hole through her head. She did her best to ignore that by raising her cup to her lips.

"I will not be tricked, madam."

He said the words so softly, so coldly, she almost dropped her cup. But her heart began to race again and she changed her mind about taking a sip. The tea was far too hot, and she would probably spill it anyway as rattled as she was. Slowly, she lowered the cup and daintily placed it on the table.

At last, she forced herself to look at him.

His eyes, as he stared into hers, were cool and direct, overflowing with a distinct forewarning he didn't attempt to hide. If there was one thing she knew about this man already, it was that no one could ever take advantage of him and get away with it.

"Tell me how you learned of the manuscript," he insisted, watching her.

She swallowed, but didn't back down. "I told you, your grace. I overheard it rumored that you had it."

His cheek twitched as his eyes narrowed. "I want the truth, Vivian."

If he wasn't so focused, so deadly calm, she'd probably waver from the oh-so-masculine way he said her name. Oddly enough, she couldn't wait to hear him say it again.

"I told you—"

"Refresh my memory," he said in a low, harsh breath.

The man was totally and utterly intimidating, even, absurdly enough, while he sat on a pink settee in a flowered parlor. She well understood at that moment why people assumed he was guilty of the crime of murder, just as something warned her he would know if she lied to him again. And as powerful as he was, he could make her life extremely difficult, probably more so than the lowly actor who knew her secrets. Still, she couldn't risk it. Never in her life had Vivian felt so caught between two horrible outcomes.

Clenching her jaw, she said, "I can *not* tell you, your grace, and that is the truth." She breathed deeply and exhaled, softly adding, "Please leave it at that."

Perhaps it was her implied trust in him not to hurt her by forcing her to reveal the facts as she knew them, but she saw a flicker of . . . *something* shadow the planes of his face. His lids narrowed; his lips thinned and the muscles in his neck tightened with an irritation he couldn't hide. But he didn't press her.

After several uncomfortable seconds, his gaze very slowly lowered to her mouth, then her breasts.

Vivian didn't move, though the heated stirring deep in her belly was difficult to deny.

"It seems we are at an impasse," he murmured, his tone thick with indignation as he looked back into her eyes.

She didn't know what to say to that.

Suddenly he leaned forward on the seat, resting his elbows on his knees, his hands, palms together, in front of him. "You don't for a minute think I'll simply sell you a piece of work signed by William Shakespeare, not without something valuable given me in return."

Vivian began to tremble inside; tears of frustration and an instantly growing fear threatened to fill her eyes as his meaning began to dawn.

Boldly, trying to keep a passionately felt anger from her voice, she asked, "What is it you want, your grace? I have very little of value to offer you."

It seemed to take a moment for him to gather the right words. Then he stared at her intensely and whispered, "*You*, madam, have exceptional value to me."

She would not cry. She would not.

"I suppose you mean my person," she stated, her voice sounding detached and distant to her ears.

He continued to regard her closely. "I do. I have lived far too long without the companionship of a beautiful woman."

Her breath caught, but for a reason unknown to her, she couldn't bring herself to slap him, dismiss him. Above all—her anger, every uncertainty—he intrigued her.

"And for my . . . companionship," she continued, her nails digging into her palms, "you will give me the manuscript."

He inhaled very deeply, holding her gaze with an intensity she could feel.

"I will," he whispered.

The grandfather clock in the entryway behind her chimed four, startling her. Vivian jumped, standing abruptly, and quickly lost her balance with her skirts pulled to the side of her so awkwardly.

Immediately, he was there, catching her before she tumbled onto the tea table. But instead of feeling embarrassed or foolish, she felt a sudden jolt of desire, thick and strong, as he caught her under the arms, his hands firmly planted on the sides of her breasts.

Stunned, she looked up into his face, noting a shock in his heated eyes to match her own. His palms lingered on her curves for several seconds, feeling like flames to her skin, until she straightened and he dropped his arms, reluctantly releasing her.

Swiftly, Vivian scrambled to the side and back where her boned skirts fell smoothly around her petticoats, closing her arms over her stomach, turning away from him so that he couldn't see her flushed face, her lust and confusion. She closed her eyes for a brief moment, placing one palm on her neck, wondering, absurdly enough, why her hand felt so cold.

This cannot be happening.

For a moment or two nobody said anything, nobody moved. Then she heard him step away from the settee, toward her.

"I will be otherwise engaged for the remainder of the week, but I would like to see you Saturday, Mrs. Rael-Lamont," he said from behind her, his voice low. "For a noon luncheon at my home."

She nodded minutely.

He walked past her, stopping when he reached the parlor doorway.

Turning his head to one side, he added, "For what it's worth, I expected nothing less between us."

And then he was gone.

He hated entering the village during daylight hours, and despised crowds with a passion. Socializing with various members of society made his skin crawl, which—aside from his very public trial and the acquittal only a few believed was just—remained the reason he lived most of the year in Penzance. He'd wondered before he made his surprise appearance this afternoon if he might shock the neighbors, and he was assured he had, as several people had seen him arrive, then leave. Of course he couldn't care any less as his reputation had long since been ruined, but he was quite certain the Widow Rael-Lamont would. Her business was at stake, and yet she'd been the one to come to him with her damned proposal. She had to know he would want more information. And did she think he was so reclusive that he never ventured from the house?

47

Will leaned back against the cushion inside his coach as his driver meandered the dirt path toward home. He'd requested an understated rig without crests and high fashion, to keep a low profile as he rode into the village, but in doing so, he'd sacrificed luxury as well. This one rattled, which did nothing for his nerves.

God, what a beautiful woman she was. She had pale, satiny skin, an oval face still free of wrinkles, stunning blue-gray eyes, and silky dark hair that he would gladly pay a thousand pounds to see brushed long and loose about her pale shoulders, down her bare back. Closing his eyes, he imagined it, thinking again how physically exciting it was to hold her, even for a few seconds, his palms clasping the sides of her breasts. Through the fabric of her gown he could feel their soft roundness, and it had immediately charged him with a lust he hadn't felt in ages. It had shocked them both, and she knew it as well. There was an energy between them, thoroughly undefined, but there nonetheless. It had been evident the moment their eyes met in the library yesterday, and in some very odd manner, he now considered it a miracle that she'd come to him with such a strange proposition.

And what of that? There was a great deal more to her visit than she'd disclosed. Will now felt certain she was being bribed, or even blackmailed. But by whom? And why? One of the reasons he'd wanted to surprise her in her home today was to get a good look, or at least a decent look, at the way she lived, her sense of style and to what social class she belonged. It had become immediately apparent that she was from good family. She treated her staff with standard distance and respect, kept her entertaining room very formal, even though her home was terribly small. She spoke in perfect English and her manners were impeccable. If Will didn't know better, he'd swear she came from nobility, or at least the well born. She certainly conducted herself well enough.

What positively fascinated him, though, was her attraction to him even with the suspicion abounding that he'd killed Elizabeth. Very nearly everybody in the country knew of the sinful Duke of Trent, feared him, suspected him of murder as well as corruption of his own trial, thought him a scoundrel in need of a good hanging—except Vivian Rael-Lamont. Why didn't she cringe from him, draw back in fear when he neared her? Hell, she even came to *visit* him, regardless of her intentions. Nothing in years had astonished him more than watching her walk up his front steps yesterday, looking dazzling and lovely with the sun on her shoulders and shiny, neatly dressed hair.

But really, all that was irrelevant, at least for the time being. What mattered now was that he find out what the devil was going on with her, how she came to know about his prized manuscript when so few in the country did. There was indeed a puzzle here in need of a good solving, and he had every intention of solving it, with or without her help, though he intended to have her in his presence frequently.

He wanted her, of that he was positive after meeting her again this afternoon. And from his best instincts, he was certain she wanted him, too. She wasn't young and inexperienced. It had been so long, so long since a woman had actually desired him, and he had seen it in her eyes. Being with her would be all consuming, a numbing of the most perfect kind. She would drug him like a fine, exotic wine.

Will fixed his gaze on the dim lighting of his home in the distance, feeling a stirring of something marvelous, deep within, that had been missing for years. He only wished he didn't have to wait until Saturday to see her again, to recall such desire one more time. But for now he had much to do. He had the beginnings of a plan.

Chapter 4

The dawn had brought rain to Penzance, but by the time Vivian ascended the stairs of Morning House, the sky had cleared so that the sun shone down in brilliance, lighting the raindrops on the surrounding brush, and making the stone walkway sparkle.

She didn't want to be here today—and yet she did. Strangely she wanted to see him again, especially after his totally unexpected visit to her home earlier in the week. And she held more than a mild interest in him, she had to admit, for he intimidated her as much as he intrigued her. He was a contradiction, a gentleman to be sure, but one with hidden secrets only barely revealed in his dark, cool eyes and uncommonly smooth, deep voice. Beyond it all, Vivian had to wonder what he had been like as a husband. Was he driven to kill by a woman he hated? Or was he simply mad beneath his cool exterior?

She quickly quashed that idea. If there was one thing she could determine about the Duke of Trent intuitively, it was that he was perfectly sane. But was it possible that such a mysteriously handsome and intriguing man really *murdered* another human being?

Vivian tried to brush the uncomfortable thoughts aside as she neared the unattractive, black front doors of the estate home. Unlike the inside rooms, the outside building front certainly needed a more inviting look. But then she knew as well as anyone that the duke rarely had guests.

Today footmen stood at attention, obviously expecting her arrival. Immediately, as she neared them, they bowed to her and opened the door, allowing her to enter without a pause in her stride.

Nervousness coiled up within her again. Not from fear of meeting the accused killer this time, but from uncertainty of the afternoon to come.

The butler met her in the foyer, obviously expecting her.

"Good day, Wilson," she said.

"Good day, Mrs. Rael-Lamont. This way if you please."

He escorted her to the same library where she'd met the duke earlier. After opening the doors for her, she stepped inside, feeling the southern sea breeze at once as it came through the conservatory windows to cool her face.

"Please make yourself comfortable, madam. His grace will be here momentarily."

"Thank you, Wilson," she replied as he closed the door behind him.

Vivian removed her bonnet and placed it over the back of the chair she'd occupied on her last visit. Just at that moment the Duke of Trent walked in through the conservatory in front of her, wearing navy pants and a casual shirt of ecru linen, sleeves rolled up nearly to the elbows, exposing dark hair on his muscled arms and strong hands free of jewelry.

For a moment neither one of them spoke. Vivian gazed into his eyes, her uncertainty conveyed by a sudden wave of shyness.

"Vivian," he drawled.

I am fighting for my life.

She swallowed, then forced a smile and did her best to relax. "Your grace."

For a second or two she could have sworn he fought a frown. She hesitated to respond any more since such intimacy disconcerted her more than he could possibly imagine.

He stepped toward her then, slowly, his hands clasped behind him.

"It's turned into a lovely day."

"Yes." She didn't move.

"I thought we would take luncheon on the veranda. The view is excellent."

"Of course," she replied, lifting her bonnet again.

"Leave it," he said. "You won't need it."

She didn't argue. "As you wish, your grace."

"Will."

It seemed so incredibly odd to her to be calling a nobleman of such high rank by his given name. But she could hardly argue when in his company, especially as they were alone.

She tipped her head toward him once. "William."

He lowered his voice, his eyes probing hers intently.

"Not William. *Will*."

Vivian clasped her arms at the elbows in some manner of defense, she supposed, having no idea why it should matter. William was indeed more formal.

"Very well, *Will*," she repeated as he'd stressed it.

Placing her outstretched hand on his forearm, she felt warm flesh covered with a soft coating of hair. It was the first time she'd touched a man's bare skin—aside from a hand or a kiss to the cheek—in more than ten years. The feeling of his heated strength brought a rush of titillating thoughts to her, all of them exciting and utterly unwanted at such a delicate time.

They didn't speak to each other as he guided her out the doors at the far end of the library and into the conservatory proper, a glass-covered extension of the house filled with the sights and scents of plants and a host of flowers, all well maintained. Two or three windows were propped open to the outside air, allowing a mild breeze to enter just enough to keep the area cool. But the view itself, reaching far across private gardens, the sandy shore, and the ocean beyond, was truly spectacular.

"It's beautiful here," she remarked with pleasure,

allowing her gaze to take in the site before her, the gorgeous backdrop to the estate glistening from the newly fallen coat of rain.

He said nothing for a moment, then, "I thought perhaps you'd appreciate the view."

She still clung to his arm, it occurred to her. Quickly glancing up to his face, she realized how close she stood to a man who only a week ago was a fantasy of a person, a shadow of gossip and intrigue. Now, touching his flesh, he'd become very, very real.

She must have blushed, for at the moment, he grinned wryly, watching her.

"You're beautiful," he said softly, almost thoughtfully.

Her eyes widened and her breath caught in her chest before she could hide that automatic response. He had to notice her sudden trepidation.

"Did you murder your wife, sir?"

His arms flexed beneath her fingers; his body instantly stilled, a flash of . . . something, shock perhaps, passed over his countenance before his jaw tightened and his lips formed a hard, straight line across his face. She'd struck a very deep chord, as she knew she would from such a question, and yet he hesitated in answering. Just watched her.

Vivian didn't move her gaze from the directness of his. Then with a twitch of the muscle in his cheek, he murmured, "If I said I didn't, would you believe me?"

There was a candidness about him that intrigued her, dug deep into her own confused feelings of a past she couldn't change. Her mouth felt dry, but she had to answer him. He expected it.

"No, probably not," she returned just as frankly. "I would have no proof."

After a moment's pause, he nodded slightly. "Ah. One is always guilty until proven innocent. A fair assessment." He lowered his voice. "And if I said I did?"

A tiny gust of air shot through the open window beside them, lifting his hair and blowing it onto his forehead and temples. At that moment, he looked young and vulnerable as he waited for her to answer.

At last she breathed in purposefully and forced herself to turn away, gazing out to the ocean beyond. "I have no proof of that, either," she mumbled a bit tersely. "I think I'd need that before I could condemn you for such a loathsome act."

"A sin, madam?"

She raised her chin a fraction. "A sin beyond measure."

"You're very brave, I suppose," he said, his tone lightening on a wave of black humor, "coming into the home of an accused killer."

She sighed. "Or very stupid."

"One only knows what I might do," he added with a hint of bitterness.

She supposed she could take that any number of ways, but decided on the obvious. "Nonsense. With servants about? And there are any number of people in the village who may be aware of where I am. Perhaps I told neighbors."

"I think, if I were a gambling man, I would bet my entire wealth on the fact that you told no one, Vivian."

He'd said that so smoothly, so darkly, she shivered inside and looked back into his eyes.

They shone with an odd mixture of intrigue, skepticism, and perhaps somewhere very far within, an emptiness brought on by years of being alone. Feeling for the sins of his past suddenly put her at a disadvantage—and made her yearn for deeper understanding.

When she didn't immediately reply, he reached up and touched her fingers, still grasping his forearm, with his own. "Why don't we discuss stupidity over luncheon?"

She relaxed, pressing her lips together to stop herself from thanking him for that. She had never appreciated a change of subject more.

Vivian lifted her skirts with her free hand as he turned, then the two of them walked side by side, her palm still laying softly on his warm arm, until they reached the opposite end of the conservatory where a meal of simple fare awaited them.

"I thought a salmon souffle seemed appropriate," he remarked formally.

Appropriate for what, she didn't know, and decided not to ask. Instead, she murmured simply, "It sounds delicious."

They talked little during the meal, and nothing of the stupidity, or rather the reason, for her being there, though Vivian was well aware that he watched her closely. Every time she glanced up she'd catch his eyes on her, or some part of her—a hand, her hair, her lips. Once even on her breasts, which, oddly enough, didn't bother her. But with such visual attention, she couldn't eat much. Being in his presence was altogether too exciting, and she had to wonder if he felt the same odd stimulation as well.

To be honest, Vivian had thought about him all night, able to sleep little, tossing and turning with the notion of all the passionate things he might do to her. And those thoughts, however outlandish, secretly thrilled her as much as they scared her. It had been so long—

"What are you thinking?"

His gentle utterance took on complex meaning when coupled with his tone of fascination and a tinge of hesitation.

Vivian almost smiled. In a manner it was somehow endearing.

"Honestly? I was thinking about us, your grace."

That startled him a fraction. She could tell by the quick lifting of his brows and the tight jerk of his shoulders. Such a reaction made her tingle inside, and her lips curved up in a grin she could no longer hide.

"I know you were once a married woman, madam, but I had no idea your thoughts strayed to the sensual during a meal."

Vivian felt her stomach lurch at such bold words. The man clearly didn't know much about women, or consider that he might embarrass her in front of his servants. Then again, maybe he simply didn't care.

"What makes you think my thoughts were so engaged?"

He eyed her frankly, sitting back a bit in his seat and placing his fork on his plate. "Only a guess."

She paused for a moment or two, playing absent-mindedly with the linen napkin in her lap. "Tell me, your grace, do you have only this one home, or are there others?" she asked, deciding to change the conversation to something more formal, and infinitely more appropriate.

He sat back in his chair and raked his fingers through his hair, a movement she found remarkably attractive in him.

"I have a cottage in Tuscany, which I don't get to visit nearly enough, and a townhouse in London, which I'm forced to visit every year."

"Forced?"

"For parliamentary duties, official and private business," he replied after a moment, his tone dropping a shade. He glanced away, squinting as he looked beyond the windows to the far-reaching ocean. "I hate the stink of the city—and going to court."

He'd said that as an afterthought, Vivian decided, and as she wasn't sure how to respond, she instead took another bite of what had turned out to be a marvelous souffle—creamy, light, and delicious. But she knew how he felt. The duties of the elite were sometimes annoying in their trivialities, sometimes aggravating in their extreme importance. She was only glad she didn't have to worry about such things living in the southern beauty of remote Penzance. He probably felt the same way.

Then again, maybe the murder trial had something to do with his hatred of court. Especially since almost everybody still believed he was guilty of the crime, even after five years.

Vivian placed her fork on her plate and patted her lips with her napkin. He turned his attention back to her, studying her for a moment, his head tipped slightly to the side, eyes narrowed.

"You said you were thinking about us?"

Her heart began to race again. Hadn't she changed that subject?

"You're certainly tenacious," she answered quickly, sitting up as straight as possible, hands now clasped together in her lap.

"Very," he admitted. He rubbed his clean-shaven chin with his fingertips. "You're nervous, though, aren't you, to be here alone with me?"

She breathed in deeply, noting how odd it was to be answering such a question while two footmen stood at attention at the sideboard. She tried not to look at them to assess what they might think. They were probably staid of expression anyway, as good servants always were.

"I'm not nervous in the least, your grace," she replied as calmly as possible. "We made a deal. I am here to honor it."

His expression never changed, though he did lower his hand back to his lap. The bell from a fishing troller tolled in the distance; the breeze ruffled the leaves on the plants surrounding them, and yet he didn't appear to notice any intrusion whatsoever, focused so intently on her. It made her squirm slightly in her seat.

"Your grace—"

"Walk with me in my garden, Mrs. Rael-Lamont?"

She blinked quickly at that unexpected turn, her lips parting a fraction. The formality of his demeanor in no way suggested he'd asked her here for a tryst, and yet they both knew he had. Suddenly she felt a bit confused.

"No dessert, sir?"

One side of his mouth kicked up minutely. "I had planned raspberries in sweet cream, but I've changed my mind."

She swallowed and smiled flatly. "Have you?"

Placing his napkin at the side of his plate, he stood and rounded the small table to stand at her side.

"Walk with me," he insisted gently, his hand extended.

She could do nothing but comply and place her palm in his. A footman immediately moved up behind her to pull out her chair as she gracefully raised her body. When he didn't let go of her hand, she smoothed her skirt with the other. "Lead the way, my lord duke."

His eyes roved over her face, and for a second in time, Vivian nearly caught a smile from him again. Then he murmured, "You are most accommodating, madam. I think I shall enjoy your company much, much more than I thought possible."

Vivian felt her face flush with keen embarrassment. And yet what words went too far when a gentleman spoke to a woman he expected to become his mistress? She had no idea. But she fumed inside from the knowledge that servants speak below stairs and word would eventually spread to the townsfolk that she was now *accommodating* the Duke of Trent. He had to know that.

With irritation, she tried to pull her hand from his. He held fast for a second or two, then suddenly must have sensed her mortification, as he let go of her without response.

Silently, he gestured for her to follow him to the far corner of the conservatory where, behind a row of potted plants, stood a glass-paneled door in front of a circular, wrought-iron staircase that led directly to the garden below.

He reached in front of her, unlatched the door, and allowed her to exit ahead of him.

Vivian clung to her skirts, but instead of placing his hand on her elbow, he skimmed her lower back, pressing his palm against her stays to balance her. Or perhaps simply to enjoy a more intimate touch. She really didn't know. But thankfully near this end of the house, and because of the angle at which they descended into the botanical midst, no one could witness it.

They both stopped short on the brick porch that appeared to stretch along the entire length of the southern facing wall of the house. In front of her, spread out in perfectly tended landscape, was an array of roses and semi-exotic flowers in every color and variety imaginable, green plants and palm trees, all cut low enough to take in the extended view of the sparkling gray-blue ocean beyond the sandy coastline.

"It's breathtaking," she said with awe, and unmistakable envy. "It's surely the most lush garden I've ever seen."

"Indeed." He paused for a moment, then added, "It's maintained to my satisfaction."

"As it should be for one of your rank, your grace."

"A title is a birthright, Vivian. What I do with my property comes from the human desire within me to relish peace and behold the beautiful."

She looked up to his face when he said that. He squinted in the sunlight as he gazed out over the water, the breeze again lifting his soft hair, which he brushed aside with his fingertips in the same manner he had before.

It struck Vivian earlier that he looked so very young when he did that, but now she reassessed that thought. It wasn't so much that he looked younger than his thirty-five years, or boyish for that matter, but that he looked so *human*—a word that had been used in its negative form repeatedly—*inhuman*—whenever he'd been described as the accused killer in newspapers across the country, and in drawing rooms across Penzance even to this day. How very . . . odd that she wasn't at all afraid of him right now, alone as they were in an enclosure of natural beauty.

He glanced down to find her staring at him. Disconcerted, she smiled faintly and turned her attention to the garden. "Shall we walk?" she asked pleasantly.

Quietly, he replied, "If you wish."

She could see two distinct paths from which to choose, and suspected there were more inside the floral array. But before she could take a step toward either of them, he reached down and covered her hand with his, so gently, his thumb grazing her knuckles. His touch surprised her, but she tried not to let that show as he began to walk forward, toward the path on the left.

"Tell me about your husband, Vivian."

She paused in her stride, which he surely noticed, but he didn't let go of her hand. After a second or two of nervous hesitation, she breathed in deeply of salty sea air mingled with the scent of flowers, and tried to relax. He couldn't know anything about her past, which only meant that he was simply curious.

"He was my cousin," she revealed, strolling beside him once again.

"Ah. An arranged union, then?"

"Yes."

When she didn't offer more, he asked, "Were you happy?"

How could she answer that? It took everything in her to try to remain calm as she continued to walk beside him. "I was very happy on my wedding day, but then most ladies are, your grace. Since my husband's unfortunate demise, I have learned to make a good life for myself and I am happy once more."

She hoped that vague reply would suffice. Apparently it did for the moment as he didn't immediately comment.

A sudden gust of wind blew loose strands of hair

from her face, and she closed her eyes momentarily to the feel of it.

"I adore Penzance, the weather along the coast," she said without thought.

Suddenly he stopped beside her, still holding her hand, and turned to face her.

Vivian looked up into his dark eyes as he studied her, her heart suddenly speeding up at their closeness, the continuing tender touch of his skin, noticing that they stood fairly well secluded from the house behind four thick palm trees.

"How did he die?"

Such a gravely asked question startled her as much as the swift intensity of his gaze. For a moment she couldn't speak.

He waited, watching her, his thumb rubbing her knuckles again in that particular way that made her face flush and her breath quicken.

"I— He had a bad heart, your grace."

He frowned almost imperceptibly. "A bad heart?"

"It's not uncommon," she murmured in quick response. "He was nearly forty years of age."

The duke nodded, thinking.

Vivian grew nervous, afraid of the probing questions almost as much as their sudden seclusion. But she couldn't move, couldn't look away. A sudden uneasiness swept over her.

And then it happened. Slowly, in shimmering sunlight and warm, fragrant air, he leaned over and faintly touched his lips to hers, just holding them there without movement.

Stunned, Vivian couldn't immediately react. Her

breathing seemed to stop as a surge of heat shot through her, making her legs weak and her insides flutter with the gnawing anticipation of a marvelous unknown.

He remained still, clasping her hand, his lips on hers, never probing for more, until a faint, deep moan escaped him and he pulled himself back.

She began shaking, though she had no idea why, and raised her free hand to her mouth, covering it with her fingers. He kept his eyes shut for a second or two as she watched him, having no idea what to say or even if he expected her to speak.

At last, he whispered, "You are so warm . . ."

Burning with fire inside, she thought, but then she really didn't understand his meaning.

Awkwardly, she attempted to pull her hand from his grasp, but he didn't let her go. He held fast to her, opening his eyes to gaze into hers.

Vivian stilled from the look of utter longing he exposed to her in those few seconds of intimate, silent contact—far more intimate than his kiss had been.

You are so warm.

That's when she knew. It was the purest touch of woman to man. A thoroughly human need to feel wanted and enjoyed, to feel accepted without judgment. No loathing, no fear. She had given him a brush of warm compassion without repulsion, and he had relished it in its simplicity.

She lowered her fingers from her mouth and smiled at him, softly. He drew a shaky breath, then dropped her hand and took a step away from her.

"Vivian," he said, his voice controlled and low, "you are ever more than I imagined."

"Imagined?"

"I've imagined everything where you are concerned," he acknowledged at once without reservation.

Her smile faded as she grew uncomfortable again, confused. "Your grace?"

To her complete astonishment, he shook his head negligibly and chuckled. "If you don't start calling me 'Will,' Vivian, I won't kiss you again."

It was her turn to take a step back. "You presume I'd want that?" she challenged.

He briefly glanced to his right, then back to her again. "I would presume."

"Your logic baffles me completely," she quickly retorted.

"As your perfect kiss did me, my dear lady."

Heat suffused her face again, but she said nothing. She couldn't possibly after that comment since he turned everything she said into something intimate.

He cocked his head to study her, though the amusement never left his features. At this moment, standing so casually in a garden of brilliant color, he looked more handsome than any man she had ever seen, and it took all that was in her not to tell him so.

"I wish you would smile more often," she confessed instead, almost contemplatively.

He pulled back in surprise. "Oh? Why?"

Was he really so dense? More likely just rarely around women.

67

She sighed and crossed her arms over her breasts. "I will consent to calling you by your given name, your grace, if you will consent to smiling for my pleasure."

He clasped his hands behind his back, his mouth curling into a smirk of satisfaction. "I think that after tasting those sweet lips of yours I will consent to just about anything for your pleasure, madam."

She stifled a gasp, pulling back a bit in surprise, which made him chuckle again. Lowering his voice, he whispered huskily, "You know you want me to kiss you again."

His teasing liquefied her but she was reluctant to deny it. "And you know this conversation makes no sense."

He took a step in her direction, his head blocking the sun as he towered over her. "It makes perfect sense, Vivian, when you consider how well you enjoyed our first very fleeting contact."

She wouldn't have called it fleeting, exactly, for the simple press of his lips to hers seemed to last for minutes. But then maybe that was her imagination. She hadn't been thinking clearly at all.

"Did *you* enjoy it?" she asked wryly, though knowing instinctively, and fully well, that he did. Vanity made her want to hear it.

He glanced down to her breasts, then back into her eyes. "You know I did."

However amused he was by his clever turns of phrase, he certainly put her in a difficult position, which he likely relished. Of course she wanted him to kiss her again, and he seemed to be more aware of it than she. How absurd.

Tipping her head back and lowering her arms to her sides, she acquiesced. "Very well, Will. I succumb to your ridiculous demands."

For a slice of a second, she could have sworn she saw relief in his eyes, and perhaps a tinge of returning desire. Then he straightened and nodded once. "I'm looking forward to your next visit then."

"And when will that be?" she asked rather perfunctorily.

"Next Wednesday, for dinner."

Her brows rose. "Next Wednesday?"

He very nearly smiled again. "Is that not soon enough for you?"

Once again the reason for their newfound association came crashing back into her thoughts, but mentioning the manuscript right now would break the lovely mood between them. This intimate moment with him suddenly, and quite irrationally, mattered to her more.

"I'm at your command, sir," she returned, her tone subdued. She felt a certain dread take hold in the pit of her stomach, yet she had no choice but to persevere. "But I must ask you now when I might be able to acquire the manuscript?"

His smile faded as he stared down upon her, his gaze holding hers for a long moment before he lifted his fingers and brushed the back side of them along her cheek, startling her with his gentleness. Before she could react, however, he dropped her hand.

"In due time. I'll look forward to Wednesday, Vivian."

He was dismissing her without answers that satisfied, and she had no choice but to leave.

"Thank you for a delightful luncheon, Will."

He nodded, very formally, hands behind his back once more. "Wilson will show you out."

"Of course." She curtsied, then brushed past him, controlling the need to touch the skin on her cheek where she could still feel him, and more than a little dismayed to be leaving his company.

Chapter 5

Clement Hastings was a rather short, round man in his late forties whom Will could only describe as squat. He sported a fairly large nose, small beady eyes, a balding head, and he wore only the most eccentric of clothing. Will often wondered how the man made a living wage as an agent of inquiry, although it appeared quite true that the wealthy and noble frequently needed some sort of pampering for which they willingly, and handsomely, paid. Or perhaps pampering wasn't the correct word. Hastings wasn't the type to pamper. The man possessed a remarkably shrewd intellect and was considered by most to be the best investigator in Cornwall. Will had used his services on occasion, though most notably before his trial nearly six years ago.

Walking into his library, Will found the man gazing at one of his shelves of books next to the mantel.
Hastings wore another atypical suit—a striped gold
and white silk shirt tucked into green and white
large, plaid pants, all covered with a lime green
waistcoat that pinched his stomach like a corset.
Perhaps this was the style in the city, Will didn't
know, but he sure as hell wouldn't be found dead in
such garb. Then again, perhaps the man's wife
dressed him and his choice of clothing was no fault
of his own.

"Have you found anything, Hastings?" he asked,
heading straight for his desk, hoping the man had
come with news today. He'd only been looking into
this matter since early in the week, so Will knew the
chances for good information were slim. Still, he
wanted a report every two days, and so far Hastings
had obliged him.

The investigator turned his attention to him and
bowed once, a thin smile displayed across his lips.
"Good morning, your grace," he said properly. "I do
indeed have something. It's not much, but it's a start,
I think."

Will gestured to the opposite chair. "Please."

Hastings nodded again and walked toward him,
arranging his plump form in the chair, his legs
stretched out in front of him as he reached into the
pocket of his waistcoat for his notes.

"Well now," he started, flipping through several
small sheets of paper, "my men in London are starting their investigation into Mrs. Rael-Lamont's

background, and about that, I have no news." He cleared his throat. "However, from my own discreet questioning about town I've learned she's lived in her Penzance home, alone aside from a small number of servants, since 'forty-four, apparently moving here after the death of her husband. There's nothing to suggest he ever came to Cornwall while still alive, although I think . . ." Hastings frowned and turned the sheet over. "Ah, yes. The property, I believe, is in her late husband's name, though that has yet to be verified. So it looks as if he purchased it without ever seeing it, and I suppose that's not too odd if he'd planned to vacation here and then died unexpectedly." He looked up to Will, his features forming a pleasant, relaxed confidence. "I'll have more information, your grace, within the week, as soon as I get news from the city. She's evidently got a trust set up there from which she's drawing income."

Will sat back in his chair, rubbing his fingertips along the top of the secretary, his mind churning with possibilities that so far added up to nothing substantial whatsoever. Except that she also drew income from selling and arranging flowers. And she had the most delicious tasting lips. "Anything else on her husband?"

Hastings shook his head. "Nothing here, sir, but again, I'll have more later in the week."

"Very good." Will moved to stand, when the investigator turned another sheet of paper.

"One last thing, your grace, and perhaps this is totally insignificant."

He remained in his chair, eyeing the investigator speculatively. "Yes?"

Hastings frowned, this time deeply enough to form creases in his forehead. "You asked me to check for people she's seen recently, and I've found one meeting she had that's rather odd and unlike the others."

Will said nothing, just waited.

Hastings looked up again. "It seems she does a good business selling flowers and floral arrangements to the local well-born, and most of them either send for her to come to their homes for consultations, or call on her for appointments."

This seemed very trivial to Will, but he decided against that remark. It was the man's job to take note of the ordinary, he supposed.

"Apparently," Hastings continued, "according to one of her neighbor's scullery maids, early last week Mrs. Rael-Lamont had a visitor whom she did not expect and who was apparently so low-born he was taken 'round the back of the cottage to meet her in her nursery. He was there only a few minutes, and when he left, she immediately closed the house up and refused visitors, customers, and social callers, and she does have a good many lady friends in the community. That was the day before she came to see you, your grace."

Will sat forward in his chair, leaning one elbow on the armrest, growing ever more intrigued. "Do you know who it was who called on her?"

Hastings scratched his jowls with wide, puffy fingers. "Well, now, that's what's so odd, sir. Seems it was an actor."

74

He could feel his heart thud against his chest. "An *actor*?"

The investigator chuckled, shaking his head as he glanced back to his notes. "I know, sir. Very odd, but yes indeed, an actor from the Shakespearean touring group—the lead actor, I believe. Name's Gilbert Montague, but that's all I know about him for now. I'm working on more information."

Will ran his fingers through his hair harshly and abruptly stood, walking with purposeful strides toward the conservatory windows. He didn't know any actors, and as far as he could remember, had never met one in his life. But Hastings was right; this meeting between the widow and an actor at her home was far too unusual and coincidental to the moment to ignore, especially since a Shakespearean actor might be well informed about Shakespearean works not generally known to the public.

"I want him checked thoroughly," he said, staring out the window to the coast beyond. "Can you look into this immediately?"

He heard the rustle of clothing behind him and it occurred to him that Hastings was no doubt trying to stand in his male corset. How utterly uncomfortable, but then again, the man's unusual taste in fashion was none of his concern.

"I can begin this afternoon, your grace. Shall I return two days from now, same time?"

Will pivoted to look at the man directly again. "Yes, and sooner if you have news of some significance."

"Understood, sir," the investigator agreed with a tip of his head. "Is there anything else?"

"No, that's all for today."

Hastings retrieved his hat from a bookcase shelf and nodded once more in Will's direction. "Good day to you, your grace."

"Good day, Hastings."

Chapter 6

```
    ~~~~~
```

The pub gradually filled with the oncoming darkness. Most of the faces this night were regulars, but from time to time a new person or two would wander into The Jolly Knights to escape the wench at home or the oppressive summer heat. He came to escape the theater, the mindless actors and all their pitiful doubts and ridiculous problems, whenever he possibly could.

Gilbert sat back in the little chair he had for himself in the far corner of the dimly lit, dank room. He'd been like that for nearly two hours, uncomfortable in a chair far too small for his large frame, wondering if he shouldn't ask the little blond wench for another jaunt to the filthy bed upstairs to relieve his boredom. He allowed himself the luxury—if one could call it that—of coming in almost every Friday evening, as he had for the last two months, now that he wasn't on stage in London and suddenly had plenty of money. He laughed again at his flawlessly brilliant planning.

"Thank you, Vivian Rael-Lamont," he said aloud in a mock toast as he raised his glass to his lips, taking several long swallows of surprisingly decent ale. He was nearly drunk already, but feeling so fine, he wanted oblivion tonight. Besides, he wasn't to perform again for two days. Who the hell would care if he slept on a bench?

His mood blackened at once as he lowered his almost empty glass to stare trouble right in the face. She stood there so casually, not two feet away, smiling down at him with complete intolerance in her pretty blue eyes. He nearly choked.

"Well, if it isn't Gilbert Montague," she purred.

"Dammit Elinor," he choked out. "What the devil are you doing here? How did you find me?"

Her brows shot up. "How did I find you? It's a pub. Besides, I'm not as frail and helpless as I look," she added, her lips curled in a sarcastic smile.

"Someone is going to see you here, you idiot," he spat, nervously looking around him. He reached out and grabbed her arm. "Sit down."

With deliberate slowness, she pulled out the chair across from him, and after rather intricate adjustments to her full, silk gown, sat on the hardwood most gracefully. "Relax," she breathed through an exaggerated sigh, "I'm covered from head to toe in these dreadful rags, as you can very well see, and nobody knows I'm here except Wayne."

Rags. To the queen, maybe. Gilbert took another large swallow of his ale, noting how very much she looked the daughter of a nobleman, especially in a place like this. If she stayed long she'd be noticed, draw attention to them, which they both knew would be a very bad thing under the circumstances.

"Where did he park?" he asked with a grunt.

"How should I know?" she retorted, glancing around. "Get me a sherry."

"Don't be stupid, they don't serve sherry in a place like this. Besides," he added gravely, "you won't be staying long enough to have a drink."

"Quit being so nervous," she threw back at him in whispered anger, "I just didn't know where else to find you."

"You could always find me at the theater."

She stared at him, aghast. "That would never be appropriate." She adjusted her sleeves for something to do with her hands. "Besides, you know I won't dare travel that far south."

Gilbert looked at her through furrowed brows. A flimsy excuse, but if nothing else, he would not allow Elinor to ruin everything now by being seen with him here. "What the devil do you want, and make it quick."

She smiled and leaned forward across the table, careful to avoid touching it. "More money," she mouthed in whisper.

He should have known. That's all Elinor ever wanted from him or anyone. "How much?"

"How much can you, a lowly actor of the stage, give me without being forced into debtor's prison, dear Gilbert?"

"How much do you think you need before being thrown out of your home and onto the street, dear Elinor?" he countered sarcastically, starting to tire of her game.

Her lips and eyes hardened simultaneously, but she avoided a retort. "Two thousand—"

"Go to bloody hell," he said as he raised his glass to finish the contents.

Elinor flashed him a crooked smile as she raised her hand, her pinkie only inches from his nose. "Remember where I have you wrapped?" she asked in a suddenly icy voice.

Gilbert wanted to reach across the table and break her little neck. Instead he offered her a rather pleasant smile in return as his eyes bore into hers, the actor in him coming out at last. "Did you know Steven is coming home?"

Elinor's entire demeanor swiftly changed, her youthful figure sagging into the chair as the meaning of that statement grabbed hold, and it took everything in him not to burst out laughing. He waited, adding nothing more, until she swallowed and took a deep breath, coming to terms with the significance of the news.

"When?" she whispered, her eyes wide with a new concern she couldn't hide, even in the corner darkness of the pub.

He reveled in that. "Soon," he said very quietly, and with intent. "From what I've heard, I think your brother misses you."

Suddenly the air around them shifted as she composed herself, straightening her rigid back, lifting her chin defiantly as her cheeks flushed with a renewed swell of anger. "There's no good in that. What sort of plan is the great Gilbert Montague concocting with the evil Steven Chester?"

Gilbert laughed again, ignoring her question. "Elinor, darling, how about five hundred now," he said as he leaned toward her, lowering his voice to a near-whisper, "and two thousand when I get the rest, for a combined total of two thousand, five hundred?"

She eyed him for a moment, suspiciously, and he knew she only tried to decide if he were hiding something. Gilbert candidly held her gaze, his lips wryly twisted, daring her to defy him again.

She hesitated, a scathing rebuttal no doubt on the tip of her tongue. But ultimately she suppressed it and leaned back again casually in her chair, folding her arms in her lap. "When are you expecting to get the rest?"

He shrugged as he finally looked away himself, toward the blond wench who laughed when a burly man with enormous hands grabbed her behind and squeezed.

"I don't know," he replied, sounding bored. "I told her I'd give her a week or two."

"What?" Elinor screeched as she stood, her chair scooting quickly back across the wooden floor, making enough noise to turn the heads of several bawdy gents.

"Sit down," Gilbert ordered with a hiss through clenched teeth.

Elinor stood her ground, her eyes glaring into his, nostril's flaring. "You said this would happen fast, that I'd have the manuscript back in my hands and that rotten son of a—"

"Careful, dear," Gilbert cut in, grinning again as he raised his glass to the barmaid, signaling her to deliver another. "That's no language for a lady."

She slapped the glass from his hands. Startled, he looked back into her eyes, now heated and overflowing with loathing.

"Do you want to hang?" she spat, her tone low and challenging. "I'm the smart one in this charade."

He ignored her question and slowly rose to tower over her, her physical beauty all but masked by a sordid personality. "Again, you're wrong, darling Elinor. *I'm* the lowly actor. Nobody cares about me. You're the one with everything to lose. Remember that."

With that whispered threat, Elinor relented, as he knew she would. She straightened her figure and took a step back.

"Just keep me informed," she warned, pulling gloves from her reticule and attempting to don them quickly. "I'll be waiting in Fowey." After a pause, she leaned toward him again, her eyes burning. "You just remember it's *my* manuscript."

He brushed over that, lowering his arms and planting his palms flat on the table.

"Don't come to me anymore, do you understand?" he warned. "I'll have the money sent to you in a few days. Now get the hell out of here before someone sees us together."

Without reply, Elinor lifted her chin high, turned her back on him, and gracefully waltzed out into the night.

Chapter 7

He knew just by being in her presence that Vivian was hoping he'd talk about himself and his past, about Elizabeth, her death and his trial for her murder. She was curious, not just in the manner as gossips from the town, but also as if she actually found it possible that he might not be as evil as society described him, wanting to judge the facts for herself. But even if that possibility warmed him inside, he still found it difficult to consider discussing it. He'd never felt close enough to anyone to bring the accusations, and his trial, into casual conversation, and as it had been the most difficult and emotional challenge of his entire life, he tried like hell to put that part of his past behind him in an attempt to forget it had ever happened. Not that his good intentions toward forgetting came to pass. Rarely a day went by that he didn't experience some reminder of that dreadful ordeal. His living nightmare. So now, for the present, he'd prefer to know more about *her*—background and past—before he disclosed his personal tribulations.

Sitting across from her now at dinner, watching candlelight shine off her hair to create a sheen on her clear, smooth skin, it occurred to him that although he'd known *of* the Widow Rael-Lamont for several years, he knew absolutely nothing about her personally. It was also quite possible that the information she offered socially to friends and acquaintances was totally fabricated, which, he had to admit, he hadn't considered before now. Of course by looking at her, daintily sipping her soup as she supped with him at his enormous dining room table that he almost never used, she bore herself so properly he had trouble envisioning her as a mere proprietor of a common flower business. No, Vivian Rael-Lamont was all sparkle and vibrant energy, a complex blend of intelligence, beauty, and secrets. An elegant lady on the outside, but with a flair that only hinted at a passionate woman within.

Will tried to concentrate on his food. He'd ordered Wilson to make sure the cook provided the best dinner served in his home in years, and the fare thus far had been outstanding. Tonight they dined on shrimp bisque, which would be followed by roasted fillet of veal in butter cream sauce, broccoli with almonds, ice pudding, orange slices, and brandied custard for dessert. A most delectable meal followed by what he hoped would be even more delectable kissing in the garden by moonlight.

They sat together quietly during the first course, making general conversation as footmen served each entree then stood in waiting by the sideboard. Will sensed that she had difficulty ignoring the servants and so he granted her silent request to keep personal topics at bay. At least until they were essentially alone. And as he watched her smile and move her hands in dramatic fashion while she spoke of something inconsequential that he only pretended to find of interest, he couldn't help but remember that brief brush of his lips to hers, his heated response to such a simple touch, and the gentle flush that had crept into her cheeks when he'd backed away. That had been days ago, and waiting this long to touch her again had been pure torture.

Now she sat directly across from him at the center of the long oak table, yet so close he could occasionally scent her perfume, watch the rise and fall of her breasts with each breath, catch the candlelight flickering in her eyes when she looked at him. She wore a simple yet elegant gown of burgundy silk, tightly corseted, with puffed, short sleeves and a surprisingly low, square neckline. She'd up-twisted her hair in some loose fashion, weaving in a strand or two of white, shiny pearls. Two simple pearls hung from her earlobes as well, but what kept capturing his attention was the one lone pearl that dangled from a gold chain to nestle itself right in the center of her smooth cleavage. Mesmerizing—

"Your grace?"

He blinked, realizing that he was staring again, and wondering, in some strange erotic manner, if she found it stimulating to know how much he admired her bosom.

"I'm sorry," he replied, sitting straighter in his chair and raising his fork to cut a bite of veal. "You were saying?"

She smirked and reached for her wineglass. "I *asked* you if you were aware of the new taxes levied this year on boats entering the harbor from abroad. They seem overrestrictive to me," she added, taking a sip.

Taxes on goods. He could think of nothing but bedding her naked body, combing his fingers through her loose, long hair, watching her eyelids close in abandoned desire as she welcomed him with arms opened . . . And she spoke of taxes. Unbelievable.

"In fact," she continued after swallowing, delicately slicing into a bud of her broccoli, "it's made it more difficult for me to get good bulbs at a decent price."

"Would you like me to attempt a change by introducing an act of Parliament for you?" he drawled, lips twisted in smile. "I wouldn't want to see your business suffer."

She jerked back a little, her eyes opening wide. "That had not occurred to me, your grace," she said at once, surprised and flustered and not at all aware that he teased her. "I mean—it was never my intention to take advantage of your station."

Will sat back in his chair, eyeing her frankly as he twisted the stem of his wineglass with his fingers.

"Advantage of my station?" he returned quietly. "That certainly sounds intriguing."

Color rose in her cheeks; that damn pearl glistened between her breasts as she squirmed slightly in her chair. To conceal her apparent discomfiture, she took a long swallow of her wine. He waited, gauging her reaction, scratching his jaw very slowly as he leaned on the armrest, enjoying himself thoroughly.

After patting her lips with her napkin and smiling politely to the footman who took her plate and offered more wine, she carried on as if he'd not spoken at all.

"I only became aware of how much this tax has risen from Vicar James, as he mentioned the difficulties imposed on all the working class during his sermon Sunday. I just wasn't certain if you'd heard—"

"I don't go to church," he said abruptly, his tone dropping a shade.

Her brow creased in thought as she tipped her head a fraction. "Whyever not?" she asked in perfect honesty.

She obviously hadn't considered it, and it made him all the more uncomfortable. He sat forward and folded his hands on the edge of the table. "Because I have sinned beyond reproach, remember? Why go to church when I am damned?"

She almost gasped. He could see the shock in her eyes as the dark pools reflected the flickering candles surrounding them. Silence reigned for seconds until one of his servants cleared his throat behind him, reminding them—or at least her—of the fact that they were not alone.

But to his utter disbelief, instead of cowering or begging his leave as any other lady would do, she suddenly sat up straighter and lifted her wineglass again.

"Nonsense," she retorted, looking him straight in the eye. "I don't for a minute believe that. I think perhaps you would do well not to listen to gossip, your grace. You of all people should set an example of your innocence, not hide from society as if you are guilty. Forgive me, sir, but you were not convicted of a crime. Staying away from church only makes you look fearful. Attending would, to all who noticed, make you look as if your innocence is beyond question. Whether you did the deed or not is irrelevant. That is between you and our Maker." With that, she took a final sip of her wine, smoothed her skirts, then muttered with a smile, "I believe I'm ready for dessert."

He hadn't been scolded like that in a long time, and in fact found it a bit staggering that she would speak so boldly to a member of his class. But more importantly, Will had a very difficult time digesting such a pronouncement, on many levels, causing him to abandon his teasing approach, his goading of her, while he considered the meaning of her words.

He had never thought of his acquittal that way, not in all the years since his trial. But she was right, he supposed. Hiding from society only perpetuated the rumors of his guilt. And yet by nature he remained a very private individual. He still could not imagine socializing with the elite, regardless of whether they thought him guilty and condemned of the crime of murder.

What stirred him internally, however, was Vivian, the woman sitting so close to him—the way she looked, smelled, acted. She was like a beautiful, haughty, elegant goddess with a sharp tongue that didn't irritate, but instead oddly aroused him. He no longer wanted dessert.

After a long, deep inhale, Will pushed his chair back and stood beside it, wondering if she would notice the fact that he was hard for her and that his pants could barely conceal it.

"I would like you to walk with me, Vivian," he said with soft insistence.

She glanced up to his face, confusion lighting her features. "Now?"

Unfortunately, she didn't appear to notice. No matter. She would know soon enough how badly he wanted her.

"Now," he repeated.

A footman was there at once to help her rise, which she did without further comment. Will walked to the end of the table where he waited for her, his arm raised, while she adjusted her skirts and then moved with shoulders erect to his side. Placing her warm palm on his forearm, he stared at her for a moment before proceeding, catching the light on her lovely face, her eyes so bright with uncertainty. Even with the ominous cloud of blackmail and mystery over their heads, it calmed him to have her there, a feeling he'd never experienced before in the presence of a woman.

Quietly, he led her from the dining room, through the music room and out the French doors to the garden where he'd kissed her so briefly only a few days ago.

"Do you know what I find strange, madam?" he asked as they walked side by side on the brick path, away from the main house.

"I'm sure I couldn't begin to guess," she replied softly, lifting her face and closing her eyes to the cool nighttime breeze.

He paused in thought for a moment, then murmured, "I find it strange that you never remarried."

He felt the slightest hesitation in her stride, but otherwise she didn't offer an explanation. And he wanted an explanation.

"I find it difficult to believe you had no suitors," he rephrased for her benefit, pushing for answers.

She sighed, stopping at last to gaze out over the expansive ocean she couldn't see at all through the darkness of night.

"I haven't wanted any suitors," she admitted at last.

He turned to face her, her expression hidden in shadow as the light of the house was behind her. "That's rather vague."

She dropped his arm and reached up absentmindedly to twist the pearl at her cleavage with her thumb and forefinger. "I suppose it is."

Will quashed his annoyance, placing his hands on his hips beneath the edges of his frock coat. "You haven't . . . longed for the particular companionship that comes from a marital union? How is that possible?"

That delicate topic made her uncomfortable, though he could only really just sense it.

"I've been busy," she said with a mild shrug.

He didn't like that answer at all. It was far too evasive and she knew it as well. "Too busy to enjoy the pleasures only a man can give you?" he asked more directly.

She took a step back, crossing her arms in front of her. "Your grace, I don't think—"

"Why do you refuse to call me Will?"

He couldn't hide the irritation in his tone, and at this point he didn't want to.

She touched one palm to her forehead briefly, with the other she continued to play with the pearl lying between her uplifted breasts. She couldn't possibly know how that mindless action threatened to undo him. It took every ounce of strength within him not to grab her and pull her into his arms.

"I don't think it's proper for me to do so," she admitted quietly after a moment.

Such a ridiculous answer made him shake his head. "You don't think it's proper when I have asked you and we are alone like this?"

She turned her attention to him, though he still couldn't read her features with the light from the house silhouetting her.

"You are a duke," she said, as if he'd forgotten that simple fact.

Roughly, he raked his fingers through his hair. "I'm also a man, Vivian."

She exhaled loudly before she replied, "I'm fully aware of that."

"Are you?"

She stilled, watching him.

Will chose that moment to make contact. Gingerly, he raised his hand and placed it over hers, covering the pearl, laying warm skin on warm skin, relishing the jolt that sliced through him when he felt the quickening of her heartbeat beneath the rise and fall of her breasts.

"You know I'm going to make love to you," he said, his voice husky and low.

She sucked in a shaky breath but didn't back down, which he found infinitely gratifying.

"Yes," she whispered.

He drew his thumb across her hot skin, softly pushing it under the edge of her gown as he pressed close to her nipple, his eyes never leaving the shadows of her face.

"But how awkward and sad it would be," he continued, his own breathing becoming unstable, "if when I take you in passion, you do not cry out my name, but my title instead."

She trembled now; he could feel a shudder course through her body. Enough of the foreplay. He'd well made his point.

Still clasping her hand with his against her breasts, Will leaned over and took her mouth with his, more forcefully than he had the first time they'd so touched. She made a soft mewing sound in her throat at first contact, but she didn't pull away.

Such shyness without reluctance, such tenderness underlying what had to be trepidation on her part, made him come alive inside. It had been so hard to hold back, so hard not to *feel*, and for now, Will allowed himself to wallow in the pleasure of being with a woman who so obviously desired him in spite of his past.

Alone in the garden, encircled by a soft sea breeze and the sweet scent of flowers, he pressed for more, wanting her to open for him and accept the beginning of the ecstasy to come. He reached behind her back, splaying his large hand across her spine, and pulled her toward him.

His mouth teased without force and she followed his lead, gradually opening for him as he gently pried. He moaned as she flicked his upper lip with the tip of her tongue, holding back the urge to lift her, hoops and all, and carry her to his bed chamber or down the path toward the sandy beach below.

Suddenly he felt her arm wrap around his neck as she gave more of herself to the moment. His tongue sought hers, grasping it faintly and sucking the edge as she whimpered and pushed herself closer into his palm at her breast.

She needed him now, wanted him fully, and as he was vaguely aware that she ran her fingers through his hair, he lowered his hand over her gown to cover her, squeezing minutely, teasing the nipple he couldn't feel but managed to imagine stood erect and sensitive in all its beauty.

Her breathing had grown as shallow as his; her urging at his mouth made him increasingly hard as he longed to push himself inside her sweet softness. He pressed her against him as tightly as possible, cursing the layers of clothes that kept the heat of her skin from scorching his own. She continued to allow him his delicate pursuit, her luscious lips assaulting his now in delicious form, in a fever of yearning she could no longer control.

He ran the edge of his thumb back and forth over the tip of her covered breast, causing her to gasp softly against his mouth as she shuddered in his arms, pulling herself against him now in growing hunger. But as she began to trace his upper lip with her tongue, he knew he could take no more from her without completion. It had been too long.

Groaning as much with frustration as passion, Will lifted his lips from hers, only a little at first to allow her to understand that he was ending the kiss, the embrace, in an attempt to tame the fire within before it consumed him and ignited what remained of his control.

She didn't want to let him go, and for several seconds after he pulled back she continued to press little kisses against his lips and chin, the side of his face.

"Vivian . . ." he whispered, grasping her shoulders, thoroughly warmed from the openness she conveyed in her sweet caress.

For a moment or two she didn't seem to hear him. And then suddenly she lowered her head and took a wavering step back, raising her hand to cover her mouth.

They stood apart for minutes as their breathing calmed, their rationality returned, listening to the cool night air rustle the leaves around them. He didn't know what to say exactly, but he refused to let her go without comment.

"When?" she finally murmured, her fingers still covering her lips.

He understood what she asked even as it surprised him that she'd spoken first. But if it had never mattered before, with this woman timing was everything.

He bit down hard to subdue what was left of his desire. "When I'm ready."

Her head jerked up as she gazed to what she could see of his face.

"When—when you are ready?" she repeated, confusion threading her tone.

He inhaled a surprisingly steady breath, then said with conviction, "When I agreed to trade the manuscript for companionship, Vivian, I meant it all. I have missed having a woman in my life for years." He reached out and touched his fingertips to her cheek, immensely pleased that she didn't jerk away from him. "I hope you didn't think I pursued you for a romp. You are more to me than the temporary enjoyment of one short bedding."

He heard her gasp faintly from the sincerity of his words, felt her shake her head minutely as if trying to comprehend the depth of his implication. And then finally she closed her arms over her stomach and took a step away from him.

He dropped his hands to his sides, a sinking feeling weighing in his gut as he waited for her to deny him.

At last she turned her head and gazed out toward the ocean. "When would you like me to return?"

The relief he experienced at that moment was utterly palpable. Trying not to grin, he replied, "I'll send word."

Seconds later, she nodded, then shook herself and lowered her arms to stand elegantly erect once more. "It's getting late, sir."

"Indeed," he returned without inflection. "I'll have my driver see you home."

He expected her to turn and walk away from him then, but she didn't. Instead, she took a step or two in his direction, pausing in front of him before she placed her palm on his shirtfront, over his heart.

Gazing up into his eyes, she whispered, "Will . . ."

And then she lifted her skirts and left him standing in amazement, alone in his huge, darkened garden.

Chapter 8

~~~~~~~~

"**M**r. Clement Hastings is here, your grace. He says it's important."

Will had been writing at his desk for what seemed like hours, and this unexpected interruption came at a most convenient time. He needed the break. And since it had been a week without news, he found himself suddenly anxious.

"Send him in at once, Wilson," he ordered, leaning back in his chair for a long stretch, then standing abruptly to receive his guest.

Moments later the investigator appeared before him wearing burgundy and plum striped pants and, oddly enough for him, a plain white silk shirt. He did cover it with a plaid waistcoat in an unfortunate shade of green, however. Will tried to ignore it. The man had remarkable taste. If one could call it taste.

"Good afternoon, your grace." Hastings greeted him with a standard smile and formal bow.

"Hastings." Will motioned for him to take a seat in his usual chair of choice, which the man did. Will chose to remain standing, feeling a bit confined and anxious under the circumstances. It had been a week since Vivian had visited for dinner, kissing him with her luscious warm lips, and since that time, he'd learned nothing of value from his investigator. He was now more than ready to move forward as he wanted a bit more assurance of her intentions before he seduced her even further.

Hastings adjusted his waistcoat and reached into the pocket for his notes—a thin, black bound book the size of his palm. Opening it, he began without ceremony.

"Gilbert Montague, aside from his work on the stage, is a rather boring character, no pun intended of course." He laughed at himself, adjusting his thick legs under the tea table before continuing. "For several years he worked as an actor on the Continent and most people believe him to be fairly talented. The productions he's been part of in Penzance, and before here, Truro, have made a little money, and his company of actors, regardless of their . . . sort have been well-received. I have yet to find information regarding his past, where he was raised, contacts, friends, or any schooling as a youth, though I've got two men working on it from the home office in London. It is entirely possible that he changed his name at some point, which I consider likely, as Montague the man, according to the few facts we've discovered thus far, simply appeared from nowhere to enter the acting circuit about seven years ago."

Hastings paused for a moment, apparently to give Will time to digest this most recent news. Will stared at the floor, fighting the urge to pace, leaning his hip on his desk as he consciously decided to draw no conclusions at this point.

The investigator cleared his throat forcefully and scratched the back of his head. "There's a bit more, your grace."

Will raised his brows and glanced at the man, who suddenly appeared hesitant. "Go on then," he urged.

Hastings pursed his lips and nodded. "One thing I did discover that I thought was rather curious, sir, and of course could mean absolutely nothing, was the fact that he left for the Continent a mere five days after the end of your . . . er . . . trial, and returned one year ago, moving very quickly into the acting circles that only toured in Cornwall. As an actor of such high esteem, the London stage would be a more likely choice, I should think, which makes the timing and his questionable employment seem somewhat peculiar, even coincidental. Again, it probably has no bearing on you, but I thought you should know."

Will felt a tremor of coldness slice through him at the mention of his trial, memories he attempted to push from his thoughts with every waking moment. Hearing a notion that this actor, Vivian, and the signed manuscript might somehow be connected to his past—even remotely so—stirred the inner self-hatred he still fought to suppress even as it ignited the remembrance of the horror he experienced during those dark days and freezing nights of what now seemed so long ago.

God, what he would give to make it all go away . . .

"Your grace?"

Will jerked his head up, looking at his agent of inquiry with the realization that he'd missed something. "Hastings. Sorry." He wiped a palm across his face, then stood erect, tense, arms at his sides as he walked toward the bookcases to his left. "You were saying?"

"Yes," the man repeated, "I saved the interesting news for last."

"Interesting news?" Frowning, he turned his attention back to his guest. There was more to this bloody nightmare?

"Yes, sir, one more thing of note," Hastings replied gravely as if reading his thoughts. "I've had the man followed every night after leaving the theater and every night for the last few days his routine has been more or less the same. He usually frequents a pub on New Street, near the harbor, called The Jolly Knights, with a *K*, where he apparently gets his fill of drink and food and sometimes . . . uh . . . lewd woman, after which he retreats to his rented room at the Regent Hotel. Last night, however, was different."

Will narrowed his eyes. "He met someone."

Hastings's brows shot up as if he hadn't thought

the duke could make such a deduction on his own. "As a matter of record, yes. That's primarily what I came to share with you, sir. I wasn't there to witness it, of course, but my man thought the meeting was highly unusual."

Slowly, Will began to walk to the opposite chair. "Unusual? Why?"

Hastings paused to turn a page in his book, "Montague sat in the same place he always does, toward the back of the room, for approximately . . . forty-five minutes, when he was approached by a lady."

"A lady? Not a common woman?"

"Yes, sir, a very small, and we believe very blond lady of some wealth who came in looking specifically for him. She wore a black, hooded pelisse—fur-trimmed, very well made—and clothing of the highest quality. Carried herself with prestige."

Will sat heavily in his chair, noting how the leather comfortably conformed to his weight. This *was* news. "Have you learned who she is?"

Hastings shook his head, his forehead creased into several deep wrinkles that well reflected his age. "No, not yet. I wanted to try and get some information on her to give you but so far we have nothing. My man wasn't able to follow her when she left, though she did appear to have her own driver." Smiling wryly, he added, "But the short conversation she held with the actor, and his reaction to her, seemed to be quite interesting. I thought, even lacking her identity, you would want to know."

Fascinated, Will leaned forward, resting his elbows on his knees. "What was said?"

"Well, we don't know exactly, your grace. They generally spoke in whispers and nobody could get close enough to hear, but they did talk as if they knew each other well and, oddly enough, for only five minutes or so. At one point Montague said or did something she didn't like and the woman stood abruptly, with enough irritation to force her chair back a foot or so. They talked for another moment or two and then she left."

"Did your man get a good look at her?"

Hastings rubbed his jowls, shaking his head in the negative. "Unfortunately, no. He couldn't see much of her face, although he said she did appear attractive and fairly young, probably less than thirty years of age. The intriguing thing, of course, was that she obviously didn't belong in a place like The Jolly Knights, meaning, I suppose, that she appeared to be a lady of breeding. She took great risk in entering the pub alone to see anyone, which in turn makes the meeting all the more significant."

Indeed it did. "Is that all?"

"For now, your grace."

Will sat in silence for several long moments, contemplating these new pieces to the puzzle that less than two short weeks ago had altered the grim reality of what had been the banal routine of his life. A puzzle that had brought him the beautiful Widow Rael-Lamont.

Abruptly he stood again, no longer able to control his desire to pace. Now more than ever he wanted to get to the bottom of things, for he was getting restless, impatient. He was also starting to worry and he didn't like to worry. Things were moving far too slowly for his taste. Turning back toward Hastings who sat quietly in his chair waiting for instructions as he always did, the duke regarded the floor in thought.

"How many men are on this?" he asked, his gaze still fixed on the plush carpet beneath his shoes.

"Four, your grace."

"I'll make it worth your while if you can double that number," he remarked, looking Hastings in the eye again.

"I can do that, sir, but I really don't want to scare the man off. I believe he thinks he's being watched—"

"What makes you think that?" Will cut in, his voice edged with concern.

Hastings sighed and slumped into his colorful waistcoat, closing his notebook and returning it to his pocket. "I don't know exactly. It's more of a gut feeling I have really. He isn't nervous and he hasn't changed his daily habits at all. In many ways I think he's . . . expecting it." He cocked his head, thinking shrewdly. "I almost get the impression that he wants to be noticed, that he's waiting for something to happen. The most interesting thing of all was his reaction to the woman. Upon seeing her, he looked around nervously as if afraid that someone would see the two of them conversing." Expelling a long breath, he concluded, "I suppose I could reasonably assume they're working together, though if that's the case, she's acting with stupidity and Montague knows it. I don't think we'll see them together again."

Will nodded his agreement. "It's possible she's using him, or paying him, to get the manuscript herself."

"Possible, yes."

"Then, Hastings, the woman is the key. She may have more answers than the actor, supposing you can find her. I want you to put four additional men on the search for her starting today."

"Certainly, your grace. A good course of action, and we'll start with the pelisse. It was quite unusual looking and very good quality. Expensive. Very few makers of clothing would get orders like that to fill. I believe we'll find that she's someone with a great deal of money, perhaps even a member of the nobility, although what a member of the social class would have in common with a lowly actor, I couldn't guess." Hastings stood at last and pulled down on his waistcoat. "I'll be in touch, your grace, as soon as we have something to report."

Will nodded in response as the investigator bowed appropriately and walked to the door of the library. There he paused, glancing back.

"Your grace, if I may be so bold?"

Surprised, Will looked at him. "Yes, what is it?"

Hastings hesitated. "Your grace, this man is very clever, and I believe he's an exceptional planner and thinker. I do not believe he's aware he's being followed right now, but I wouldn't be so quick to assume the man hasn't thought you might hire someone to watch him. If that is the case, he could very well lead us to false ends. I'd watch my step if I were you, sir, and remember one last thing, this man makes a living on pretense."

A living on pretense.

"Thank you, Hastings. Keep me informed."

With that, the investigator took his leave.

In deep thought, Will walked to the windows, gazing out across the far-reaching ocean without seeing.

Every time someone mentioned a small, blond woman he was overcome with images of Elizabeth, making his heart ache and his mood darken with despair. Someday he hoped her tragic death could be remembered without the bitterness of lies. Someday he hoped to move on.

Suddenly Vivian's serene, mature beauty came to mind, and he smiled.

Someday . . .

Chapter 9

Vivian sat as daintily as possible in the hot humid air, tucking her skirts in as close to her body as possible to allow more parishioners to squeeze in beside her on the hard wooden pew at St. Mary's Church. She didn't particularly want to be here this morning, and it had little to do with the heat. Today's sermon would no doubt be long and tedious, at least for her, because, annoyingly enough, she found it so incredibly difficult to concentrate on anything but the taste and feel of Will Raleigh's lips against hers. And there had to be something horridly wrong in thinking of it in church. That didn't seem to stop her, though. Surely God understood the frailties of human nature.

The organist began to play a somber piece she

didn't recognize, and she closed her eyes, pretending to all who noticed that she was simply either deep in prayer, or wallowing in the beauty of the music. Only a glance to her hands now clutched in her lap would lend any indication that she was tense, her thoughts on darker subjects.

She hadn't wanted to attend this morning, but forced herself to since she would be meeting with Vicar James and his wife this afternoon regarding flower arrangements for their daughter's wedding next month. In her position, she couldn't very well be ill for one and not the other.

Just as the choir began the final number before the beginning of the service, a murmur or two began around her, growing in resonance with each passing second. Vivian opened her eyes. The music continued at a quicker pace, until a gasp escaped the suddenly dropped mouth of Mrs. Trister, the organist, as she hit a wrong key. The music faded. Immediately everybody, it seemed, twisted their necks to look to the back of the sanctuary, mouths gaping, at which point Vivian realized the Duke of Trent had arrived for early Sunday Mass.

She didn't turn around, and no doubt that was a mistake since everybody else in the crowded church did. It also dawned on her, moments later, that he would attempt to sit as near to her as possible. Quickly she took a glance down her pew, four from the front, to notice, thankfully, that it was entirely too full for anyone to squeeze in comfortably beside her, especially a large man. Then again, he was a duke. He could very well sit anywhere he pleased, and it would be expected for him to go to the front. Somehow, though, she knew he wouldn't do that.

The rumblings from the crowd increased, and Vivian could no longer contain her curiosity. She had to look at him.

Straightening her back for confidence, she turned and gazed to the entrance of the church.

His appearance took her breath away.

He stood tall and stately at the top of the center aisle, in front of the waiting processional of the vicar and altar boys, his handsome face clean-shaven, hair combed back from his lovely hazel eyes which exuded confidence and an inner— almost defiant—strength. He was dressed entirely in navy, save for a honey-colored shirt, in a suit of expensive silk expertly tailored to fit his large form beautifully.

Hands clasped behind him, he acknowledged Vicar James with a slight tip of his head, then once more faced the obviously discomfited congregation before he began to make his way down the center aisle to find an appropriate seat.

Vivian swiftly turned back to the altar, not certain whether she wanted him near her or not. True, she'd been the one to encourage him to attend church, if *encourage* could be the right word. But then she didn't exactly want the attention from social acquaintances should he choose to speak to her. How the gossip would spread!

She could hear his shoes on the wooden floor even over the sound of the organ, which had resumed its play, however irregular and out of place it sounded now. Suddenly, without looking, she realized he stood just behind her. She didn't move.

With a sudden rustling of skirts and bodies, she became ever more aware that he would be sitting at her back, though she was undoubtedly the only one who realized he did that on purpose. It was just the sort of spot for him to watch every move she made, and where she couldn't help but be aware of him.

He knelt to pray—or perhaps just to tease her with the shocking closeness of his presence—and Vivian caught a quick whiff of his cologne, could absolutely feel his warm breath on the bare skin of her neck, making tiny hairs stand on end with his steady exhalations. Then, through the faintest of whispers at her ear, she heard, "If only I knew what I'd been missing . . ."

Vivian wanted to crawl under her pew, because everyone, absolutely *everyone*, continued to stare at him while pretending not to. She felt the heat rise to her cheeks at once, her palms begin to perspire as she clutched her fan more tightly in her lap, hoping to God nobody had heard him, or noticed just how close he was to her exposed flesh. But she refused to respond to him, or glance over her shoulder just yet.

The music took on a more somber note as the processional started, the vicar and altar boys slowly making their way down the aisle toward the altar to begin the service. As soon as the vicar passed, the duke sat back in his seat, and she forced herself not to show her relief by letting her shoulders droop and her body sag into her corset.

The music continued until everyone was seated

and the vicar stood at the podium, Mrs. Trister playing in earnest, likely just as shocked as everyone else, hoping in some measure to impress such a high-standing member of the nobility.

At last Vicar James cleared his throat, and with a tip of his head, acknowledged the acclaimed guest. "Your grace, we welcome you this morning."

There were vague murmurs from the congregation, but the duke said nothing in response.

For three quarters of an hour, Vicar James droned on about sin and redemption, a thoroughly inappropriate topic considering the status of their all-important noble resident, and the vicar well knew it, as he stumbled once or twice and appeared flustered through most of the sermon.

Vivian did indeed have trouble following it, and the usually decent choir seemed to fare little better with their sense of key. It was simply a profound hour in the recent history of the Penzance community, and everybody knew it.

At last the final song was played, the final admonition and prayer given, and the congregation allowed to exit. Vivian had no idea what to do.

Will watched the entire spectacle with some amusement. Of course he knew what the reaction of the townspeople would be once they realized who he was and took note of him. He couldn't begin to care. His only interest was in shocking Vivian, though he wasn't at all sure why he wanted to do that either. He just did.

But reluctantly, he had to admit he was nervous,

and had been since he'd awoken this morning with the notion of attending church of all places. Still, it gave him the perfect opportunity to observe the Widow Rael-Lamont in action, so to speak, meaning, he supposed, that he wanted to watch her move in her circles. Or maybe he just wanted to look at her.

He'd also found it quite amusing that she made herself openly obvious to him when she was the only member of the entire congregation who didn't turn around to gawk when he appeared. For some unknown reason he gravitated to her. And he only hoped she liked his nearness as much as he liked hers.

Of course he met with Vicar James on occasion, but always at his home, never here or in town. The fact that the man had so much difficulty in blurting out his message today had to be due largely to Will's presence in the congregation and to the subject of overcoming one's sins. Such a common topic seemed to be directed to him this day, quite obvious to everyone. How unfortunate.

Of course Will had learned to adjust his thoughts regarding how the general public accepted him. He was a murderer in their eyes, and nothing he could do, no acquittal he might win, would ever prove his innocence to them.

But Vivian had come to him, besting her fear, if she had any at all to begin with, and he had enjoyed her company more than that of any woman in years. He supposed she was the draw this morning, not the vicar, guilt, or repentence, and certainly not the message. He was more or less on display, and he hated it. But he also managed to seat himself behind her so that for nearly an hour he could watch her slight movements, take note of the line of her smooth neck and shoulders, and even catch the slightest trace of the scent of her—all warmth, perfume, and woman. The thrill of the moment with her right now did nothing short of arouse him. And that, he supposed, was probably a greater sin in church than that which he'd ever done to his wife.

After what seemed like hours and hours, the choir sang their departing hymn and the congregation rose to leave. After dressing and taking the time to come here today, he refused to allow the moment to go to waste.

Swiftly, as he stepped from his pew, the surrounding people backed a bit away from him. Whether that was due to his title or their continued revulsion to him, he couldn't guess, but fortunately it did allow him to take up the space between Vivian and her best exit should she try to escape him.

At last she turned so that he could see her face. For the first time that morning, he had to hold back a smile of satisfaction.

His presence here had shocked her, he could plainly see that now. Her cheeks were flushed a dewy pink, her hair pulled up into a loose bun of curls with tendrils plastered across her forehead and neck from the irritating heat. But her eyes held his in the most peculiar way. Bold, intimidating and yet intimidated, they entranced him.

He could read anger, surprise, and even a touch of gladness in her expression. If there was one thing he enjoyed, it was making Vivian squirm.

"Madam," he said softly, raising his arm in her direction.

One or two of the ladies to his side gasped; Vivian's eyes simply opened wider as she realized he wanted her to take his arm and exit the church with him. And considering his rank and her position in the community she could hardly refuse. Nor would she.

Inside a cluster of bodies making their way toward the entrance of the sanctuary, Vivian Rael-Lamont walked beside him, her arm interlocked with his. She was tense, and none too pleased to be more or less forced into this position, and yet she made every effort to smile to those around her as if nothing was out of the ordinary. He had to admire her for that.

The bright sunlight hit them squarely as they paused on the front steps of the east-facing church. At last he leaned over to whisper in her ear, "Thank you for that."

Immediately she jerked her head to the side to glance up to his face, the irritation he read in her eyes dissolving as quickly as it was replaced with sympathy. He didn't need that, nor had he expected it exactly, but he tried his best to ignore it.

"Well, Mrs. Rael-Lamont. So good to see you here this lovely Sunday morning."

They both turned together at the intrusion. Evelyn Stevens stood in their path, one step below, gazing up to them with interest and a bit of malicious humor in her pale blue eyes.

Vivian dropped her arm from his as quickly as if she'd been shocked.

"Mrs. Stevens. How good to see *you*," she remarked congenially, as if standing next to one of the most famous accused murderers of their decade were nothing significant whatsoever.

He just stood there, and after a few long seconds, several other women surrounded them like chickens drawn to tossed grain.

One by one, they curtsied as they should, all eyeing him with various expressions of amazement, concern, and sheer inquisitiveness. But their curiosity over his obvious friendship with the Widow Rael-Lamont had them fidgeting in their stays.

Will groaned inwardly, but otherwise said nothing, only nodded to each one who acknowledged him with the appropriate formality.

Vivian came alive with confidence as a sort of vague conversation began among the women, their husbands standing off to the sides either in deep discussions with each other, or uncomfortable in the moment, hands in pockets as they tried in vain to pull their wives from the scene. Not one, however, chose to speak to him, and Will simply accepted that for what it was.

"I noticed the roses on the altar this morning were in high bloom. Were they from you, Mrs. Rael-Lamont?"

A rather trivial question, but they all managed to look at Vivian with a measure of intense interest, including him, mostly to see how she would handle such an awkward situation.

"Yes, indeed they are from my stock, Mrs. Stevens," she returned with a pleasant smile, "purchased by Mr. and Mrs. Weston for services today. I thought they were most appropriate for a sunny, summer morning."

"Of course," Evelyn Stevens agreed, her lips pulled back into a flat smile. "You obviously have excellent taste."

"It is her . . . means of employment, Evelyn," piped in a very plump Elizabeth Boseley, who managed to take up two steps with her large frame and full skirts.

Nobody said anything to that, although it couldn't help but be known that such a comment about a woman and her occupation was intended to be cutting.

In a soft tone laced with charm, Vivian countered, "I find working with flowers and plants to be rather exhilarating as well, Mrs. Boseley. It's refreshing to be outside, work with one's hands, and have others in the community appreciate one's effort."

Everybody more or less nodded in agreement, mostly, Will surmised, because they would be expected to be gracious, especially just coming from church.

Grace Tildair fiddled with her parasol, having some trouble opening it, and they all watched her as if thoroughly fascinated, trying their blessed best not to stare at *him*. Frankly, he didn't give a damn. The only thing he seemed to be aware of at the moment was the smell of Vivian's perfume as it drifted toward him in the breezy air. Not being able to appropriately touch her was suddenly killing him.

Someone cleared a throat. Then, "Your grace, you seem . . . well."

He lifted a brow and looked into the eyes of a

woman he didn't even recognize as someone he had ever met before.

"Thank you," he said laconically.

Murmurs around them began to cease as church-goers gradually departed the front step, making their way home for Sunday dinner. He, Vivian, and the immediate ladies remained standing where they were, however, as if their curiosity was so thoroughly piqued by his presence they couldn't move.

Finally, Mrs. Tildair got that damn parasol up and faced him once again with a full, false smile on her aging lips.

"Well, then," she piped in.

They all looked at her.

"And how, may I ask, are you acquainted with the Widow Rael-Lamont, your grace?" she asked without reservation.

Will could feel Vivian tense at his side. He drew in a long breath, clasping his hands behind him. "She supplies the flowers for my estate, naturally."

"Oh, naturally," someone mumbled.

Mrs. Boseley chuckled. "How very brave you are, Mrs. Rael-Lamont."

With that comment lacking any kind of social refinement, someone gasped. The air turned chilly, even with the summer sun beating down on their exposed skin.

Will didn't know exactly if the woman had meant her words maliciously or not, though he suspected she had. He had grown weary of such rudeness over the years, but he bloody hell didn't appreciate it in front of Vivian. If he hadn't been so intent on seeing her reaction to him in public, conversing regally with her peers, he wouldn't have shown up in so public a place. He now realized just how colossal a mistake he had made. He should never have come today.

"I'm sorry, Mrs. Boseley," Vivian said in all sincerity, "but I don't understand. In what manner am I being brave?"

That rebuttal shocked everybody present, including him. Mrs. Tildair's parasol fell back and she made a great effort in righting it again; Evelyn Stevens took a step to her side and looked at the ground as if she'd dropped something; the woman he didn't know coughed, covering her mouth with her hands; someone else's husband tapped her shoulder and said, "I'm starved, my dear." She brushed his hand off her shoulder without looking at him, engrossed in the conversation.

Silence lingered for more than a few seconds as Will glanced down at Vivian, his mind filled with distracting thoughts of her luscious body coupled with a sense of amazement at her ingenuity, taking particular note of her neatly combed, mahogany-colored hair, shiny in the sun, wondering at her thoughts. For everything she said and did, he *liked* this woman.

Mrs. Boseley, realizing her gaffe, chuckled with a sudden awkwardness, placing a plump hand covered with expensive rings on her chest defensively.

"Of course I didn't mean to be unpleasant," she stated with forced conviction. "It's just that I've not seen his grace at any social function in perhaps years, and here he is today, escorting you."

117

Vivian fell in line with the woman's weak explanation. "Oh nonsense, Mrs. Boseley. I've met him before as I've delivered flowers to his home, and as it happened, he simply sat behind me this morning in a crowded church. That's all."

Will found it absolutely astonishing that they spoke of him as if he wasn't even there. And he had no intention of interrupting. It was becoming all too amusing in an oddly uncomfortable way.

"But with all due respect, Mrs. Rael-Lamont," the woman continued, "today's lesson from the pulpit seemed particularly . . . appropriate under the circumstances."

Vivian pulled back a little and shook her head daintily. "Under what circumstances?"

Mrs. Boseley had the courtesy to flush with hot color. "I'm sure I don't have to tell you the vicar discussed sin, Mrs. Rael-Lamont. Were you not listening?"

"We have all sinned," Vivian returned at once, her voice now dripping with disdain. "Would you dare to cast stones, madam?"

Mrs. Boseley gasped loudly, her mouth dropping open as she dramatically clutched her neck. The other ladies simply gaped at Vivian, stunned at her boldness and unable to move or speak.

Will finally decided it was time to interrupt, reminding them all that the sinner stood amongst them.

He cleared his throat and rubbed his neck of perspiration brought on by the increasing heat.

"Is it not true, ladies," he began very slowly, "that

if God had not given us the ability to sin freely, we would not recognize it, thereby never learn from that recognition?"

It was as if he had appeared from a ghostlike state right into the center of the Ladies' Society for Better Interpretation of Biblical Scripture or some other such well-intended meeting of female minds. They all stared up at him silently with varying degrees of horror.

He smiled in satisfaction, adding, "Would it then be fair to say that a true child of the universe learns how it is to be Godlike from actually partaking in sin and being fortunate enough to observe it in others? We are only redeemed when we recognize sin in ourselves and beg forgiveness. I would submit to you, then, that sin is a natural product of the universe, created by our Lord, intended to teach."

That shut every one of them up, including Vivian, who now looked at him in astonishment as the others did. He almost laughed.

Vivian was the first to recover herself. With the straightening of her spine and the clasping of her closed fan with both hands in front of her, she gazed up at him, thoughtfully looking into his eyes as she daintily shook her head.

"My lord Duke, I had no idea you were a philosopher."

The other ladies simply gaped at her.

He tipped his head once to her. "I have little else to do but read, Mrs. Rael-Lamont."

"You'd do well to be reading the Good Book, your grace," Mrs. Boseley admonished.

His brows lifted. "And who's to say I'm not, madam?"

The whole lot of them seemed to twitch in their stays from that comment.

He glanced down to Vivian again. A slow grin widened across her mouth.

"Indeed, sir," she said pleasantly. "Would you care to walk me to my doorstep, your grace? I only live around the corner and I would enjoy hearing some of your philosophic interpretations of our holy book."

She asked him politely and yet dared him with her eyes. He couldn't begin to assume what she felt at that moment and decided not to try.

"I'd be delighted, Mrs. Rael-Lamont."

"Good." Turning back to the women of her acquaintance, she nodded once to them. "I shall see you all on Tuesday for tea at Mrs. Safford's cottage."

One by one, they curtsied to him, without response, likely due to the fact that they'd been made speechless. For him, after all these years of solitude, it was a priceless moment.

"Good day, ladies," he remarked. Then he offered his arm to Vivian once more, and she took it without reservation. Together they began to stride down the street, turning more than one head with the very odd look of a local widow who makes a living selling flowers clinging to the forearm of the Duke of Trent. For Will, it felt marvelous, a feeling of freedom he hadn't experienced in years.

They strolled silently at a relaxing pace until they rounded the corner onto Pillar Street. At that point, when they were at last out of range of prying eyes, Vivian sped up a bit, releasing her grasp of him as she more or less hurried to her house.

Will grew mildly perplexed at her change in demeanor until he crossed the threshold of her porch that intentionally hid the front door with clinging vines and pots of sweet-scented flowers.

Suddenly she whirled around to face him, her eyes flashing an anger he had never seen in her.

That stopped him abruptly. "I suppose you're mad at me."

Her lips drew back into a thin line as her lids narrowed. "Of course I'm mad at you!" she seethed in whisper. "When I suggested attending church as a way to redeem your character and good name, I didn't mean for you to purposely seek *me* out *this* Sunday." She closed her eyes and placed her palm on her forehead in an attempt to calm herself. "Do you have any idea how your attention to me this morning could very well cost me my social status in Penzance? I rely on that, sir, for my well-being. God, how all of that must have looked."

That statement struck him hard at gut level. His mind went numb as his blood turned cold. When he said nothing in response, she opened her eyes again, noticing immediately how her words had affected him. Her mouth opened slightly and her shoulders sagged. "Your grace . . ." Her voice trailed off and she simply looked at him, confusion on her brow melding with a hint of sorrow and regret.

"You have no idea why I sought you this morning," he stated, not expecting an answer.

She just continued to look at him, dumbfounded.

His jaw tensed as he clasped his hands behind him. "And all this time I was hoping to kiss you. I think I shall find my driver instead. Good day, Mrs. Rael-Lamont."

He turned on his heel and left her.

Chapter 10

She'd had enough of being used.

Vivian sat lazily on the settee, hands folded in her lap, staring at the ceiling in her parlor as she took note of the wallpaper: fat little cherubs, golden scrolls, intertwining vines and pink roses. It was perhaps a bit flowery, some might say meretricious, but this was *her* room, *her* house, *her* life to choose the style in which to live it. She had demonstrated that numerous times, to friends and those who loved her. But in the course of three weeks her very secure world had been turned upside down—first by a devious actor, of all people, and then by *him*.

Vivian closed her eyes and shivered as she remembered with clarity the feel of his large hands on her back, his lips on hers, his gravelly sigh as he pulled her tightly into his arms. He was a man who wanted her, probably needed her for more than her sexuality, and yet there was so much else involved, so many hidden issues to be resolved. So many secrets.

"Mrs. Rael-Lamont, this just came for you."

Vivian opened her eyes and stood quickly, acknowledging her housekeeper who had entered the parlor to hand her a note.

"Thank you, Harriet," she said, taking the plain white paper from the woman's outstretched fingers.

Harriet nodded once, then turned and left the parlor.

There was no indication of its sender from the purple sealing wax on the back, so Vivian used her finger to pull it apart. Instantly, she felt herself go numb.

I am leaving Saturday for Thuro. You have six days. GM

Gilbert Montague . . . A man who would destroy her life as surely as if he wielded a knife and cut her heart out with the skill of a hunter.

And with that vivid thought, the most amazing thing happened. Along with sharp feelings of betrayal, helplessness, and rage, she also unexpectedly felt a burst of renewed energy course through her, threatening to bubble over, forcing a dose of absurd laughter to escape her. Seconds later her eyes began to water from her now uncontrollable fit of giggles, and she covered her mouth with her palm should Harriet think she'd gone mad.

But it was all too suddenly, intensely funny for her sensibilities. How, dear God, had her ordinary, simple life become so twisted? How did she come to allow two totally different men to control her destiny? Why was she at *their* mercy? She had never been one to shrink from difficulties, but to face them with dignity. At that moment she came to the realization that it wasn't these two powerful men, so diametrically opposite each other, who'd caused the problems she now faced, but rather her reaction of cowardice in allowing them to use her. Finally, it was all too apparent what she had to do.

With her palms together in prayer position in front of her face, the simple note resting between them, Vivian kept her eyes closed for several long moments, forcing herself to calm. Then with deep resolve, she crumpled the note in her fist and tossed it into the wastebasket beside her writing desk as she walked to the parlor door.

Enough self-pity. It was time for her to act.

Will sat at his writing desk, attempting to concentrate on the correspondence before him. Try as he might, there was just no comparison between the settling of estate taxes and the vivid memory of Vivian's luscious lips, the color of wet rubies. God, how incredible they would feel wrapped around his—

"Your grace, Mrs. Rael-Lamont is here to see you."

Wilson's interruption startled him and he jerked upright at his desk. "Show her in."

"Immediately, sir."

Will raked the fingers of both hands through his hair, closing his eyes and wishing, *wishing* for his erection to subside, at least for now. He had so much to discuss with her, he supposed, and she probably wanted to offer an apology for her anger this morning, which was no doubt why she'd come calling on him only hours after he'd left her at her doorstep.

He groaned, then stood to greet her, a certain nervousness seeping in, which, under the circumstances, thoroughly annoyed him.

He turned to face the door when he heard her approaching footsteps on the marble floor in the hallway, leaning his hip on the side of his desk and crossing his arms over his chest. He wouldn't begin to determine if that were a defensive measure or not. He did it more or less without thinking.

Then for the second time that day he stood before the beautiful widow, who now appeared much calmer in his presence. She no longer wore her formal attire but instead had changed into a simple yet presentable gown of peach muslin, cut low in the neckline but hung rather loosely at the bodice. Actually, for the heat of the afternoon, she looked cool and refreshed, striking really, with her ivory skin and shiny upswept hair that simply begged to be wrapped around his fingers.

Her expression remained unreadable as she walked toward him, her gaze holding his almost defiantly. Will could very well expect that she was still angry, though at this point he suspected *he* was madder. Why she was here after the argument they'd had, he couldn't begin to guess. He decided then to let her control the meeting, for now.

"That will be all, Wilson," he ordered, even as his

butler retreated, shutting the double doors behind him.

They stared at each other for several long seconds, their standoff disquieting.

"Your grace," she said stiffly.

"I'm surprised to see you again so soon, madam."

Her brows arched minutely. "Are you."

It was a statement rather than a question. "Indeed. You must be overheated from the walk."

She pressed her lips together. "That's irrelevant, really."

"Is it."

What a remarkably stupid conversation. "Why are you here, Vivian?" he asked quietly, his body tense.

She drew a deep breath, though she never looked away. "I'm wondering when I might receive the manuscript," she admitted forthrightly.

Her directness was enough to give him pause. And her change of approach honestly puzzled him. "When I'm ready to give it to you, I suppose," he replied.

She lifted her chin a fraction. "You'd said you wanted companionship in exchange for it, and I'm beginning to wonder why you haven't taken it."

Will began to feel his heart beating in his temples, an incessant pounding that increased by the second. He remained composed, his body calm on the outside, though, lest she realize what thoughts of taking her were doing to him. Even now, as standoffish as she was. "I thought that's what I'd been doing all this time," he maintained bluntly, "enjoying your companionship, that is."

That confused her for a moment as she studied him, her forehead creased ever so gently. Then, hugging herself tightly, she bravely acknowledged, "But you have yet to take *me*."

He breathed so steadily, so slowly, he knew she had to be wondering if her words affected him at all. She merely had to glance down to notice how very much he desired her. And almost intuitively he decided she kept her eyes focused on his because she was afraid of what she'd see. Widow or not, she understood the attraction he felt for her, and most amazing of all, she didn't back away from it. Undaunted, she stood before him with the will of a woman who once knew lovemaking and desired it again. It took everything in him at that moment not to take two steps forward, grab her around the waist, lift her skirts and plunge deeply.

"It is . . . what you want, isn't it?"

Those quiet words of unsureness shook him from his reverie. God, if she only knew.

"I thought I'd made that clear, Vivian."

Instead of faltering, she straightened her spine and narrowed her eyes. "You're still angry."

He quickly caught himself from very nearly gaping at her. "I don't even understand that."

"Naturally." She finally glanced away, taking one palm and patting the uplifted hair at her neck. Clearly exasperated, she added, "I will never understand men, either."

Now he was amused. Unfurling his arms, he placed his palms flat on his desktop behind him and stretched out his legs, crossing one over the other.

"I'm not sure what I've done that's so terribly difficult to understand," he countered. "Perhaps you can explain it to me."

"Explain it to *you*?" She lifted both arms heavenward and turned her back on him. "I'm the one who's suddenly baffled."

He was getting to the point where he couldn't even begin to remember what they were talking about.

"Vivian—"

"What are you waiting for, Will?" She moved farther away from him, toward the settee. "I need the manuscript; you need me."

The trees rustled from a sudden gust through the windows; a foghorn sounded off the distant shore. Neither of them noticed the intrusion.

"Tell me what you need my prized manuscript for, Vivian," he insisted very quietly. "And why you need it now. Today. That is why you're here, isn't it? Not because you're so anxious for me to bed you."

She didn't respond to his bold statement because they both knew she didn't need to. She turned her profile to him and brought both of her hands up to her face, clasping them together at her mouth. Just from that gesture alone, Will could easily detect her frustration and annoyance.

After a moment of silent tension, she eyed him sideways, watching him with a frown upon her brow. "I need the manuscript. I offered to buy it—"

"It's not for sale."

"And yet I am?"

That caustic reply made his blood boil, and he fisted his hands on the desktop. "From the beginning, madam, I asked you to tell me the truth. You've denied me the advantage of knowing why you came to me with such a ridiculous proposal in the first place. Now you're here and you're desperate. Why?"

She dropped her hands and faced him fully again, her cheeks turning pink, her lips thinning with her willfulness. "I'm not desperate."

"Yes, you are."

That made her thoroughly mad again. He could see it in her set jaw, her ramrod stiff posture, the way her lovely hazel eyes flashed at him hotly. Oh yes, he'd hit a nerve. It was suddenly a very real confrontation between them, with revelations lying just below the surface.

Will stood erect again and slowly began to walk toward her. "You came to me from the beginning, Vivian, with your half-truths and riddles. I'd finally like some answers. I'd finally like to know what scares you so, *who* scares you so."

Her mouth dropped open. "I'm not scared."

He cocked a brow as he neared her. "Oh? Then why are you so anxious to spend your time with an accused murderer? Obviously something frightens you more than I do."

She had no answer for that, though she looked ready to slap him. Seconds later he towered over her, impressed that she stood her ground without tears or claws.

With trepidation flowing through her soft voice, she fairly whispered, "Has it not occurred to you, sir, that I might want more from you than your treasured manuscript? That this might only be an excuse? That I might simply desire you as a man?"

For the first time in his adult life, William Raleigh, Duke of Trent, nearly fell to his knees in front of a woman. Astonished, and likely unable to hide it in his expression, he peered down to her beautiful face, her dewy soft skin now moist from a combination of heat and tightly wound anger.

She smirked, knowing she'd stumped him, which conveyed to him how perfectly proud she was of it.

And that's when he finally understood. She was using him—a pure, animalistic man—just as all women used men, appealing to their needs and base desires. Oh, how desperate he must look to *her*, must have seemed to her when she first appeared on his doorstep only three weeks ago.

Nostrils flaring, he reached out and firmly grasped her neck with his palm. Startled, her eyes opened wide and she pulled back a little. He held to her tightly, letting her know, in no uncertain terms, that he was in control.

"You expect me to believe you made up this entire scheme because you desired me physically?" he murmured, his fury bleeding from his words.

She attempted once more to break free of him, to no avail. "That's not what I said."

"No, it's what you didn't say, my darling Vivian. How foolish I must look to you. How arrogant. Just like a gentleman who is not gentle. A man who killed his wife, who is shunned by society, who is not fortunate to have the charms of a lady at his fin-

131

gertips." Through clenched teeth, he added, "What a challenge."

She began to tremble. He took that as a sign of guilt and mounting anger rather than fear. If there was one thing he knew absolutely, it was that she was not afraid of him.

"I desire you as a man, your grace," she spat, her focus quickly shifting to the doorway and back again. "Why can you not believe that?"

Through a bitterness he felt very deep within him, he replied, "Because of all the things I am, stupid isn't one of them."

She swallowed; her wide eyes shined with brilliance as she locked them with his.

"Of all the things I have ever said to you, your grace," she countered, "implying stupidity on your part wasn't one of them."

His cheek twitched even as he rubbed his thumb along her jawline, lowered it to feel the quick pulse in her neck. "If you were so attracted to me as a lover would be, Mrs. Rael-Lamont, why do you continue to avoid using my given name?"

She raised one hand and clasped his forearm, though she didn't try to lift it or push it away. She just held on to him as if unsure what her next move should be. In some very odd manner, Will found this battle of wits with her unbelievably arousing.

"Because," she said succinctly, lips tight, "I didn't expect us to be so intimate emotionally."

He almost laughed. "After the . . . exchange of the manuscript?"

"Yes, well—before and after."

132

"How frightfully absurd."

Her eyes widened a little as if she'd only just considered it. "Perhaps," she agreed after a moment, drawing her chin up and away from his thumb. "But the point, sir, is that we had an arrangement."

That made his blood boil. "An arrangement? Do you think that's all this is? Do you think I enjoy being used?"

She faltered with that, blinking quickly as her gaze shot to the closed double doors once more. "I'm not using you—"

"Why would you risk everything to be with me, Vivian?" he cut in, his voice thick and strained. "You were so angry when I appeared today at the church, in your very ordered world, embarrassed to acknowledge me in front of friends. And it was *you* who came to *me*. You're here now." He leaned toward her, nearly nose to nose, clutching the back of her neck to keep her steady. "Tell me why you're here."

For a slice of a second he saw hesitation in her eyes, a quick calculation of whether to offer him the truth, explain her underlying worries, or continue with this game of deceit. It was all he could do not to grab her by the upper arms and shake her—or make love to her to distraction.

As if reading his mind, she suddenly relaxed and exhaled softly, lowering her lashes. "I'm so sorry."

Such softly spoken words gave him pause.

Then she whispered, "Please, Will . . ." and tilted her head, gently kissing his palm that still rested beside her cheek, over and over with lips of rose-petal softness.

133

Eventually, he supposed, he would sit back and wonder about this day, about the first time he took her, about the reasons for their initial meeting that led to a decision to be with her, to give her so much of himself when she offered so little. But for now, he realized, he could no longer refrain from a consequence of action they both desired, regardless of the reasons behind it.

For now, she had won. Just as she knew she would because he was a man.

With a surge of primal lust—a lust fused with a heightened sense of fury at the futility of it all—he grabbed her jaw firmly and lowered his lips to hers, wrapping his free hand around her to pull her against him in a crushing embrace.

She gasped from the initial contact, then moaned as he immediately deepened his kiss, as his tongue invaded and searched for hers.

Raising her arms quickly, she clutched his shoulders firmly and pulled him even closer, her breasts flattened against him, teasing him.

For a fleeting moment, Will realized she'd changed into a gown without hoops, a decidedly convenient asset for them. And then she began to caress his neck, brushing the hair at his nape with her fingertips, following his lead as she seemed to melt into him, her tongue flicking across the inside of his top lip as she kissed him back with a passionate fervor he hadn't felt from a woman in years. Suddenly all reason within him vanished.

He groaned, tightening his grip on her waist, pushing his fingers up into her hair. In an instant her breathing grew as rapid as his; his heart pounded

134

against his chest, as she very nearly began to claw at his shirt.

She needed him. Wanted him. Will could only hope that she'd dreamed of him as he had of her.

With a sigh, she pulled her mouth away and began to kiss his jaw and cheek in quick pecks, pushing into him with the weight of her body. His lips skimmed her neck; his hands began to caress her back in strokes timed to the rhythm of his breathing. He didn't worry about anyone intruding; his staff had strict orders not to interrupt when he was alone with her—a fact about which she seemed concerned as she glanced for a third time to the door.

"Vivian . . . don't worry," he muttered as his tongue found her earlobe and flicked it.

She moaned a sigh, and at last he felt her yield to him, her warm breath on his neck, her fingers laced through his hair as she held firmly to his head, her hot lips to his warm skin.

God, he wanted her, had wanted her for so much longer than she knew. And yet to hold back now . . . He had never in his life been so tempted to give in to an unquenchable desire.

With gentle urging, Will pushed her down onto the black leather sofa. Her gown fell around her as she followed his lead, leaning her head on the thickly padded armrest and pulling at his shirt, urging him silently to join her. He hesitated in climbing on her, for her skirts were bulky and her bodice tight. He knew that without testing it.

Instead, he knelt beside her, his knees resting on the thick oriental rug as he pushed the tea table

135

away to give himself more room. He searched for her lips again, cutting her off with a full and searching kiss should she try to speak.

She didn't. She whimpered softly when he slowly lowered his palm along her leg, over her skirt, moving deliberately toward her ankle. Her breathing grew uneven, her hands on his back, clutching him tightly, pulling him into her. Will could feel her breasts rising and falling with each fast breath, her hips starting to rotate independent of thought as the passion within her grew. He shoved his engorged member into the side of the sofa to temper his lust, afraid he'd come from simply hearing and feeling how much she wanted him at this moment. It was all he could do to stall his reaction.

Through a faint whisper she murmured his name, barely heard, and it made him groan as his palm began to glide along her leg, moving higher beneath her skirts as he caressed her over fine silk stockings.

His mouth devoured hers through staggered breathing, through the steady rocking of her hips, through the urgent pounding of his heart in his chest. He teased her lips, plunged his tongue inside the hot, dewy depths that beckoned him. Her hands clung tightly to his back, his shirt bunched in her palms as she kneaded his taut muscles. She strained her barely concealed breasts into his chest, and at last, with the upward drifting of his hand, he finally found the center of her desire, hidden oh so tantalizingly beneath a thin layer of satin.

She inhaled a sharp, quick breath when he touched her intimately, her head jerking back in response.

"Please . . ." she begged through a gasp, her words scarcely heard.

He moaned against her mouth, his lips skimming her jaw and the deep crevice of her neck as he began to lower them.

"Ah . . . Vivian . . ." he breathed, "let me give you what you need . . ."

She whimpered again, moving her palms up to cling to his head, her fingers threading through his hair. He didn't think she heard him, or comprehended what he'd said, so lost was she in his wondrous assault on her delicious body.

With concentrated gentleness, he began to brush his fingertips up and down along the ridge of silk that thinly covered her feminine softness. In seconds, she'd found his rhythm, moving her hips steadily back and forth against his caress.

He lowered his lips to her perfectly molded collarbone, inhaling the scent of lavender on her skin, tracing the lace at the top of her breasts, seeking the delicate, rosy tips still covered in fine fabric. Due to unfortunate timing, he couldn't actually feel *her*— her hard, aroused nipples, her sleek entrance, how wet he'd made her and how her naked form reacted to him. But it would have to be enough for now. He wanted to get her *there*.

He ran his chin across the swell of her lovely hidden breasts, sought one raised tip, nipped it with his teeth through the shear fabric of her clothing, and coupled with the quickening of his fingers between her thighs, she immediately neared the crest of orgasm.

Will raised his head and looked at her face, concentrating on every beautiful contour, listening to every sweet, feminine whimper, focusing on the heat he generated with each thrust of her hips against his hand. She still clung to his head but she was in another world, enjoying it as he gave it, her eyes squeezed shut, her breathing shallow and fast, her brow creased with intensity as the marvelous tightness coiled within her.

And then her lashes fluttered open.

She was nearly there.

Reaching down with his left hand, Will touched himself over his pants. Suddenly, and without stroking, he'd reached the point of no return.

God, just the feel of her, the look and sound of her, had made him come . . .

In that magnificent instant, she gazed into his eyes and whispered, "Yes—oh, yes . . ."

He let himself go.

Groaning deep within, Will captured her mouth as she cried out, as her fingers dug into his scalp and her entire body shook and trembled and found its ecstasy. He shoved his own hips into his palm, pressed to the side of the sofa, one hand at her hot center, the other feeling himself pulsate with his own explosion of pleasure.

Never had an orgasm hit him so hard and at such a sweet moment.

Never had it been like this.

"Vivian . . ." he breathed, fitting his face gently at her neck, lips to hot skin, slowing the moments he made with her and for her.

What you've done to me . . .

"Take—" She swallowed a harsh gasp. "Take me, Will. Please."

It took seconds before he realized she didn't know it was too late for that.

Jesus.

"Vivian," he whispered after a moment, unsure what to say and not ready to back away, to look into her eyes and expose himself completely. Not yet. In soft murmur, he added, "I don't want our first time . . . to be like this."

After an agonizingly long pause, he thought he felt her nod, her chin brushing his temple negligibly. She trembled beneath him until her breathing began to even, though she never said another word.

Time stilled for them, for now, for several lingering minutes as an afternoon rain began to fall atop the roof, stirring the vegetation in the conservatory beyond. William felt his pulse slowing to a normal, steady pace as he listened without thought to the pattering of rain and the steady beating of her heart beneath his cheek.

Everything would be more complicated now. She would demand the manuscript and he wouldn't provide it, had no intention of providing it, for in truth they hadn't consummated anything. A nasty play of words would likely now ensue. Unless, he considered with an unusual flush of warmth, she'd want him again, with greater intimacy. For now, he awaited her response.

At last she squirmed a little beneath his chest, drew her hands to his shoulders and pushed him away with soft force. Reluctantly, he raised his head and sat up a little, gazing down to her rosy, satisfied face.

She kept her eyes closed, her long, dark lashes creating a striking contrast of shape and color as they formed half-crescents across her clear, pinkened cheeks.

God, she really was a beauty of a woman—vibrant of personality, warm, colorful, intelligent. And a physical appearance that stirred his blood and heated his desire every time she cast him even a trace of a smile.

He reached up and lightly ran his index finger over her brow. The muscles of her forehead twitched once, though she still didn't acknowledge him. Then she turned to her side, placed her palms on the sofa's armrest, and pushed herself to a sitting position.

Will raised himself up and sat beside her, hands clasped together, feet planted on the floor, and, although he was loathe to define its cause, feeling rather nervous. For a moment she did nothing, just stared at the tea table in front of her. Then, with the elegance of a high-born lady, she stood and arranged her skirts, taking a moment to fix her hair and pat loosened strands back into place. She never even glanced at him.

Awkwardly, he raised himself to stand beside her. "Vivian—"

She cut him off immediately by placing her hand on his chest, shaking her head minutely. And then with a subtle lift of her chin, shoulders erect, she stiffly walked out of his library.

Chapter 11

Clement Hastings lowered his body into his usual chair of choice across from Will's secretary and reached into his coat pocket for his small book of notes. He'd come with news, sending an abrupt correspondence early this morning requesting a few minutes of the duke's time so that he could relay some important, recently acquired information. A bit on edge, Will had been able to think of little else aside from his first intimate encounter with Vivian yesterday afternoon, so this diversion came as a bit of a relief. If it weren't for the fact that the entire relationship between them centered around that damn manuscript and whomever was behind its desired possession, he'd concentrate solely on her and pleasing her to distraction. As it was, he found it increasingly difficult to think of anything else.

"Thank you, Hastings," he said, motioning with a nod as he leaned back in his rocker. "What have you this morning?"

"Well," Hastings began as he crossed one chubby leg covered in purple and yellow plaid over the other, "my men and I have discovered some rather peculiar things about Montague's past."

Will slowly leaned forward in his chair. "Go on," he urged when Hastings paused for several seconds to flip a page or two in his notes.

"His real name is Gilbert Herman. He's the great-grandson of a Bohemian Jew who immigrated to England during the outbreak of the Seven Years War in seventeen fifty-six. His great-grandfather and great-grandmother, who was pregnant with Gilbert's grandfather at the time, came here looking for work and eventually started a small merchant business on the east side of London, near the river we believe. In any case, the great-grandfather's name was . . . er . . . Isaac, yes, Isaac Herman."

Will watched Hastings stretch out a bit in an attempt to get comfortable in the chair. Herman . . . he'd never heard the name before.

"They named the child she carried David, which was also the name of Gilbert's father," Hastings continued gravely. "David Herman the second, Gilbert's father, was apparently an extremely bright and very interesting character. He took over his grandfather's merchant business—after his father tired of running it—when he was twenty-two, quickly building it into a solid shipping company—"

"What's the name of the company?" Will asked, cutting in, quite certain he wouldn't know anyway, though it seemed a decent place to start.

Hastings frowned and shrugged negligibly. "We really don't know, your grace. He sold the company only three years after he acquired it. He made his money fast and got out quickly as far as we can tell. He married a woman by the name of Mary-Elizabeth Creswald when he was twenty-seven, a rather plain creature from Northampton whose father owned a small bank. With the money he had and a father-in-law with banking influence, he became, after several years, a rather affluent banker himself in London."

"When was Gilbert born?"

"Er . . . let's see . . . oh, yes, in eighteen twenty-two, two years after his father married Miss Creswald." Hastings drew his brows together, looking hard at his notes. "He was an only child, as his mother apparently had a very difficult birth and was told never to have more children. She died of a lung ailment only two years after that. Gilbert was raised by his father to succeed him in the business, but at some time in his youth he was told he had no sense of numbers and would never make it in banking. At that point, I'm guessing, he decided on acting as a profession. The rest you basically know."

Will leaned back in his chair, eyes narrowed in puzzlement as he tapped his thumb on his desktop.

Hastings relaxed as well, closed his notebook, and waited for questions or instructions as was usual. What the devil did the son of a Jewish banker have in common with Vivian? And how could he have possibly learned about his prized manuscript?

"Is either David Herman senior or Herman junior still alive?" he asked, although already speculating on the answer.

The investigator shook his head. "No, your grace, the senior Herman died of natural causes some years ago; Herman junior died in a fire in his home."

"I see . . ." Will drew in a long, deep breath. "Did he die before his son left for the Continent?"

"Yes, your grace, the banker died nine years ago. He did, however, leave Gilbert a nice little package of wealth when he went, although most everything is gone now. The actor himself doesn't have any money to speak of unless he's keeping it tightly hidden. We haven't found a trace of any substantial wealth in his name, or his father's."

"So," Will speculated out loud as he slowly stood and began to pace the oriental rug, "two Jewish immigrants come to this country, set up a business, have a son and grandson who, in turn, sells the business at a young age. The grandson marries a plain, ordinary woman whose father happens to own a bank. With the banker's influence, and his money, he goes into business for himself, making a nice little income. His wife dies and their only child, who is half Jewish, becomes a Shakespearean actor who suddenly turns up in Cornwall, has one rather unusual conversation with a local widowed florist,

who, in turn, attempts to extort a priceless manuscript from me."

"That about sums up what we know so far, your
grace."

Will stopped pacing in front of his enormous man-
telpiece, gazing thoughtfully at two fine Chinese
vases that, if sold, would render him more cash than
the manuscript ever could in a free market. To the
average subject, the sonnet was useless.

"Why Vivian?" he heard himself asking. "How
does she play into all of this?"

"I've no idea," Hastings answered honestly. He
cleared his throat. "But I think it's plausible that a
Shakespearean actor, regardless of where he came
from, would desire to possess a manuscript signed
by the master himself."

Will nodded, shoving both hands in his pockets
and turning to face the investigator. "Indeed. But
why use Mrs. Rael-Lamont?" *And why would she put
her work, name, and future at risk by coming to me?*

Slowly, taking extraordinary care with his words,
Hastings tapped his fingers together in front of him
as he replied, "I would suspect, your grace, that he's
got some hold over her. And yet we're not even certain what his intentions are. The change of his name
from Herman to Montague might have no malevo-
lent meaning at all. It could be because of his work
on the stage, or more likely because Herman is a
Jewish name."

Will very well understood the role anti-Semitism
might play in one's career, within the city or outside
of it, and still, Gilbert Herman's name change

seemed most convenient. Everything in him told him there was much more involved. There were simply too many questions.

"I don't like it, Hastings," Will said, staring now at the floor. "It smells of something else and I want the connection."

"We'll find it, sir," the investigator said with assurance.

"What about the woman at the pub?" he asked, glancing up as it occurred to him.

Hastings sighed. "Nothing, so far. We've tried with the pelisse but as yet she's still a mystery."

The *entire* mystery absolutely confounded him, which in turn made him angry. If there was one thing Will couldn't stand it was being played for a fool.

"What do a blond, attractive woman, a banker's son turned Shakespearean actor, and an inconsequential widow living perfectly well on her own in southern Cornwall have in common?" he asked aloud, though not really expecting an answer. He should have known that Clement Hastings was, if nothing else, the foremost expert on propriety and so felt obligated to respond.

"Well sir, I still believe the answer lies with Gilbert Montague, or Herman, as it were. It all starts with him. I don't have any information as yet on Mrs. Rael-Lamont being anything more than she claims to be, though I've got two men checking her background, and that of her late husband's. If there's something she's hiding, we'll find it."

"Very good," Will muttered.

Hastings stood as if knowing this was his cue to leave. "I'll be in touch with anything new, your grace, especially if we uncover something about the woman, or Mrs. Rael-Lamont."

"Yes, thank you Hastings. That will be all."

The investigator bowed once and took his leave.

Will stood where he was for several long minutes, staring at the floor, at the intricate weaving of the outrageously expensive oriental rug beneath his feet. It struck him how odd life was when he could afford such luxuries as this, any luxury he wanted, and yet, at this moment, he didn't feel important, or worthy, or a man of unlimited wealth. He missed Vivian, the verbal witticism they shared with a strong sense of enjoyment, the moments of passion that seemed to possess the two of them when they were together. But mostly, at this second in time, when it felt as if there was no one in the world he could trust, he just felt lonely.

Chapter 12

I f only the intimacy of married life had been so
utterly incredible, she thought wryly, trying not
to let the memories of the past bring tears to her
eyes. If only her husband had wanted her physically.
If only he had made love to her with a completion of
passion that satisfied them both. If only, if only . . .

Dear God, *why* did she have to keep dwelling on it?

With irritation borne of stubbornness her father
had constantly accused her of possessing to her
detriment, Vivian dug into the large pot of soil with
both hands, uncaring how dirt sprayed up onto her
arms and coated her work apron. Truth be told, she
was far more furious than upset, far more determined than confused.

If only he had taken her . . .

"Arggg," she voiced, teeth clenched, tossing the soil with a force so great much of it spilled over the side of the ceramic pot. She'd done it on purpose, of course. Right now she felt like *throwing* dirt, and why not? It was late, nearly time for her bath and bedtime. It would feel good to get dirty, and to the devil with men.

Digging deep, she fisted her hands and, with purposeful glee, pulled out two very large clumps of potting soil and tossed them into the air above her.

"Hello, Vivian."

She gasped, whirling around to face the sound of his voice as waves of fine dark soil fell on and around her. Her entire body froze on the spot, eyes opened wide as the Duke of Trent stood in all his beautiful, manly, male . . . ness, three feet from her on her torch-lit backyard patio.

For a moment she gaped at him, unable to speak. Then vanity overcame her as she realized she looked atrocious.

Her dirty hands flew to her cheeks. "Your—grace."

He sighed and took a step toward her. "You're—dirty."

She actually had to stop herself from giggling. Squeezing her lips together, she dropped her hands to her sides and stood very straight. "I was working."

He raised his brows as he glanced up and down her body. "Were you."

She didn't answer, though she now felt thoroughly embarrassed by her appearance in an old gown of brown muslin. He, on the other hand, looked positively marvelous, dressed so casually he hadn't fastened the top three buttons of his linen shirt. She'd never seen him looking so relaxed before, so less like a peer of his rank.

"Messy work, too, apparently," he added lightly. "You must have to bathe frequently."

She cleared her throat and swished a bit of remaining dust in front of her face. "I bathe daily."

A slow grin crept across his mouth as he eyed her candidly from forehead to waist and back again. "That's very good to know."

She had to wonder if he was teasing her, trying to pass the time with idle discussion that had to have nothing whatever to do with his reason for being here, or perhaps just trying to imagine her in her bath, a shocking little notion that sent waves of heat through her body. Suddenly it occurred to her that the last time she'd seen him he'd made her—

"What exactly are you doing out here so late in the evening, Vivian?"

She swallowed, hoping it was too dark for him to notice how fiercely she was blushing. "I was working."

He remained grinning as he took another step toward her. "So you said."

"Actually, I was planting bulbs," she expounded as if it mattered.

"Ah."

For seconds she didn't know what to do. Softly, she decided just to get to the point. "Why are you here, Will?"

He smirked and reached over to caress her ceramic pot with his thumb. "I think we need to talk. Really talk." Scanning his surroundings, he added,

"I thought perhaps an enclosed, informal place like this, free of prying ears and eyes, might get you to open up to me."

She clasped her hands in front of her, refusing to appear affected by his frank statement or to back away. "We've been talking. Talking is not our problem."

For a moment or two he said nothing. "I told your staff we weren't to be disturbed."

She snickered at that. "I have a staff of two, your grace."

"And they'll leave us in private if they want to remain employed in Penzance."

Smiling, she crossed her arms beneath her breasts. "My, sir, but you sound arrogant."

He shrugged, eyeing her directly once more. "I'm a duke. It's in the blood."

She cocked her head a fraction. "Or perhaps just a benefit of the title?"

"Perhaps."

"I would expect nothing less from you, Will."

He moved ever closer to her so that he stood only inches away, gazing down to her flushed and grime-covered face. "I will always be honest with you," he fairly whispered, his voice husky.

She blinked from his immediate change in mood, unsure how to respond. She'd been teasing him, more or less, and without any warning whatsoever he'd closed in, his expression as grave as his tone.

"It's time to *talk*, Vivian," he repeated.

Nervously, she chanced a quick glance to her right, to the corner of her house.

"We're alone," he added in reassurance, noting her hesitation.

She rubbed her palms over her upper arms. It seemed so odd to be standing next to him now, isolated in her humble backyard. No servants, no prying society eyes, no appointments to be kept, no rigorous formality and pomp. Just the two of them alone in her nursery by fading dusk and torchlight. On any other night, with any other man, it might seem . . . romantic. Only one thing remained to unsettle her. "Did anyone see you arrive?"

"Would that matter to you?" he asked.

She paused to consider it. At last, she murmured, "Honestly? No."

She noticed a very slight easing in his shoulders, in his countenance, as he let out a long exhale.

"I have something to confess to you, Vivian," he admitted quietly, reaching out to run his index finger from one button to another down the front of her gown.

The intimacy of that action made her belly tighten. He seemed different to her tonight, in a manner she couldn't begin to decipher.

"Perhaps I should take a few minutes to freshen up, so we can discuss this rationally in the parlor—"

"No," he cut in. "If I'd wanted that, I would have called on you formally."

True, she decided. "So what is your confession?"

He drew in a long breath, standing so close to her now she could feel the heat from his body through the still evening air.

"I want there to be total honesty between us," he maintained, voice low and cautious.

She gazed into his lovely brown eyes, now hinting of secrets and hidden feelings. Vivian had to fight herself from reaching out and touching his face in tenderness.

"I believe we've always had relative honesty between us, sir," she mumbled, her mouth going dry as the conversation grew even more personal.

His lips twitched. "Relative honesty? You have not been entirely truthful with me, my darling Vivian, and you've truthfully admitted it."

His play of words annoyed her even as it warmed her very deep within. *My darling Vivian . . .*

She raised her chin a fraction, noticing, oddly enough, how quiet it was outside tonight—no wind, no rain, no insect creatures buzzing around the torches. And not a sound from her house.

At last, she murmured, "I told you that I can't tell you everything, true, but it's imperative that I—"

He reached out and placed his fingertips on her lips, effectively cutting her off. "Let. Me. Help. You."

For the first time in her life, Vivian thought she might break down from nothing more than a demand of trust revealed so intensely, so empathetically, at a time when she felt she had no one in the world who would understand.

Closing her eyes, she kissed the tips of his fingers that he held against her, brushing her lips across them. He inhaled in a shaky breath.

"Vivian . . ."

"Make love to me, Will," she pleaded in a whisper. "Make love to me, and I will tell you everything. Please."

For long, aching moments, she waited for him to respond, wondering at his thoughts, why he *really* came to her tonight.

Finally, he said, "You know how much I want you."

Vivian felt heat rush into her face, her legs liquefy. She nodded negligibly.

"But you also know that once I take you, that would be the end," he continued, his tone gruff. "And I'm not ready for this to end."

The end. She hadn't considered that. If he consummated their "companionship," he would then be obligated to fulfill their agreement; Vivian never for a moment doubted that he would. Suddenly she understood. "That's why you didn't take me yesterday."

With all the things he could have said to her, she never expected him to chuckle.

Raising her lashes, she gazed at him by torchlight, taking note of his handsome face, his thick, dark hair, his hard, masculine features aligned in perfect planes, complementing even his unpredictable amusement.

"I'm sure I don't see the humor in any of this," she said a bit curtly.

He leaned toward her, looming over her. "I didn't take you," he revealed in whisper, "because my attraction to you is so strong, Mrs. Rael-Lamont, that by the time you asked, it was already too late."

His explanation perplexed her for a second or two.

Then his meaning struck, and as embarrassment flooded her, her initial thought was that she couldn't believe he said something so utterly . . . personal. She continued to stare at him, her body growing hot, afraid to let him know that although she was fairly certain she understood what he meant, she was more impressed by the fact that he told her of it without showing any apparent discomfiture.

But alas it was his eyes that held her interest. Always his eyes . . . so bold, speaking so clearly of a strong male desire, openly expressing his concerns and longings. Always so honest.

Reaching up with both hands, she captured his fingers between her palms, caressing his skin with soft thumb strokes. Bravely holding his gaze, she whispered, "This will only end if you want it to."

His smile wavered; his brows drew together as he assessed her. And then he lowered his head and kissed her, teasing her lips with his, stroking them with his tongue, invading the softness of her mouth.

Passion quickly enveloped them. He pulled his hand from hers and reached around to run his fingers through her hair, loosening her coiled braid so that it fell down her back.

She pulled away from him a little. "Will—" she gasped. "Not here—"

"Here," he insisted with a groan against her mouth before capturing it once more, his tongue probing, finding hers, sucking.

She moaned when he raised a hand and gently began to knead her breast over her thin work gown, playing her nipple till it rose to a peak.

Wrapping her arms around his neck, Vivian remained only vaguely aware of her surroundings as he pulled her away from her wooden work table to guide her toward the side of the nursery where a cushioned, wrought-iron bench lay waiting in the far shadowed corner.

Beneath a canopy of ivy and starlight, he gently urged her to climbed on top of him. Through mingled breath, rapidly increasing heartbeats, and caressing hands, Vivian felt the swelling ache between her legs as she lifted her skirts then allowed them to fall around both of them as she gently lowered herself onto his lap, her inner thighs caging his hips.

She felt his erection the moment she eased down on him, its thick hardness shocking her sensibilities at first—until she began to relish the feel of his desire for her, yearning to experience him skin to skin.

He moaned very quietly when she nestled herself onto him. He continued to assault her lips with his, pressing both palms against her breasts and faintly caressing.

It wasn't enough for her.

Vivian reached up and began to unbutton her gown from the neck down until she'd loosened it enough to expose her cotton shift.

He continued to kiss her, increasing the momentum, hunger escalating, his fingers tugging at the top of her shift until her breasts came free of the loose material. Almost instantaneously he dropped his head and took one pointed nipple into his mouth. Vivian nearly screeched.

Clasping his head, fingers raked through his soft

hair, she tilted her head back and closed her eyes to the wondrous assault. He kissed her nipple, sucked it gently, nipped at it with his teeth, stopping only to move to the other one, giving it equal time.

For ages and ages, it seemed to her, he tormented her with his mouth, breathing heavily as he sucked and kissed, clasping her back as she gasped and moaned and whimpered. Finally, of its own accord, her body began to rock against him, allowing her to feel his rigid erection as intimately as possible against her still-clothed body. He caught her rhythm immediately, pressing her to him with his hands at her waist, his tongue tracing circles on the tight tips of her nipples.

"Will . . ." She breathed without real thought, fearing she was drawing near the loss of her sanity. She was so close, moaning incoherently now, ready to reach the peak of passion and tumble over that exquisite crest.

Just as she neared it, he lowered his palms to her hips and forcefully stopped her movement.

"Not yet," he said with short, raspy breaths. "Wait for me . . ."

She squeezed her eyes shut and tried to calm the thunder rolling through her body.

And then she felt his fingers under her skirt, fumbling with his pants, grazing the most intimate part of her unintentionally as he tried to free himself.

God, it was happening.

And I'm ready . . .

She raised her hips up an inch or so, giving him better access. He kissed her mouth once or twice, quickly, concentrating on freeing himself. Then his fingers again touched her between her legs and she whimpered when he found the tiny slit in her drawers, spreading it as wide as he could.

Vivian opened her eyes and looked down into his. He was watching her, his face, partly in shadow, intensely focused on her pleasure, on what he was doing to her.

And then she felt him touch her at her heated, moist center, and she gasped his name.

He shuddered beneath her. "Wet, soft, perfect," he whispered, voice strained, his gaze still locked with hers. "I knew you would be . . ."

Vivian thought she might explode when he began to stroke her there. She drew a shaky breath, closed her eyes once more, and began to rock her hips against his fingers.

It felt so good, so good . . .

"Sit on me," he breathed, placing both hands on her hips again.

She complied, lowering herself until she touched the hot thickness of his rigid shaft, smothering the length of him with her own heated center.

"Don't move," he said, his words almost imperceptible, his hands grasping her tightly to hold her still. "I'll come if you move."

Vivian had never heard anyone speak so openly about what they were now doing. But instead of embarrassing her, it made her positively crazy with need.

"I want to move," she murmured, squeezing her thighs against his.

He inhaled deeply and kissed her nipple. "I know, I know, sweetheart," he replied as his lips circled the tip. "Give me a minute."

She pushed her fingers through his hair, feeling the quick pounding of her heart, listening to his harsh, rapid breathing, noting just how hard he felt between her legs.

Suddenly his fingers sought the nub of her desire and a tiny sound of pleasure escaped her.

"Raise up a bit, Vivian."

She did his bidding.

He lifted until the edge of him began to slide into her.

They were both panting now, both engulfed in an overwhelming fever, both oblivious to everything around them save each other, the intensity, the charge of accelerating bliss. The knowledge that they were about to become one and find satisfaction together.

He settled himself just within her heated walls. Vivian braced herself, closing her eyes, her hands gripping his shoulders.

"Mmmm . . ." He moaned, eyes squeezed shut, his hands back on her hips to better guide her. "You are so wet, so—tight."

Her thighs tensed; her breathing wavered; a flicker of fear washed over her. But as soon as he began to make small thrusts upward, she nearly climaxed from the feel of him easing his way inside her.

He drew a nipple into his mouth again and she gasped aloud, trying desperately to focus on holding back as she knew he was. It hurt a bit more than she expected, felt so incredibly tight, and for seconds she worried that he might not fit. He pressed harder, faster, pushing ever deeper with each thrust until at last the uncomfortable constricting gave way to an exquisite sense of fullness deep inside.

He stilled his movements when at last her body consumed all of him, his mouth to her breasts, his hands kneading the soft flesh, his tongue flicking the tips.

Vivian couldn't breathe, thought she might heat to bursting. Then the faintly glimpsed sensation to move became overwhelming.

Slowly, she began to rock back and forth against him, switching to small circles when she found her rhythm and a pace of her choosing. He matched it, a slight groan escaping him as he let her make love to his body.

"Yes," he whispered between sharp breaths, "God, you're so good, Vivian."

She whimpered, clutching his shoulders, quickening her pace, nearing her peak with each tiny rotation.

"Come for me, sweetheart . . ."

She opened her eyes and glanced down to him. He lifted his hands to her breasts again to knead gently, then looked up into her eyes, his thumbs flicking over her nipples. His concentration on giving her such enjoyment put her over the edge.

"Oh, yes, Will," she breathed, moving faster, digging her fingers into him. "Oh yes, oh yes . . ."

She very quietly cried out as she exploded within, feeling every pulsating wave of exquisite pleasure flow through her and rhythmically caress the thickness of him deep inside.

"God, I feel you," he said huskily, leaning his head back and squeezing his eyes shut. "Don't stop. Don't stop—"

He shoved his hips up once, twice, while she continued to move against him faster, harder, wanting him to experience every sensation with her, because of her.

"I'm coming, Vivian . . ." he whispered seconds later.

She whimpered from that, rotating her hips steadily against his. Suddenly he leaned forward and wrapped his arms around her, hugging her close, his face in her breasts as he groaned and jerked into her.

She felt the slightest pulsations within her, knowing now that he had spilled himself deeply. In many ways, Vivian was to contemplate later, the notion that he risked so much to be with her thrilled her more than anything had in years.

She slumped against him, his cheek still against her chest, his warm breath teasing her nipple with each fast exhalation. She held him securely, listening to her own rapid breathing, noting how they were both now perspiring in the humid night warmth.

The outside remained still, remarkably silent, making her feel as if they were the only people alive. Resting her cheek on the top of his head, she stared at the rows of tulips to her left, their brilliant color softly illuminated by faint torchlight. The night air surrounding them smelled of plants, earthy soil, which still coated her skin and hair, perhaps the faint traces of a coming rain, and of him—a seductive musky scent that was all male, all Will. She knew now that she'd recognize it anywhere.

For minutes they stayed joined, neither saying a word. Finally she felt him slip out of her, effectually terminating the act that had bound them so intimately. He continued to cling to her silently, though, as if he were somehow afraid she'd vanish.

Vivian decided at that moment that he needed her. She'd never felt that way about a man before. Through the years men had wanted her, certainly, had tried to bed her, use her for status, befriend her, enslave her—or so it felt—but never before had she sensed an almost insatiable *need* from any man that included far more than just the physical. Right now, enclosed in her small patio garden, she sensed that Will felt more for her than he'd probably even realized. That frightened her. If there was one thing she knew positively could not happen between them it was a lasting relationship. If he got too close emotionally, she was afraid she might grow to love him.

Slowly, she began to ease off of him. "I'm sticking to you," she whispered.

He nuzzled her breasts for a final time. "Mmmm . . . A marvelous heat."

On shaking legs, she pushed against the back of the bench to help herself stand, her gown falling down around her legs to properly cover her. He ran his fingers through his hair, and with that she turned away from him to button her shirt and allow him privacy to do the same to his pants.

"I have something to confess," she said after a moment, glancing to the house again to notice with great relief that it remained closed and in darkness.

She heard him stand, adjusting his clothes, so she walked a few steps to her work table, into the torchlight again, and began to tidy up from her dirt toss earlier.

"I'm anxious to hear it," he maintained, standing quietly where he was.

At his contemplative tone, she paused very briefly while brushing loose soil into one hand with the palm of the other.

"Stop working, Vivian, and look at me."

Her heart began to race again, though this time it had more to do with nerves. But she did as he bid, straightening and turning to face him boldly.

He continued to stand in the shadows, and although she could tell he'd crossed his arms over his chest, she couldn't read his expression. She supposed she should feel glad about that.

"I—I'm not sure what to say."

He inhaled, then murmured, "You're ready to tell me everything, to let me help you, to confess who Gilbert Montague is and what information he has about you that has you willing to sell your soul to the devil."

She fairly snorted. "That's a bit dramatic."

"Is it?"

An instant concern overwhelmed her. She didn't

expect him to be so . . . reserved. Or at least it seemed as if he were.

"What's wrong?" she asked in marked hesitation, clasping her hands in front of her. Then a surge of heat swept over her. "Was I—not—"

"You were magnificent," he replied, his tone gruff.

She positively marveled in that. At any other time she would have grinned and embraced him. But the mood had subtly changed.

"Will you be honest with me?" he asked after several silent seconds.

She swallowed. "As honest as I can be."

He turned his head to the side, thinking, then gazed back at her. "Vivian, I have been with several women."

Confusion enveloped her. "Are you expecting me to be shocked by such a confession?" *Or maybe jealous?*

He ignored her question as he began to stride in her direction. "Of those few women, I'm almost positive only two were virgins. One was my wife when I married her; the other was you."

Oh, my God . . .

She nearly collapsed. A small sound of horror escaped her as her hand shot up to her throat.

He stopped directly in front of her, staring down at her, his expression grave. "Would you like to explain that to me, sweetheart?"

She could hardly find her voice. When she did, she completely ignored everything he'd just said. She refused to discuss it.

"I have a proposition, your grace," she mumbled, mouth dry, body trembling inside.

A flicker of surprise crossed his face. "A proposition?"

She forced a smile. "I propose that we work together. We get a reasonable copy made of the manuscript and—"

"Vivian, what the hell are you talking about?"

She blinked. "You're certainly not going to give me the original, I realize that now."

Slowly, he began to shake his head. "I don't care about the manuscript at the moment. Tell me why—how—were you a virgin?"

"I'm not a virgin," she said, sounding rather more defiant than intended. She simply would not discuss it, and he had to understand that.

He chuckled snidely, running a palm over his face. "You're certainly not now."

A warmth oozed through her again as the memory of the last perfect hour filled her mind. If only he would concentrate on that.

"You never had intimate relations with your husband, did you?" he tried again.

Taking a long, deep breath, she replied, "My past is irrelevant."

"No it's not," he countered, moving one step closer. "Not anymore."

Her brows shot up. "Yours is."

That bold statement stopped him cold. In an intensely quiet voice, he murmured, "Don't play games with me, Mrs. Rael-Lamont."

For a long, drawn out of moment she held his gaze, wishing a hundred things could be different between them. But she refused to consider the pain.

Finally, she whispered, "Please don't make me talk about it, Will. I can't."

She watched a stream of emotions pass over him—disbelief, anger, even a marked hurt. Then he backed up a step, dropped his arms and narrowed his eyes with contempt. "I suppose there is nothing more to say. Good night, madam."

He turned his back on her and left through the side gate.

Vivian stood where she was for a long time, staring at the spot where he'd made love to her, hearing nothing, feeling everything. At last she went to bed when the rain began to fall.

Chapter 13

Wilson had said she'd find his grace on the beach, and no sooner had she left the garden trail—the expanse of a turbulent ocean spread out in front of her—than she saw him, sitting alone on a patch of long grass, just above the shoreline. He wore casual clothes just darker in shade than the color of the sand, the sleeves of his shirt rolled up to his elbows that now rested on his raised knees.

Vivian paused for a moment a few feet away, studying him from behind. The memory of two nights ago was still so fresh, so erotic to her, she'd had trouble concentrating on anything except him since he'd left her standing alone in her patio. It had made yesterday's tea at Mrs. Safford's home quite uncomfortable, especially with the nosy, invasive questions flung her way regarding last Sunday's debacle at St. Mary's Church. If she wasn't careful, there would soon be rumors swarming all over town suggesting that she and the Duke of Trent were associating improperly, even intimately. She couldn't have that with her social status and livelihood at stake. And yet, here she was, calling on him again at his home and meeting him privately. At least this time they were more or less out in the open, in relative view from the house. They needed to talk to each other, really talk, and she had vowed to herself, before she'd left the confines of her home, that she would do everything in her power to keep their physical attraction to each other at bay. At least long enough to get some things said.

"Are you going to approach me or just stand there and stare at my back?"

She smiled at the forced roughness of his tone as she began to walk toward him. "I was thinking."

He picked a blade of grass and twirled it between his fingers. "Well I hope you weren't thinking of murder."

Vivian supposed she could be offended by that, but she knew instinctively that he was in a manner teasing her with shocking words underlining perhaps a small degree of self-pity. But the fact that the comment seemed so personal warmed her heart immediately. He always seemed to have a way of doing that.

She moved slowly down the grassy slope until she stood directly behind him, wrapping her arms around her waist to ward off the cool afternoon breeze as she gazed out to the gray and choppy sea. "I wouldn't dream of murdering you right now," she replied evenly. "Eventually, maybe, but not now."

"I won't give you a copy of my manuscript, then, until I've hired sufficient protection."

"Ah. Well, no one would kill for a copy, your grace, but perhaps for the original."

He chuckled softly, tossing her a sideways look. "Sit, madam, and tell me why you've sought me out here on this dreary day."

Of course she did as commanded, adjusting her hooped skirts out around her to her right, which allowed her to fix herself in appropriate closeness to him at her left.

She didn't immediately speak, either, since being next to him like this gave her an odd sense of comfort she wasn't ready to lose to an argument. And they had much to discuss that could lead to irritation, though she intended to do her best to avoid it.

"It is dreary, isn't it?" she agreed at last, gazing out over the waves, colorless save for white crests, the visible ocean free of vessels and fishermen. "Why are you here when there isn't much of interest to see?"

He sighed aloud. "I was thinking as well."

When he added nothing more to that, she said, "I would assume a man of your position would have more important things to do."

"Yes," he agreed, nodding slowly, "but my position also allows me to organize my time as I please. The masses will follow regardless of what I do or where I do it."

She couldn't stop herself from laughing. "The masses?"

He shrugged and shot her a quick glance. "Haven't you been privy to the masses, Vivian?"

"What masses, pray tell, are we discussing, your grace?"

"The masses who live for gossip and form opinions based on not one shred of reasonable evidence."

Smile fading, she leaned back a little, resting her forearms on the soft grass behind her. "I've tried for the last fifteen years to live as privately as possible, not sharing parts of myself on purpose in every attempt to avoid gossip."

"And yet," he remarked, "when you least expect it, it's flung back at you, rearing its ugly, misinformed presence for everyone to observe and be drawn toward without resistance or restraint, like little ants to a marvelous picnic luncheon."

Vivian wondered for a moment how he wanted her to interpret that, deciding he meant social talk regarding both of them, not just him alone. "You're referring to Sunday when we stood outside St. Mary's?" she asked.

The side of his mouth twitched up. "Exactly. Fortunately for you, my sweet Vivian, most of the people in our quaint town have tired of gossiping about the Duke of Sin who murdered his poor, tortured wife."

Poor, tortured wife.

She exhaled slowly, afraid of saying something inappropriate when in actuality, more than he could possibly know, she understood his feelings so very well. At last, she murmured, "I've learned to draw my own conclusions about others, Will. Most people of any worth do the same."

He turned to look at her, his eyes roving over her face, taking note of her features so intently she felt a bit of heat rush into her cheeks.

"What, then, are your conclusions about me?"

Such a grave question asked in so brusque a manner made her hesitate. To lie to him now would surely be disastrous, for if nothing else, Vivian felt strongly that he knew her thoughts and motives almost as well as she knew them herself. He would instantly see through a deception.

With only the slightest doubt remaining, hidden beneath the surface, she revealed, "I don't believe you killed your wife."

For several long moments he gazed into her eyes, his lids narrowed in assessment. She refused to look away, to back down, even if, for only a second or two, she sensed an inner trepidation as it dawned on her why he carried such a dark reputation—so masculine, so brooding, so strongly intense. But strangely it was also those very same qualities or quirks of personality that she found so positively fascinating about him.

Finally he lowered his gaze to her lips, then reached out to touch them tenderly, his expression void of emotion. She didn't draw back but instead, very gently, kissed his fingertips.

He swallowed somewhat harshly, seemingly perplexed by that reaction, then dropped his hand and looked back out over the roaring ocean.

"I didn't kill her. My wife had a . . . condition, Vivian. Her name was Elizabeth, the second daughter of the Earl of Stanwynn. When I married her she was beautiful, two weeks shy of her eighteenth birthday, and so in love with me, which at the time I found amusing because our marriage had been planned by our parents nearly twelve years earlier."

How could she not be? "And your feelings for her?" she prodded nonchalantly, controlling her own insecurities from slipping into her tone.

"I loved her," he answered at once. "She was such a delicate thing, soft and considerate, blond and pretty. I truly had hopes for a compatible marriage, for several children and an old-age companion. But it took only months of living with her to realize I didn't know her—or at least her inner personality—at all."

Vivian refrained from reply, not wanting to interrupt a long-awaited disclosure. A gust of wind swept around them and a shiver ran through her, but she refused to give in to the cold when the man had suddenly become so revealing. She sat up and crossed her arms in front of her, rubbing them with her bare palms to stay the chill that blasted inland from the sea.

He picked another blade of grass—a long one—and began to play with it, attempting unsuccessfully to tie it into a knot. "The first year was difficult, but then I assumed all marriages have some difficulty in the beginning as couples try to adjust to each other and their new relations. But she was often irrational. I didn't know how to view that."

"Irrational?"

He picked another blade of grass. "She would be so . . . energetic, so happy and full of excitement, so overjoyed with life sometimes, Vivian, that she had trouble sleeping, sitting still, even for meals, concentrating on the simplest of tasks. Her mind constantly seemed to race with new thoughts and ideas of how to use her position as my wife to better society. During these times of high enthusiasm she made great plans for her future, spent my money without restraint or care. She once bought every female member of my staff at my London townhouse a pair of ruby earrings."

Her mouth dropped open. "You must be joking."

He shook his head. "I'll never in my life forget how astonished those women were to receive such a gift. Jesus, Vivian, they had no need for rubies, and Elizabeth very well knew that. Where on earth did she think they'd wear them if they wanted to? Regardless of the fact that I paid them well, have *always* paid my staff well, these women were born and raised in a world where they worked for money to buy food and necessities. I've no doubt every one of them sold the earrings on the street for pennies of what they were worth, thankful to the Duchess of Trent for giving them an opportunity to stash a bit away, clothe their children in new fashions, and put a rare side of beef on the table."

Vivian fully sympathized with his concern, knowing perfectly well what it was like to live by modest means, yet fully understanding how such a ridiculous act must have looked to everyone who knew what the duchess had done. "Did that incident bother you?"

"You mean did I get angry? Of course." He tipped his head a fraction and eyed her candidly. "It didn't bother me that my wife cared about others and desired above all else to please them. It bothered me that she would do these irrational things so ... spontaneously, without ever consulting me." He ran his palm quickly over his face. "As the wife of a nobleman, it's one thing to help the needy by donating old clothes, visiting the sick and the poor, and filling soup bowls. It's another to think you're so important you're going to save the underworld. Elizabeth truly believed she alone was going to save the underworld."

A gull dropped low on the sand in front of them, pecked a few times, then took flight once more, heading south over water.

"How did she die?" Vivian finally found the courage to ask.

He hesitated for a moment or two, inhaling deeply as he concentrated on tying the two blades of grass together.

"There were other times, dark times, when she wasn't herself," he disclosed, his tone low and taut. "During these times, Vivian, it was as if she ... became ill, absorbed not in herself and her power to do no wrong, but fearful, anxious, so overcome with despair, crying until there were no more tears to cry, then growing angry and even cruel to me. She would throw books or candlesticks or teacups at me—whatever was available and at her fingertips—

if I didn't say or do that which she deemed appropriate and reasonable. She used language no lady
should use, treated servants who had been under my
employ for years with such suspicion they were genuinely afraid to go near her when she entered "the
mood" as they called it. God help me, but I never understood it. Her physician said it was normal for
ladies to get . . . emotional during their monthlies,
but this was . . . I don't know, pronounced. Extreme.
And it wasn't at all predictably based on her female
cycle, either. She would sometimes go for months
with incredibly high energy, then sink so low into
desperation that for weeks she would rarely leave
her bed." He raked his fingers harshly through his
hair then threw the knotted blades of grass out on
the sand in front of him. "After a while, because I
had no idea what else to do, I retreated physically
and emotionally from her, which proved to be the
beginning of the end."

Vivian watched the wind lift the knotted grass
and carry it off across the sand and down the beach-
front. She remained motionless, fairly speechless,
and found it terribly difficult not to reach over and
caress his cheek, then pull him against her in a loving embrace.

"The night before she died, we had a terrible argument," he continued, now seemingly lost in remembrance. "She'd come to the conclusion that I no
longer cared about her, and it didn't matter what I
said to the contrary. She had been in her bed for two
weeks, unwilling to leave it. Her sister had just come
for a short visit, and she more or less accused me of

175

not giving Elizabeth enough attention, which I think had the negative effect of putting ideas in her head. By that point I felt helpless, I suppose, and refused to speak to either of them. Her sister left on Saturday, and the next morning, a beautifully warm, sunny Sunday, Elizabeth's body was found floating in a nearby lake. The following weekend, her relations accused me of murder." He squeezed his hands into fists. "The only reason I'm not dead or imprisoned now is that I had friends, members of the peerage, to testify on my behalf, and there was never any solid proof that I did anything to her at all. In her despair, which she could not handle, my wife drowned herself. In the public's mind, however, the suspicions still exist, will *always* exist. I have committed the ultimate sin, for which they will never forgive me." He lowered his gaze to the ground in front of him, staring without seeing. "If I've learned nothing else, it's that life is not only difficult, but sometimes unbearable and only rarely fair. If not for the faint glimmers of sunshine and hope at the top of each hill we climb, I think we would all give in to it."

For a long, long time after he finished his disclosure they sat in silence, listening to the ocean waves crash upon each other as they pushed toward shore, an occasional squawking bird, the whistle of the wind.

"Who are these friends who came so readily to your defense?" she asked sometime later.

Without pause, he replied, "One is Samson Carlisle, Duke of Durham, the other is Colin Ramsey, Duke of Newark. Our families are all distantly related, of course, but the three of us have been more like brothers since early childhood."

"I met his grace, the Duke of Durham a few years ago," she confessed after only a second's hesitation, "at Lady Clarice Suffington's coming-out soiree." Uncertain whether it would be wise to admit it, Vivian decided the encounter had been so brief it wouldn't matter. "I recall that he was very handsome in a rather distinctive, melancholy way, and very tall, though I don't suppose he would remember our brief introduction. The man had seemed so positively bored—*that* I do remember well about him."

Will glanced sideways at her, smirking. "A fair assessment of Sam, I suppose." His gaze skimmed her face. "Why were you there?"

Her eyes widened. "At Lady Clarice's coming out?"

"Yes."

Think fast.

"As it happened, I was standing in the library, with Lady Clarice's mother, reassembling one of the floral arrangements, when he walked in to get a moment's peace, or so he said." It wasn't a direct answer, but one she hoped would suffice. Reaching down to avoid his penetrating contemplation of her, she pulled a handful of long grass up by the roots and tossed it out into the breeze. Truthfully, she had been an invited guest at the party, and had gone into the room with the countess to advise her on floral pieces for her older daughter's upcoming nuptials, when she'd been introduced to the man. But she didn't want to give Will too much information, leading to more questions she wasn't prepared to discuss. Instead, she kept the conversation focused on his friend. "I do remember that he seemed annoyed to be there, and rather contemplative."

After a moment she chanced a glance back at his face.

He watched her, assessing, then offered, "Sam is quiet, and he despises parties."

She nodded, smiling faintly. "And your other friend? The Duke of Newark?"

He continued to study her for several moments. Then he brushed windblown hair from his forehead and turned his attention back to the churning waves. "Colin is everything Sam isn't—self-assured, gregarious, flirtatious to a fault. Colin is . . . colorful."

"And the ladies adore him?" she guessed, knowing the type all too well.

His mouth turned up slightly in wry humor. "An understatement. Even as a child, swarms of little girls would stand around him and giggle incessantly at the things he would do and say. Sam and I would roll our eyes and run from such nonsense. Colin absorbed it like butter on toast. Still does." He snorted. "He needs female attention in constant supply to feed his excessive vanity."

"You're just jealous," she asserted through a small laugh.

"Probably then." He looked into her eyes. "Not anymore."

That warmed her from the inside out. Vivian found

it fascinating to consider the apparent differences between the three, friends from childhood whose personalities remained unique through the years. She imagined it must have been amazing to those who witnessed the Duke of Newark and the Duke of Durham, two distinguished gentlemen of such high noble rank, standing in court, before a judge and jury, defending a man's character. She surmised that Will's future—his entire fate—had for a time rested precariously in their hands.

"They saved your life," she said softly.

"They did," he agreed after a deep inhale. "Without them, and their unswerving testimonies, I probably would have hanged."

Vivian felt her heart swell with compassion and she made a concerted effort not to break down in front of him. How horrible his life had to have been, not only while married to someone he couldn't understand or reach emotionally, but experiencing the humiliation of a public trial, and especially these last five years when society had judged him evil and beyond redemption. She had to wonder if this was the reason why he'd moved to Cornwall, why he spent his money on rare and exquisite items of beauty to decorate an estate he rarely left, a marvelous home he shared with nobody save a few loyal servants. She was beginning to understand his actions and thoughts, his confusion over the years his wife suffered, only to realize she ended her life in such terrible sadness, such emotional torment about which he could do nothing. His frustration and grief must have been as great as his guilt. No wonder he remained a recluse to this day. No wonder he seemed so alone.

Without clear thought, Vivian reached out and placed her hand on one of his, clasping it firmly, holding on tightly should he attempt to pull away. Instead, he tenderly began to brush his thumb across her knuckles, back and forth, in a calmly shared intimacy he seemed to relish.

After a long while of contentment, she pulled his hand up and lightly kissed his wrist. "You may find this incredible, Will, but my husband was very much like your wife. Not because of an emotional imbalance, but because of an addiction so strong it took away all that he was in personality before it destroyed the best of his life."

She paused for a moment as he continued to gently caress the top of her hand, saying nothing, waiting for her to carry on at her desired pace. Vivian instinctively knew his curiosity about her very personal history had to be as great as hers had been about his. In that she felt strangely comforted.

At last, throwing caution into the moist, sea-salted air that enveloped them in a world of mutual confidence, she gathered her fears and began to disclose her perfectly veiled past to the one person she suddenly trusted above all others.

"My husband was a man of some means," she started quietly, with only the slightest remaining reservation. "I've told everyone that he was a cousin, to avoid unwanted questions, but he wasn't. He was a longtime family acquaintance, and I fell in love with him the instant we met. But not only was I young when I got to know him, I was also extremely naive. I married him just before my twentieth birthday, and I, like you, was filled with good cheer and hope for a decent future of laughter, companionship, and children. Unfortunately, on my wedding night, my world took a tumble into the realm of the unimaginable."

Vivian closed her eyes and lifted her face skyward, noticing the familiar coiling of tension inside of her that always appeared when she remembered that other life. A life she hadn't discussed with a soul in more than ten years.

"My husband, Leopold, had an opium addiction, Will. He smoked it daily, hidden from everybody, and it became a nasty obsession that slowly tore away his reason to live, ate away everything he was." Lifting her lashes, she gazed straight ahead into the dull grayness of early afternoon. "On our wedding night, I dressed myself to please him, readied myself for the consummation that would take my virginity and make me his. I loved him, you see, and wanted him to love me in return."

Vivian drew in a shaky breath, feeling his eyes on her but afraid to look at him, unwilling to expose just how deep her anger had carved its way inside her mind and tender heart of so long ago. Still, though, she clung to his hand, the tether that joined them in past and destiny. Above everything, she needed to touch him now.

"I was naive, as I said, so young and unaware in my sheltered upbringing that I couldn't believe someone of my husband's prestige in the community, a man of relative wealth and education, a noble subject with a sterling reputation, could become so addicted to a substance that eventually everything good in his life held no meaning. He lived each day, from morning till night, for what he conveniently termed his *medicine*."

Will lifted her hand to his mouth and kissed her knuckles softly, though he didn't interrupt. Finally she turned and smiled at him faintly. His eyes had narrowed as he watched her with a gravity she could feel to her bones.

She lowered her voice to a soft whisper heard just above the wind. "You asked me why I was a virgin. The truth is my husband couldn't sustain an erection. Oh, he tried, and when his . . . when he didn't—respond physically, even to my touch, he blamed me for his own inability."

She watched his reaction to that news carefully as his brows drew together with an apparent confusion. Then he remarked, "His addiction was so all-consuming that it made him impotent and he considered it *your* fault?"

Heat suffused her, but she held his gaze with strength. "I was his wife and I couldn't satisfy him, which was naturally a terrible blow to his pride as a man and husband. In the beginning he didn't blame anyone; later, as he grew more and more frustrated with his physical inabilities, he blamed me—I suspect, because he refused to blame himself. And it was so much easier than blaming the opium, which he needed, at that point, for survival. He couldn't bed me and after a while it obsessed him. In time, he no longer cared."

For moments Will just stared at her, his contemplation of her confession almost visible in his handsome, sculpted features as he digested the information. Strangely, she felt neither embarrassment nor repulsion in revealing her very private affairs for the first time in a decade. In a manner of speaking, what she really felt was a sense of relief.

Finally he stretched his legs out casually along the grassy slope, crossing one ankle over the other as he angled his body in her direction, never letting go of her hand.

"How did it make you feel?" he asked soothingly.

Her mouth opened a bit in surprise. Although it was true that fewer than a handful of people knew of her marital woes, nobody had ever asked her to express how she personally felt about them.

"I—I suppose in the beginning I was unconcerned. I mean—I really didn't understand it. Later I felt hurt, especially when I tried to be a good wife, attractive to him personally, and still couldn't get him to respond." She sighed and gazed out over the water again. "In the end I got angry. He loved his smoking more than he loved me, preferred to spend time in seedy dens where he could dispose of his income and share his habit with others so inclined to throw life away. Not once did he care that others viewed me with pity. Not only was I married to a man who was obviously addicted, I also couldn't conceive, which everybody assumed to be *my* fault. At least, in society's eyes, a child would have kept me occupied and able to ignore his vulgar, dark side." She swallowed harshly, keeping fresh tears restrained. "I didn't tell anyone that he couldn't be stimulated into response. I didn't know how to discuss it."

Will exhaled loudly. "Did you consider an annulment? At least it would have given you a chance to start over—"

"I suggested it once, six months after we were married," she cut in, facing him directly, her eyes flashing a bitterness she would never be able to conceal. "He slapped me so hard my head hit a wall and my jaw was bruised for two weeks. It was my word against his, he informed me, and he would not be humiliated socially or ruined professionally by any charge of mine. I never mentioned it again. Five years later, my husband departed my world, and I moved to Penzance to forever forget the lonely nightmare that was my so-called marriage."

His expression darkened considerably as a muscle in his cheek flexed, his lips thinned.

"Bastard," he murmured, looking past her out to sea.

She turned her attention to the grayness beyond as well, answering him simply in whisper, "Yes."

A calmness settled over them, a soft and comforting cocoon of shared appreciation for mutual anxieties and shattered dreams. She faintly squeezed his hand, beginning to think she needed him more than air and sunshine, grazing his fingers with her thumb, back and forth in a sensuous motion of complete contentment. But for this day, at least, the two of them were all who mattered in the world.

They sat together for a long while, mollified by the companionable silence. Far in the distance she noticed a lone fishing boat being tossed about on large, cresting waves, a violent ocean attempting to thwart its hopes of finding its destination safely. So like the worries that engulfed her now.

"Who is blackmailing you, Vivian?" he asked in a gruff whisper.

Without pause or prevarication, she replied, "Gilbert Montague, a gifted Shakespearean actor performing in town for the season. He has in his possession a copy of a note I sent to my solicitor in London years ago in which I requested information about my erring husband. It was quite detailed. Montague knows my secrets and is threatening to reveal them to any who might be interested in a bit of gossip regarding the well-respected Widow Rael-Lamont." She exhaled through her teeth, her jaw tightening once more in fury. "In essence, he could ruin me."

Will released her and sat forward again, elbows on knees. "Did you consider going to the magistrate?"

She scoffed. "Of course." Sitting primly once more, hands folded in her lap, she added, "But what good will that do? I have no proof of blackmail, and he's got proof that could damage my reputation beyond repair. I've worked too hard to build a solid position in this community only to see it disappear at the hands of a scoundrel."

He thought about that for a moment. Then, "I could have him arrested."

She shook her head. "That won't work. I need the letter he has from my solicitor." With disgust flowing through her tone, she added, "I can't imagine how he got that."

"With enough money and persuasion, one can buy almost anything," Will replied matter-of-factly.

"Which makes no sense if Mr. Montague is a lowly actor."

He looked at her, a faint smile playing across his lips. "Very astute, madam."

She pulled a handful of grass and flung it at him.

He chuckled and lifted his hand to ward off the attack.

"Which means he's using someone else's funds, or he's not who he says he is," she related as other possibilities began to invade her mind.

"Do you know how badly I want to make love to you, Mrs. Rael-Lamont?" he said very softly, leaning back on one elbow again. "Just looking at you, talking to you, arouses me to unbearable heights."

She fairly giggled at that, at the very male way he changed the subject to one of intimacy, at the ease in which he confided his desires, at the manner in which his words and inflection made her heart jump and a surge of tingling heat flow through her past her better judgment. The Duke of Trent, she realized at that moment, possessed a wicked way of arousing her with feelings of complete contentment.

He gave her a lopsided grin. "If you weren't wearing hoops, I'd take you now."

She smiled wryly in return. "And cause more scandal? Nonsense. Besides, we can be seen from your home, your grace."

"Wilson has terrible eyesight."

"And the rest of your staff are blind, no doubt."

He shrugged lightly. "They are if I say they are."

Her smile faded. Seconds later, she admitted, "Do you know how desperately I want to feel you inside of me again, Will?"

His eyes narrowed as he studied her. "Not that I care in the least, but are you serious or teasing, Vivian? Never in my life have I heard a lady say that to me."

She thought she might have caught a trace of concern in his quieter tone.

Reaching out, she pressed her thumb to his lips. "You'll have to discover that on your own next time."

He kissed her soft skin gently.

She pulled back with a smile—until he grabbed her wrist and placed her hand, palm down, on top of his pants where she couldn't help but feel the length of his shaft, swollen and pressing against her.

"That is how much you stir my blood, Vivian," he admitted very softly. "Never doubt that I will always want you."

Her breathing grew instantly shallow as a wave of desire hit her strongly. Instinctively, she rubbed him, minutely at first, but certainly enough for him to feel the hesitant, intentional motion.

Suddenly a hunger lit his eyes. "Yes," he whispered.

She lay back on the grassy slope as best she could with her hoops at her back, next to him by mere inches, her head in her hand as she rested her elbow on the ground. He watched her, held her gaze with a startling strength of will as she began to stroke him through his clothes.

"I like touching you," she murmured, feeling the aching swell between her own legs. "I like the way you look at me . . ."

He drew in a shaky breath, never closing his eyes as he placed his head in one palm, his other hand on her breast.

"One day we will do this where I can see all of you," he murmured huskily, his thumb searching for her nipple through soft muslin.

She felt her entire body come alive, wishing desperately she could climb on top of him. "Yes . . ."

He let her find her rhythm against him, never moving himself, just letting her trace him up and down with fingertips, nails, her entire palm, stroking him steadily.

"Are you wet for me, Vivian?" he asked, his voice raspy, his eyes glazing over with his mounting desire.

"Yes."

"One day I will taste you there."

She inhaled sharply through her teeth. "How does this feel?"

"Perfect," he whispered, tenderly pinching her pointed nipple through her dress.

"Will . . ."

"If you continue," he said, his breathing labored, "I'll climax like this."

She swallowed, witnessing the passion in both his voice and the building tension in his expression, the tightness in his jaw and the muscles of his neck. He was straining to hold back.

"I want you to," she said with a dare that astounded even her as she spoke the words, moving her hand steadily over his erection. "Do you know how this excites me? I want to watch you."

"God, Vivian . . ." Suddenly he closed his eyes and pushed into her hand. "Make me come, sweetheart."

He clutched her breast now as she realized he was almost there. She, in turn, relished the moment, the feel, and the knowledge that they were the only people on earth who knew how familiar they were with each other at that moment.

She leaned over and gently brushed her lips against his. In a second of sheer recklessness, utter abandonment, and without clear thought, she whispered, "Come into my hand, sweet Will . . ."

Startled, his eyes opened wide. And then he groaned and jerked his hips against her two or three times, gritting his teeth as he leaned forward and placed his forehead on her chest. She continued to stroke him through his pants, unsure, until she felt him grab her hand, stilling her movements.

They lay very close like that for several minutes as his breathing calmed and balance of mind returned to both of them. He still pressed her hand against him, though she could feel him gradually soften. In a manner, Vivian felt so content, so free of restraint right now, knowing that if onlookers could see them, they would appear to be two fully dressed people relaxing side by side at the ocean front, close enough to be in deep conversation. Never could anyone guess they'd just been overrun with passion, that she'd said those things . . .

Deeply ashamed of a sudden, Vivian pulled back and sat up a little, looking away from him toward the house. "I—I don't want you to think I'm—"

He grasped her jaw with his hand and forced her to face him. Searching, he stared into her eyes.

"I think you're beautiful."

She offered him a tepid smile, slumping a little into her stays. "I didn't want to shock you."

"Shock me?" he frowned. "Vivian, what you just did to me, what you just said to me, made this one of the most satisfying, quick romantic interludes I've ever had. If I seem *shocked* it's because I can't believe how incredible it was to experience it fully dressed." He grinned devilishly. "I only wish you weren't wearing those blasted hoops."

She smacked him lightheartedly in the chest, though she knew her cheeks were flushed with acute gratification at his confession. "It's still embarrassing to me. I was overcome with . . . with—"

"Passion for me?"

"Yes," she whispered.

His smile faded a fraction. "Nothing we do privately is wrong as long as we both enjoy it. Understand?"

She nodded negligibly. "Will you give me the manuscript *now*?"

He dropped his hand from her chin, laughing out loud as he rolled onto his back, fingers interlocked over his stomach.

Eyeing her mischievously, he said, "You do so know how to wound a man, my darling, Vivian."

She pressed her lips together to keep from breaking into her own fit of irritated laughter.

He sighed with pure exaggeration. "First you tease, then torture me with pleasure, then demand. What, pray tell, should I do with you?"

She leaned over him, her face only inches from his. "Will you help me?" she asked very softly.

His expression became contemplative as his gaze roved over her face. Then he reached up and gently touched her hair. "With every need, until my dying breath."

Vivian stilled inside as clarity washed over her. She couldn't move, couldn't utter a sound in response as she choked back tears. Never had a man said anything quite so precious to her. Never had any man meant so much.

She glided her fingertips across his cheek. "Let's get Gilbert, my darling Will."

Chapter 14

Lady Elinor Chester took a long, deep breath then walked sensually to the full-length mirror near her bedroom window to study herself with a critical eye for the first time in years.

She really did look quite good for a woman now almost twenty-six years of age. Her long, silky blond hair was piled on top of her head while little ringlets framed her face. Her light blue eyes were delicately outlined with almost invisible lashes, but of course Elinor was an expert in the art of concealing minor flaws. She lightly applied bits of kohl to her lashes to make them darker, and skillfully rubbed rouge on her cheeks and lips to give them color. To her chagrin, Elinor found herself prone to occasional blemishes of the skin so she sometimes brushed powder on her face to absorb the oil.

Nevertheless, she was quite lovely, everyone thought so, and attracting men had never been a problem for her. In fact, it had been almost effortless until just recently when she began to notice that many of the eligible men were getting married to other women. This in itself was starting to bother her, for she only just realized that she was getting old. Not old in the aging sense but old in the marrying sense, and she absolutely refused to die unwed. During the last several months she'd slowly come to the conclusion that she was very nearly on the shelf in terms of marriage, and when she coupled that with the fact that she was running out of money, she was left with few reasonable choices. Now, at least, she had a plan.

Elinor stared hard at her reflection. Critically, the only flaw she possessed was her figure. She'd been built like a boy, a tad too slender, having no curves to speak of, and worst of all, cursed with an inexcusably small bosom. Most men in her experience didn't tend to care all that much, however, for she presented herself to the gentlemen in society with a sensuality that overcompensated for her somewhat unfeminine shape. Yes, Elinor Chester certainly knew how to please a man in bed and that in itself was worth thousands.

A slamming door from the landing below pulled her out of her thoughts as she realized Steven had returned home at last. She'd received a note from him yesterday informing her that he'd be arriving today before noon, and although it had been years since he'd stood on the grounds of their estate, she was ready, more than ready, to face her brother again.

"Elinor!" he bellowed from the entrance hall.

She sighed, rolling her eyes before lifting her skirts to walk with a purposeful stride to receive him. She knew without a doubt he'd be waiting for her in their late father's study. It's where he'd always felt important and superior.

"There you are, little sister." He half-smiled for her benefit.

Elinor stopped short in the doorway and literally gaped at him, astonished by the change in the man. "I wouldn't have recognized you, Steven," she said with a touch of awe in her voice as she looked at each feature of his face. "You look so utterly different."

His reddish-brown brows rose with indifference. "It's been a long time since I stepped foot in this pig pit," he replied with a disgusted chuckle. He sat heavily in a large winged chair, taking quick note of its dull gray leather, dry and cracking beneath his legs. "Don't we have any nice furniture anymore, Elinor? Where the devil does the money go—"

"You're one to talk, you swine of a brother," she cut in with increasing agitation. "You run away from here to God knows where, spending whatever you like, then you return years later and wonder where the money is going? Why don't you give me a little of what you and the great Gilbert Montague have stashed away?"

He only laughed harder at that, sinking further

into the chair, stretching his long legs out in front of him and crossing one ankle over the other.

Elinor could feel her anger bubbling at the surface from his rather relaxed entry back into her life, but because her brother remained in control of the situation, and more importantly the money and the manuscript, she had no intention of ruffling his feathers. Not too much, anyway. Instead of saying what was on her mind, she smiled prettily at him and sat down on the matching settee across from him, drawing her small legs up underneath her dress.

"So, Steven, how long will you be with us this time?"

"We're getting the manuscript back," he fairly whispered as he gave her a sideways glance, his good humor now changing to a wry grin.

Her eyes narrowed. "We?"

"You didn't think it was just yours, did you?"

Elinor stared at him, confused, saying nothing for a moment as she tried to ascertain the meaning of his words. Then suddenly the cloud lifted and shock took over as her eyes widened in horror.

"You can't sell it," she nearly choked out.

He snickered again, his tone abounding with ridicule.

Her stomach lurched but Elinor, ever restrained, refused to let her worries show.

"You're only trying to make me angry," she stated succinctly. "So typical of you." In a tone dripping with caution, she reminded him, "But the manuscript is *mine*, Steven."

He ignored her warning, looking now at his

hands. "That manuscript belonged to Elizabeth. She's dead."

Elinor felt her bones grow cold. "That is the point, dear brother," she spat. "It belongs to *me* now, and I want it back."

"For what purpose?"

That simple question caught her completely off guard. Seething, she squeezed her hands together in her lap, eyeing her brother candidly, amazed that he hadn't seemed to age a day in the last five years. Nor had he changed. He was as despicable as ever.

"What I want it for is not your concern."

He chuckled again, though this time it appeared false, forced.

"It's always my concern," he remarked casually as he absentmindedly picked imaginary lint off his shirt. "With Gilbert in charge—"

"*Gilbert* can rot in hell," she threw back at him, "and you damn well know it. That is *my* playing card, Steven."

His gaze shot up to her again, his eyes black with a fury he refused to contain. "Now, now, that's not proper language for a lady like yourself, dear sister," he replied, his voice softly grave.

Her body felt instantly charged with an odd mixture of its own rage and a cold rush of fear, though she sat composed, thinking furiously. She shouldn't have said that. It would do her no good at all if he walked out now. She would never see him—or her manuscript—again. And as appalling as it felt, she needed them both.

Drawing a long breath to help ease her agitation,

she lowered her lashes quite submissively and brushed her palms down her gown, freeing it from wrinkles it didn't have.

"If you must know, I believe the Earl of Demming is a collector of fine artifacts and essays—"

Her brother's burst of genuine laughter cut her off. Feeling her cheeks burn, she asked, "What is so amusing?"

"Good God, Elinor, the man is ninety years old if he's a day."

Her lips thinned. "He's only a tad over fifty, dear brother, and frankly that's irrelevant." She sat straighter on the settee and folded her hands in her lap. "He's got unlimited wealth, and he needs a wife."

Steven looked positively baffled in his continued amusement. "He doesn't need a wife, and I doubt very much that he wants one, being, as it were, a man who, shall we say, hunts on the other side of the meadow."

"I'm wondering how exactly you know that, Steven," she remarked bluntly.

His eyelids thinned to slits. "Don't toy with me."

She ignored that. "The point is, he will marry me if I offer him the manuscript in exchange for vows. Then *we* will live comfortably for the rest of our lives."

Frankly, Elinor couldn't care less if Steven—and Gilbert for that matter—disappeared forever from her world. But she wanted the assurance of a good life, and this was a nearly certain way to get it. Appeasing her brother's own desire for a rich and easy existence seemed a decent way to guarantee some cooperation at the very least.

Suddenly Steven drew his legs in and leaned toward her, hands clasped together as he rested his elbows on his knees.

"I don't think you understand something, Elinor. The point *actually* is that you don't know for a fact that the Earl of Demming will marry you, that *anyone* will marry you in exchange for a signed Shakespearean sonnet. Once again you're thinking too far ahead." He snorted, waving a hand in front of his face. "We don't have the manuscript in our possession yet."

Steven, in all his arrogance, forever knew how to counter an argument to bring her back to reality. She hated when he did that.

Sighing, Elinor acquiesced. "So what do you propose we do? Why are you here?"

He smiled again to reveal succinctly, "Our friend Gilbert has already begun a brilliant plan and this one is even better than the first."

He paused after that, attempting to tantalize her with his silence. She wasn't amused. He disgusted her.

"Oh, splendid, another great plan," Elinor retorted most sarcastically. "I suppose he wants to murder the woman then abscond with all her flower money."

Steven raised his brows in mock appreciation. "Very clever, Elinor. But actually, she's quite wealthy in her own right. God knows why she plays with dirt." He lowered his voice. "And apparently Will Raleigh has taken quite a fancy to her."

Elinor stared at him, startled at the implication. "How do you know this?"

He smirked. "I know everything."

She refused to counter that boast because she knew him well enough to understand that he'd already thought of a marvelous comeback. She refused to give him the satisfaction of making her feel stupid.

Suddenly it struck her that he hadn't denied a desire for murder, and with that frightening thought, all other considerations vanished.

"She doesn't know anything, and never will, Steven," she warned in a deadly quiet voice, sitting forward on the settee and watching him carefully. "Get the manuscript back and leave her alone."

He flattened his palm on his chest. "Goodness, such concern, Elinor."

She positively hated him. "So what *is* the plan, dear brother?"

For the first time since his arrival, she noticed a rather grave look shadow his strong features.

"She sent a note to the theater yesterday, requesting a meeting Saturday afternoon to exchange the manuscript for the original letter I purchased from her solicitor. Gilbert, of course, agreed and selected his regular pub, The Jolly Knights for the exchange because it would . . . assure her that she would be safe in a public place."

Elinor watched him, her eyes narrowed suspiciously. "You and Gilbert, you and Gilbert . . ."

He relaxed in his chair again. "As a team, he and I work far better than you and I ever did."

She brushed over that as well. "So I don't understand the need for violence. We get the manuscript back and she can go back to planting flowers none the wiser."

For a moment or two he just glared at her. Then his lips turned down snidely as he slowly shook his head.

"You're so goddamned stupid, Elinor."

Immediately, she became incensed. "How dare you insult me," she hissed, jaw set, fisting her hands at her sides to keep from lunging at him. "Getting the manuscript back from the evil man who murdered our sister was *my* idea—"

In the flash of an instant, he cut her off by springing from his chair and towering over her, planting his large palms flat on the chipping tea table between them.

"Plans change," he murmured very softly, his face only inches from hers. "Ideas are often faulty. You of all people should know that the Duke of Trent would never simply give that manuscript away for a toss or two in bed, nor does he need the money he would gain by selling it. What he'll offer instead, through the lovely Vivian Rael-Lamont, is a very grand forgery." Quickly he stood up again, pulling down on his fine waistcoat as he leered at her with nothing short of contempt. "But he likes the woman, Elinor, and for *her*, he might pay."

It only took seconds for her to come to full term with her brother's intentions. "Nobody needs to die, Steven," she said again quietly, as a calm river of dread for the woman, for all of them and what was at stake, began to course through her body.

His expression went flat as he clasped his hands behind his back. How very odd that at that moment, Elinor decided he looked quite like the gentleman he was born to be yet rarely revealed.

"Listen to me well, dear sister, for I'm only going to say this once." He continued to look down at her, his voice low as it held a cautious note. "We are no longer playing by your rules. I am in charge from this moment on."

She said nothing, but neither did she look away. He evidently took her silence as a form of agreement.

"If you stay out of this," he continued, "we will end up with more money than you can comprehend." He took a step toward her, his finger pointing at her for emphasis. "If you do as I say, this time next year you will be relaxing on the sunny coast of any country you choose with any man you desire." Again, he grinned wryly, looking her up and down. "Or of course you can attempt to wed and bed the pretty Earl of Demming. I frankly don't care. Just leave well enough alone and let Gilbert Montague do what he does best."

With that, he stepped over her skirts and walked to the door of the study. Pausing, he turned and gave her a lovely, heartfelt smile. "It's good to be home. Tell Wayne to take care of my horse, will you? I'm in desperate need of a nap."

Elinor sat on the settee for a long time, staring vacantly at the cold, clean fireplace, all the while picking at the fraying fabric of the cushion with her nails until the aging feathers inside began to poke through.

Chapter 15

Stretching out on his cool, cotton sheets, Will stared at his bedroom ceiling, painted dark green and brown to match the foliage design of the textured wallpaper. It struck him so strangely at that moment to consider that if Elizabeth had lived here she wouldn't have approved of such a dark ceiling, but Vivian most certainly would. He didn't doubt that for a minute, though how he knew such a fact, he couldn't be sure since she'd never been inside his private bed chamber in Morning House. Knowing things instinctively about another person was simply one of those oddities of life, he supposed. And lately he'd begun to realize he knew many things, intimate things, about the Widow Rael-Lamont.

He'd awakened with a strong erection this morning, thinking of her and of the erotic way she'd willingly touched him three days ago. He'd thought of little else since that afternoon by the shore. This morning, however, he'd been dreaming of her hands on him, stroking him as she'd done, arousing him beyond sanity, bringing him to climax. When he woke only a few minutes ago to an empty bed and brilliant sunshine, he actually felt regret. He wanted her here, with him, and most shocking to his sensibilities, it made him consider what it might be like to wake up with her by his side every single morning. He couldn't begin to imagine that sort of contentment after years of being alone, but after her reaction to him and his desire for her days ago, he was beginning to believe she would welcome the closeness herself. And she wouldn't care about the dark ceiling.

Groaning, he turned over onto his stomach and shoved his arms under his pillow. The hands on his mantel clock read half past eight. He hadn't slept so late in years that he could recall, but the dream of her and her nude body teasing his had kept him deep in the realm of fantasy. Yet Clement Hastings would be here in less than an hour and he needed to wash, dress, and get his thoughts in order before meeting the man. He'd received a note late last night by messenger informing him that his agent of inquiry had urgent news he needed to relate in person, but couldn't be here until after nine this morning. So although Will's marvelous thoughts consisted of the pink-tipped perfection of Vivian's breasts, he knew he had to concentrate on the more important matter of the moment.

Finally he rolled onto his back again and sat up, running the fingers of both hands through his hair.

He'd already decided it wasn't fair to compare Elizabeth to Vivian, for they were so different in every way imaginable. Yet he found it difficult not to do so. They were the only lovers he'd had in his life who mattered to him more than a quick and mutually enjoyable bedding.

Elizabeth had been sweet and young, innocent and soft, beautiful, starkly feminine, and temperamental. Vivian was mature, bold, luscious in her beauty, and although just as outwardly feminine, she was inwardly smarter, her thoughts controlled by a wisdom that certainly comes with age. Yet she was far from old. She carried herself with so much dignity and grace, so much passion for everything— from the mundane planting of flowers, to touching him intimately just for the thrill of watching him respond. Elizabeth had been well-bred and graceful, but Vivian was the epitome of charm and dazzle. Loving Elizabeth, at least in the beginning, had been a joy, an easy attachment to sweetness, a pursuit of discovery, a feeling that required no effort. But loving Vivian . . .

Will swung his legs over the side of his bed, rubbed a palm harshly down his face with an aggravation borne of confusion, then opened his eyes to stare at the blandness of his oakwood floor.

God, if he loved Vivian, and she loved him in return, it would enrich their lives like the gift of laughter. It could be the ultimate discovery for both of them, the final enchantment, the *best* effort. Not *a* joy, but *the* joy. Yet why did that seem so much better to him than the love he'd once felt for his wife? As he considered it now, he realized that in a very strange sense, loving Elizabeth had been the beginning of what should have been a delightful journey; loving Vivian would be like . . . coming home, the journey's end. And nothing was ever more comforting, more satisfying, more marvelous than that.

If he loved her—and she loved him back.

Clement Hastings had already taken a seat in the library when Will arrived, clean-shaven, bathed, and dressed in a morning suit of deep blue. Hastings, on the other hand, wore a suit of plum and tangerine, standard attire for him, actually, especially with the corsetlike waistcoat in purple plaid. Will no longer found it worth his contemplation. The investigator simply had strange taste or an even stranger valet.

He decided against sitting at his secretary this morning, instead choosing to relax on his sofa where he could pour himself a cup of tea. Hastings, he noted, had already drunk a cup and sat nervously on the edge of the cushion, a piece of paper in hand.

The investigator cleared his throat to speak even before he was asked.

"Your grace," he began, "there has been some news."

He knew that, of course, but didn't repeat it.

"Yes," he replied simply, adding a trace of cream to his cup.

"Actually," Hastings continued, "news on two fronts. I'll start first with Gilbert Herman."

Will took a sip of the steaming tea, freshly brewed and delicious as always. "Proceed."

Hastings adjusted his rotund body in the chair, looking now to his notes. The man kept meticulous notes.

"I've had Herman followed for the last two weeks, sir, on your orders," he started, delving into the matter at hand. "As you know, his routine is rather ordinary, though for the last week he's been working late nights at the theater in preparation for their final few productions before the theater closes and the troop declares its hiatus for the coming winter season."

Will nodded and leaned back against the soft cushion, lifting one leg and resting his ankle on his knee. This was all very predictable. "Go on," he pressed, taking another sip.

"Well, sir, at your request, I observed Mrs. Rael-Lamont after the production of *As You Like It* three nights ago, where she met Mr. Herman, or as she thought, Mr. Montague, to inform him she would be presenting him the manuscript. She appeared a bit agitated, which was to be expected, and he seemed his usual calm and arrogant self. They spoke only for a moment or two, then she left."

"Left the theater?"

"Yes, your grace. She left and went home alone where she remained for the rest of the evening."

"I see," he responded matter-of-factly.

Hastings pulled at his collar, loosening it with two fingers as he looked down once more to his notes, forehead creased in concentration.

"Now, sir, Mrs. Rael-Lamont was followed by one of my men; I followed Mr. Herman. He stayed at the theater until nearly one in the morning, where he then proceeded to The Jolly Knights. He met with the usual barmaid of his choice, drank two glasses of ale, and followed her upstairs."

"Isn't that rather typical of him?" Will asked.

The investigator nodded. "Yes, sir, although he's usually not so late in arriving."

Frowning, Will leaned forward in his chair and placed his feet flat on the rug. Elbows resting on his knees, he held his cup and saucer in front of him and stared down at the remainder of his tea. "I'm not sure I see the importance of this, Hastings."

"Yes, of course, sir. I'm getting to that."

For a few seconds the man studied his notes. Then unexpectedly, and quite surprisingly to Will, he folded them and tucked them into his coat pocket. Leaning forward to face the duke directly, Hastings followed Will's lead by sitting with elbows on knees, hands clasped in front of him.

"Your grace," he maintained, his tone grave, "there are two things I'm going to tell you that you may find to be a bit disturbing."

The investigator eyed him for a moment, his thick brows drawn closely together with concern as he waited for a response before continuing. Will suddenly began to feel a tinge of uneasiness settle into the pit of his empty stomach.

Gradually, he leaned forward and placed what remained of his tea on the table between them. "Tell me everything."

The investigator nodded negligibly, lowering his gaze for a moment to study the plush carpeting at his feet, then raising it again, his eyes sharply focused, his face pulled back in a grim line of determination.

"I and one of my men were in The Jolly Knights, watchful of the interactions around Herman and the other . . . patrons. The pub was crowded, certainly, but I wasn't neglectful of my duty by any means—"

"What happened?" he interrupted, his own concern threading his words. He'd never seen his agent of inquiry so unsettled before.

Hastings cleared his throat again. "Well sir, it seems as if Gilbert Herman, for a short time anyway, disappeared from under our noses."

His eyes slowly narrowed. "What do you mean, 'disappeared for a time'? I'm not sure I follow."

Hastings began tapping his fingertips together in front of him. "Your grace, precisely fifteen minutes after his arrival and the completion of his ale, Gilbert Herman took the barmaid upstairs with him, but he never came back down. For a time we thought little of it, until we began to wonder what—if you'll forgive me—was taking so long. Finally, after more than an hour, one of my men went looking and he simply wasn't there. There were no windows, and only two extra rooms for the women to entertain guests, I assume, and both were windowless and empty as well. Timmons, my man, found the barmaid asleep on a cot and when he questioned her, she rudely informed him that Herman was only with her for fifteen minutes."

Hastings paused to take a deep breath then looked directly at him once more. "As I said, the pub was very crowded last night, your grace, but the fact still remains that there was absolutely no way for that man to get past us on the main floor without us noticing, and yet that's exactly what he did, sir. He had to have walked right out of there without our knowledge, right under our noses." He finished his statement with emphasis. "The man simply vanished."

Without clear thought, Will replied, "He's an actor."

"Yes, indeed," Hastings shot back quickly in agreement, "and the oddest thing about this, your grace, is that he was back at the theater for another performance the following day." He scratched his side whiskers. "If I may be so bold, I'd like to suggest the man is working with someone else, one or both of the men are wearing disguises, and together they have planned this blackmail for months, maybe more than a year, and very, very well."

Seconds passed in silence. Then, placing his palms flat on his thighs, Will raised himself quickly and began to pace in front of the fireplace. "But what you're suggesting, Hastings, is that Herman purposely paid off the barmaid to stay upstairs for a time to dupe you, then changed his clothes, maybe his appearance, and left for a short time only to . . . do what?" He turned to the investigator and paused in his stride.

"I don't know. Meet with his accomplice? Confuse us because he knows we're following? But I do think we're being manipulated, either for pure enjoyment or some more sinister reason."

"I see. Then that's the proof that he knows he's being followed."

Hastings nodded. "I believe so, yes. As I was afraid of, sir. He's toying with us."

Toying with us.

Will shoved his hands into the pockets of his morning suit and started walking again, head down. "He's enjoying himself."

"I think he is, yes."

"Could his accomplice be the blond woman?" he asked after a moment.

Hastings leaned back in his chair. "I've considered that possibility, but I don't think so. When I saw them together the first time at the pub he was clearly disturbed by her presence." He shook his head. "No, she may be involved, but this is a complex scheme planned by men, and probably men who don't want her talking. I think that if it got ugly, she would be a liability."

"As Mrs. Rael-Lamont could be," he murmured.

The investigator hesitated, then said crisply, "As Mrs. Rael-Lamont certainly *is*, your grace."

He stopped pacing at once and stared down at the man, feeling a chilling dampness break out on his neck. "You think she's in danger?" he asked, his voice low, controlled.

"Yes," the man replied without prevarication. "Not imminent danger because there hasn't been a transfer of property or information. She is the manner or means that he's chosen to achieve a goal, to get

210

something he wants or feels he needs, and he hasn't received it yet." Hastings nodded again minutely. "But ultimately, yes. She is in the way."

Will suddenly felt as if he were thinking in a circle of fog, confusion blending with certainty, theories mingling with facts, and all of it getting them nowhere while they groped in the darkness, perilously closer to the edge of some great abyss.

"Your grace, keep in mind that right now he has the upper hand, he's smart, he knows he's being followed, knows we can't accuse him of anything because there is no proof that he's done anything even socially improper, much less illegal. He knows he's being followed and not only does he not care, he taunts us. It's a most careless thing to do, and yet I can't help but think he knows this as well, and that it's some point he's attempting to make. He's purposely shown us incredibly abrasive and reckless behavior on his part."

Hastings leaned on one leg and pointed to the ground to make his point. "The important thing to remember then, your grace, is that he's overconfident in the extreme. If we proceed with caution, plan our moves very well from this moment on, as he's done until now, he'll eventually make a mistake. They always do. And when he trips, we catch him as he falls."

Such a reassurance seemed arbitrarily vague, and it was no real comfort either, Will thought, staring now out the conservatory windows to the blue sky beyond. But the one thing of which they could be absolutely certain was that Herman had no idea how much they'd guessed about his plan. Will just hoped to God they weren't missing anything. Hastings was the best in the business, but even he had been outwitted by a man who made a living on pretense.

Will inhaled deeply, closing his eyes for a second or two before turning around to face his investigator again.

"We'll have to assume he'll suspect I'm giving him a forgery," he said.

The man's eyes narrowed shrewdly. "Indeed. It's imperative that we attempt to think like he does, and suspect as he would suspect. We can't know his motives, or his intentions, your grace, but we're smart, too." He smirked. "We're smart, too."

"I want to be there when Mrs. Rael-Lamont hands over the document."

Hastings's smile quickly faded. "I'm not sure that's a good idea."

"Why?"

"We don't know what his goals really are." He tapped his fingertips on the padded leather armrest. "For all we know, he could expect that and be planning for it."

Will felt his shoulders tense. "For what purpose?"

"That's just the point, sir, we simply don't know the details in his mind, or the mind of his accomplices. My experience tells me to continue playing the role he has assigned to us, using every caution, absorbing every detail, until he makes that one mistake—"

"And if he doesn't?"

Without hesitation, Hastings articulated, "He will.

In the meantime, we watch his every move and protect Mrs. Rael-Lamont. That is our prime objective."

He considered that for a moment, then shook his head and murmured, "I don't like it."

"I'll continue to keep my men on him, sir. I assure you if he changes one moment of his routine before his meeting with Mrs. Rael-Lamont, you'll be the first to know."

He supposed it was the best that could be done. Nodding once, he replied, "Very good." He straightened and clasped his hands behind his back. "Thank you, Hastings."

As clear as that dismissal came through, the investigator hesitated in standing. For several seconds he rubbed his thick chin with the fingers and thumb of his left hand, then said, "One more thing, sir. About the Widow Rael-Lamont."

"Yes?" he replied gruffly.

Hastings scooted forward in his seat a little. "I had mentioned earlier that there were two disturbing things I needed to convey."

He didn't like the sound of that at all. "Go on."

The investigator now made a great effort to scratch the back of his neck.

He's stalling . . .

"What is it, Hastings?" he asked very formally, the urgency and power of his position more than obvious in his tone.

The older man's plump cheeks turned a reddish hue, most unbecoming when contrasted with his purple and tangerine attire. But very telling.

213

"Forgive me, your grace, but—I do realize you've grown quite . . . fond of the Widow Rael-Lamont."

Will said nothing, feeling an instantaneous heat to his own face—and a bolt of foreboding slice through his body.

Hastings rubbed his palms along his pants. "You see, sir, as I said before, I've had some of my men working in London, and as you requested, did a bit of checking on Mrs. Rael-Lamont's family."

"Yes," he murmured, trying to control the steady beating of his heart.

"So far we haven't been able to trace her past before her marriage to Leopold Rael-Lamont, a French aristocrat roughly the rank of a baronet, we believe."

Vivian married a French aristocrat.

Hastings sighed. "Your grace, her husband was apparently a renowned opium addict, who lived off a substantial income he received from her dowry—"

"Her *dowry*?" he repeated, now admittedly baffled, and thoroughly intrigued.

The investigator pulled down on his waistcoat with both hands. "Yes, sir. Although her family is not from London, and still remains a mystery, or rather, we haven't found them yet, we do believe that she comes from a home of considerable wealth."

Will began to stride forward, toward the tea table again, noting oddly enough that his legs felt weak. Something about this was not right.

"Why is she living so . . . frugally here?" he asked, more to himself.

"Your grace," Hastings explained, his tone now quiet, sober, "in our investigation we've learned that not only is she living on her own income and not her husband's, she in fact has claimed that her husband died some ten years ago."

Stopping short of the sofa, Will stared down at the man, small and round and appearing so very uncomfortable in his ridiculously tight suit jacket and tapered waistcoat. His forehead beaded with perspiration, his jowls hung over the neck of his shirt and pinching necktie, and as he squirmed in the winged chair, he looked utterly uneasy.

"Her husband died more recently than that?"

Hastings cleared his throat. "No sir, actually just the opposite."

His earlier sense of dread exploded, rocking him back on his heels.

"Your point," he demanded too sharply.

Taken aback by that forceful charge, Hastings's eyes opened wide. He licked his lips and clarified, "We have reason to believe her husband is still very much alive, sir, and living in France. There has been no recording of his death. Mrs. Rael-Lamont is still married."

It took hours, it seemed, for that revelation to sink in past a brick wall of stubbornness and disbelief. Then at last, in unequivocal shock, he reached out with both arms and clutched the sofa back with tightly flexed fingers.

"Still married . . ." he repeated, his mouth going dry with incredulity.

"Yes," Hastings returned, never looking away.

Jesus. "I don't understand."

Hastings finally stood, rather awkwardly under

the circumstances, so that they now more or less faced each other, the sofa and tea table between them.

"To be quite blunt, your grace, after careful investigation, we've come to the conclusion that Mr. Rael-Lamont did not die, but that he and his wife came to a mutual arrangement regarding their separation. Under these conditions, they would have signed a legal separation agreement, which would entitle her to the money she brought into her marriage." He paused to let the startling information sink in. Finally, he added, "I've no idea why the man would go to France, aside from the fact that he was raised there. But such a situation does explain why Mrs. Real-Lamont is presenting herself as a widow and living in Cornwall. I don't know how much information you have regarding separation agreements, but they're binding by law. She can live as a divorced person would, I imagine, in charge of her own funds and without complete social disgrace, but she can never remarry."

Never remarry.

It had been years since Will had felt such a devastatingly personal blow at such an unsuspecting moment. Even now as he recalled it, learning of the death of his wife at her own hands had been less of a surprise. Still, with his suddenly paralyzed mind, he was nevertheless forced to admit that this situation was not about him. This had nothing to do with his power as a duke, his sensibility as a man, or his worth as Vivian's lover. This was about a long-held secret, an enormous deception, by a woman he was growing to care for deeply.

Never remarry.

Will bit down hard, jaw tight as he continued to clutch the back of the sofa with both hands, staring blankly at the leather seat. His investigator remained standing across from him, waiting.

He hadn't really considered marrying her. Not in specific terms. But now that it didn't appear to be an option at all, he felt a crushing bitterness within, a disappointment for an unrealized lifetime of peaceful dreams and loving companionship. And all along she had known they could never be together as husband and wife, with each kiss, each tender touch, each look from her beautiful eyes. In a roundabout way she had lied to him. That probably hurt the most.

Suddenly, he stood erect, clasping his hands behind him once more in stately bearing. "Do you think this is the information Gilbert Herman is using to force her into blackmail?" he asked, his voice oddly subdued.

Hastings frowned, nodding slightly. "I do, sir. Either he has very good sources, or he has somehow obtained a copy of the separation agreement. Difficult to get, but not impossible with the right persuasion and funds."

"I see." Will forced himself to breathe steadily, to allow his racing heart to still, to force his mind to *think*. At last, he said pointedly, "Thank you for your thorough work, Mr. Hastings. I'm sure I need not remind you that Mrs. Rael-Lamont deserves her privacy, and that the unusual information you've uncovered is nobody's business but her own."

Hastings gave him a half-bow. "Absolutely, your grace. I am in your service, and it shall not leave this room."

"Good."

A rapping at the library door startled them both.

"Come," he fairly bellowed.

Wilson entered, his features as prosaic as ever, reminding Will that nothing in the outside world had changed as he had in the last half hour.

"Pardon me, your grace," Wilson interrupted, "but his grace, the Duke of Newark is here."

Will almost smiled with relief to know Colin Ramsey, one of his most trusted friends, was here at last—and that his forger had arrived.

Chapter 16

❝**H**is grace, the Duke of Trent, is here to see you, madam.❞

Vivian stood up from the chair at her writing desk where she'd spent the better part of the afternoon working on lingering correspondence and sifting through personal financial accounts, thankful that he'd finally arrived. She hadn't been able to concentrate on anything anyway, knowing he'd have the manuscript copy ready and that by this time tomorrow their shared nightmare would be over.

"Thank you, Harriet. Send him in," she acknowledged with a tip of her forehead, wishing she had a moment to freshen up before he entered. The best she could manage was to shake out her silk skirts and smooth down several strands of stray curls that had loosened from the plaits she had wrapped around her ears.

Seconds later she heard his footsteps in the hallway, followed by his majestic presence filling the doorway. The sight of him never failed to take her breath away. This afternoon he wore a formal suit in dove gray, exquisitely tailored to fit his large frame, white silk waistcoat and black Byron tie. He'd combed his hair neatly away from his face in a manner that added distinction to his perfectly sculpted features and dark hazel eyes.

Faintly, she smiled at him. "Your grace."

He nodded once, minutely, and stepped into her parlor. "Mrs. Rael-Lamont."

She cast a quick glance to her housekeeper who followed him in. "That will be all, Harriet."

The older woman curtsied once and replied, "Yes, ma'am." Then she closed the door behind her, leaving the two of them alone.

For a few seconds neither spoke. Vivian's first instinct was to throw herself into his arms, to kiss him, embrace him, love him. But something held her back. In an instant she became aware of a change in him, from the tight line of his mouth to the subtle look of formal distance in his eyes. Such an unexpected turn unnerved her.

"I—would you like to sit?" she asked, palm outstretched as she motioned him toward a chair across from the pink settee.

He drew in a long, deep breath. "Thank you."

She swallowed, unbearably anxious of a sudden,

watching him closely as he turned and stepped around the settee. Lowering his body into the chair, he tossed a plain white folder of sorts onto the tea table in front of her.

Vivian stared at it, realizing at once that it contained a copy of the signed Shakespearean manuscript. She desperately wanted to open it immediately, but restrained herself because of his unusual demeanor. What surprised her was that she cared more about him and what he was feeling at the moment than she did about the opportunity to clear her good name. That was dangerous.

"I'm not sure what to say," she remarked, studying every nuance of his face.

He leaned casually against the armrest, his fist at his chin, scrutinizing her candidly. "I have something to confess, Vivian."

Her eyes widened a bit. "Confess?"

"Why don't you sit down."

She didn't like this change in him at all. "What's wrong, Will?" she asked very quietly.

He thought about that for a moment, then said again, "Sit down, Vivian."

Her heart began to race. She couldn't think of a single thing she'd done to make him angry with her, and yet he didn't seem angry exactly. Just . . . distant. Formal.

Shoulders erect, she stepped around the tea table and did as he bid her, arranging her skirts with precision then placing her hands in her lap.

"I'm going to say some things to you that you may not like," he maintained, his gaze locked with hers.

"When I'm finished, I want you to explain some things to me."

Confusion lit her brow. "Explain what things? Did something happen?"

He lowered his fist, rested his elbows on the armrests, and folded his hands across his stomach. "I'm sure you understand that from the first moment you stepped into my home weeks ago with your unusual . . . proposal, shall we say, I was under obligation to protect myself."

"Protect yourself?"

"From any potential threats—to my good name, my finances, my property."

She began to shake her head, now completely stupefied. "I'm not sure I understand."

He offered her a twisted grin. "I hired a private agent of inquiry."

It took seconds for her to grasp that disclosure, and when she did, her eyes opened wide in shock. "You had Gilbert Montague investigated?"

His lids narrowed to slits as he held her gaze. "Yes. And you."

And you.

Vivian felt her heart stop, the blood drain from her face. Dazed, she whispered, "Wha—what?"

Shrewdly, he repeated. "I had you investigated, Mrs. Rael-Lamont."

She couldn't breathe.

Oh, my God . . .

Blinking quickly, she looked around her, her fingers clinging to the cushioned seat of the settee, deathly afraid she was about to lose her stomach, or faint. The room reeled before her, the sudden heat oppressed her, and still he sat across from her calmly, watching her.

He doesn't understand.

On shaking legs, she tried to stand, uncertain where to go, what to do or say. She couldn't think.

But he knows.

Her palm flew to her mouth as a rush of tears filled her eyes. Tears shed mostly because she was starting to love him. And now he knew.

It was over.

"Why didn't you tell me?" he asked in a husky whisper.

Trembling, Vivian walked around the settee, one hand over her mouth, the other clutching the fine fabric of her gown at her belly. For a minute or so she tried to steady herself, to concentrate on what he said to her, to keep from looking at him until this moment of crazed weakness in her passed and she could think about these implications rationally.

She kept her back to him, resting her bottom on the sloped arm of the settee, hugging herself now for her own sense of protection.

"What did you learn?" she asked at last, her tone raspy and low as she stared at the tiny pink flowers in the wallpaper.

She heard him adjust his body in the chair but she didn't turn around. She wasn't yet ready to face him.

"I learned you're still married."

She closed her eyes. "I suppose that's true."

He grunted. "You suppose that's true? Do you have any idea what that means?"

How could he ask her that? "Of course I know what that means, Will. I am fully aware of all the implications. But there's much about the circumstances you likely don't understand."

"Explain it to me," he gruffly demanded.

Her eyes popped open as a fast irritation struck her. She whirled around to glare at him. "Don't you dare think you can come into my home and present yourself as the mighty Duke of Trent, ordering me to explain things to you that, in fact, are none of your concern. I'll tell you what I choose to tell you."

He pulled back just enough for her to realize she had jolted him with that bold and unladylike assertion.

"That's right, darling Vivian," he remarked caustically, and very slowly, "I can't order you to do anything, can I? I am not your husband."

The idea of Will Raleigh as her husband simply stunned her—and made her tingle all over with a heady need unfulfilled. Oh, if only it were so . . .

She pressed a shaky palm to her forehead and closed her eyes again. "You of all people should understand that I was never married in the complete sense of the word—"

"Goddamnit, Vivian, that's irrelevant." He bolted from the chair, turned, and walked swiftly to the window, staring out to Mrs. Henry's petunias next door.

"It's not irrelevant," she countered furiously, "and you should understand that after I told you the cold and horrid facts about my husband and our relationship. Everything I told you was the truth."

He pivoted to face her once more, his arms crossed over his chest. "The fact is you are married, Mrs.

Rael-Lamont, not widowed, and *that* you never told me," he enunciated in whisper. "You knew it when you let me make love to you."

Her mouth dropped open as she fisted her hands at her side. "Let you make love to me? Were you not a willing participant?"

His eyes flashed daggers. "I was not a willing participant in adultery."

"In my mind, your grace, and by law, it was *never* adultery," she seethed, her tone low and daring him to counter. "I have a separation agreement signed by Leopold. You know it's as good as a divorce."

He shook his head in wonder. "A divorce. *Nobody gets divorced!*"

His blatant fury and lack of understanding brought tears to her eyes again, but she remained steadfast in her stance, her gaze locked with his. Softly, she murmured, "No they don't. Not in our world, Will. But he used me for my money, married me for my name, then couldn't provide me with companionship or children, and refused to grant me an annulment because of how it would reflect on *him*." She inhaled a deep, trembling breath, then added in whisper, "The separation agreement was all I had. Without it, I would have had no life worth living, Will, and above all things I wanted a *life*."

Will just stared at her, caught in a turbulent storm of raw emotion. If there was nothing else he understood about life it was that it must be *lived*. He had nearly lost his through no fault of his own, and for the remainder of his years on earth he vowed to fight if his survival were ever again attacked. As he witnessed Vivian expressing her own desire for personal justice, he couldn't help but be enamored of her passion, her elegant beauty and strength of will that allowed her to establish herself as a woman of independence and charm when the alternative for her would have been certain boredom, regret, anger, and eventually suicide, whether real or emotional. She had risen above it the best way she could. Will identified with every word she spoke, and even as livid as he was with her now, he knew at that moment that he was beginning to love her.

He shifted uncomfortably from one foot to the other, afraid that she would suddenly notice his own revelation. "But you can never remarry," he mumbled thickly.

She laughed as she wiped a lone tear from her cheek with the back of her hand. "Remarry? What on earth would make you think I'd want to?"

He tried not to let that irk him. "Maybe for love?"

She faced him directly, hugging herself again with her arms crossed over her breasts, chin lifted and eyes shining with a mixture of determination and outright sorrow. "Just as nobody gets divorced, nobody marries just for love, Will," she returned softly. "It's an illusive thing, with or without the legal documents."

He felt like crawling out of his skin. Remarkably, on the outside, he remained composed. "Have you never been in love?" he asked quietly.

She took a staggered step back, then lowered her gaze to the floor and shook her head. "I can't discuss this now," she said, lifting a palm to her throat.

"Can't discuss it? Why?"

"Please," she begged in whisper. "It doesn't matter. Don't make this harder, Will."

God, she frustrated him! Raking his fingers harshly through his hair, he turned his back on her to stare out the window again, seeing nothing. She couldn't marry even if she wanted to, wouldn't divulge her innermost feelings to him. They were at a standstill.

For several long minutes silence reigned in the pink, flower-filled parlor. Then at last he heard the rustle of her skirts and realized she'd sat on the settee again.

"Tell me one thing more," he said without looking at her.

Seconds later, she replied, "If I can."

He considered his words, choosing them with care. "You said he married you for your name and money, and yet he is a French aristocrat, thereby surely possessing his own. What, then, did you mean by that?"

She took so long to answer, remained so quiet, he finally had to turn to see if she was still in the room, still breathing. But as his eyes fell upon her lovely form, in her teal gown of costly silk and hand-stitched lace, her composed manner even in the midst of heart-rending discord, her regal posture, dignity, and elegant beauty, he very nearly smiled as a shudder of incredulity passed through him.

"Who are you, really?" he asked, his gentle tone of concern imploring her to reveal what she'd been so long trying to hide from everyone.

Without moving a muscle, without taking her eyes off the ceramic pot filled to the brim with dried daisies in front of her, she breathed, "I am formerly of Northumberland, the eldest daughter of the Earl of Werrick."

And that's when Will grasped it all. "Lady Vivian," he stated through a softly spoken sigh.

She closed her eyes. "Always . . ."

It had to be the most appalling thing, Will surmised, to pretend for years to be something you are not, or in Vivian's case, a member of the nobility and unable to shine as one of them. The cold darkness of Northumberland was far removed from the sun and flowers of Cornwall, yet her entire life had paralleled his in almost every other way. She had been raised as he had, educated by the finest tutors, given every opportunity to advance socially, likely spoiled with riches, and married to the best. Only in her case, the best had turned out to be her worst nightmare. Just as his had.

"Why are you living here?" he asked in a hoarse whisper, hoping his own confused emotions would remain in check and unobserved.

After a moment of thought, she lifted her face and opened her eyes heavenward. "You of all people should understand how it feels to be shunned, to be turned away by one's peers."

That cut him deeply, but he stayed silent.

She swallowed with considerable effort, her forehead creasing from an inner pain.

"I have two sisters, Will, and no brothers. As the oldest, I was expected to be the one to achieve excellence first, to set a good example, and indeed, my father arranged a magnificent marriage for me to Lord Stanley Maitland, Viscount Shereport. Unfortunately for my father, I didn't much care for aged, widowed Lord Stanley and all four of his children, even if his property did border Werrick and would eventually become part of our family's estate." She lowered her head and stared at her hands as she wrung them tightly in her lap.

"I met Leopold at a masked ball several months before my wedding and quickly became enamored of him. He was French, true, but he was also exotic, handsome, and charming to a fault." She snickered bitterly, shaking her head. "You asked me if I've ever been in love? Well, I was in love once, Will, with Leopold Rael-Lamont, and he in turn loved my dowry and everything he could buy with it, including trips to Nice with hired ladies, very fine wine, expensive suits, and of course his opium, always that. I was deceived by an expert, and the hardest thing of all was admitting to my father in the end that he had been right. I should have married Lord Stanley. I may not have been loved, but I would have been needed. With Leopold, I wasn't even needed."

Her voice had started to tremble when she finished her divulgence of past mistakes and difficult memories. Will absorbed every word of it, both fascinated and intensely moved, wondering at the strength of the human spirit that above all else must be free and must feel worth. Vivian had found that freedom, that self-worth, by leaving a husband who deserted her on their wedding night. But at what cost?

"I think you are very brave," he whispered huskily, wanting to embrace her but holding back because he instinctively knew she'd dismiss it as coddling. She was not, and never would be, a woman to be coddled.

Recovering herself, she straightened and offered him a faint smile. "You're kind to think so, but I'm probably just the opposite, your grace."

He began to stride in her direction, though he stopped as he reached the chair across from her, placing his palms flat on the high back.

"I suppose that in the end, your father did not approve of the separation, either."

Gracefully, she stood to eye him at his level. "I think you know that he wouldn't have, Will," she said softly.

"And that's why you chose to live in Penzance, far away from home."

She hesitated, then amended, "Far away from disgracing my family. I have two sisters. They've made good marriages, but scandal would cost them. I've chosen to live out my life here in Cornwall, the relatively wealthy widow of Mr. Rael-Lamont, while my family lives in Northumberland, claiming I'm in good aristocratic company living with my husband's family on the Continent."

"And your husband?" he had to ask, even as the question left a knot of coiled tension in his chest.

She clasped her hands behind her back. "I paid him handsomely to sign the separation agreement. I haven't heard from him in more than ten years, though it's been rumored that he's enjoying my funding in the sunny south of France."

He shook his head in amazement. "Were you the

230

one to come up with this arrangement, or did someone else?"

"I did."

"And you both win."

"Yes, in a manner of speaking."

"In a manner of speaking," he repeated.

She raised her chin a bit higher. "I do still communicate with my sisters, but only by post. I enjoy my freedom here, Will, my social position and business, for which I've worked so diligently all these years, and I suspect I'd do just about anything to preserve them."

Suddenly, with those carefully guarded words, the initial reason they were brought together in the first place came crashing back into the solemn interlude they'd just shared.

After a brief moment of studying her, Will stepped around the chair and moved toward her. She didn't back away this time, but remained resolute in bearing, steady in her stance.

When he stood inches from her, he gazed down to her beautiful face, noting the determination etched into her features. Placing his palms on her cheeks, he held her, watching her, until he felt her shiver.

"I will forever guard your secret, Vivian."

She lowered her lashes, then once each, he kissed her eyes.

"Will . . ."

He faintly pressed his lips to hers, held them there for several long seconds, then released her.

Damn.

"The forgery is in the envelope," he said softly against her forehead. "What time is the meeting?"

She raised her hands and placed her palms flat on his chest. "Seven o'clock this evening, at a pub behind the theater on Canal Street."

He frowned. "The Jolly Knights."

She backed up a bit. "You know of it?"

"Yes," he answered without explanation, then added, "He's chosen wisely in meeting at a public place."

She nodded, reassuring him. "There will be others nearby. I shouldn't have to be alone with him at all, at any time."

Will wasn't altogether certain she could know that, but he would be taking precautions, something he chose not to mention to her.

He drew in an unsteady breath. "I'll be watching; my investigator and his men will be watching." Pulling back, he cupped her chin and jaw in his large hand. "Most importantly, you watch yourself. I don't want to lose you now. I have no other florists."

She looked into his eyes a final time, managing a half-grin, though her gaze conveyed a trepidation that made his heart melt. Always together, forever to be apart. In a husky whisper, he assured her, "I'm not going anywhere, Lady Vivian."

Her gaze softened with tenderness. "Thank you—for everything."

He smiled reassuringly, gently squeezed her chin. With a parting, soft touch of his lips to hers, he turned and walked out of her parlor.

Chapter 17

～♡～

Will remained standing on her porch for several long moments, hands shoved into his pockets as he stared out at the beginnings of a light rain that tapped the thick stone slabs of her walkway to the street, distorting the beauty of her small front garden like the blur of a watercolor painting. It all seemed so clean and peaceful. Such an illusion, he thought bitterly, feeling his mood darken by the second, his emotions churn in turmoil, an unsuppressed anger at himself rising to the surface.

Why the hell was he more concerned about her feelings for *him*, for their unusual and seemingly hopeless relationship, than he was for her overall safety? And yet as he considered it rationally, that

233

wasn't the case at all. He didn't think he'd ever been so worried about another human being, and it had been years since he'd felt so helpless to alter a situation. Perhaps the truth existed in the one overlapping the other—her longings to persevere mixed with his longings to have her; his desire to protect her as they both knew he had no legal right to do; their mutual attraction that would likely never go away, even as they continued to live in the same community day by day, year by year.

Will rubbed his aching eyes, wishing he'd brought an umbrella, then deciding he didn't care at all if he got wet. He would be drenched anyway if he stuck to his plans, and stick to them he would. Vivian would be meeting Montague in less than two hours. What she didn't know, what even his investigator didn't know, was that he refused to be a pawn, to sit at home and wait for news as Hastings had suggested, had even insisted. He would be there for her, protecting her at all costs. Nothing else mattered. He and his friends, Samson Carlisle and Colin Ramsey, would insure both her safety and the arrest of the actor. Ultimately, he trusted no one else.

Will took a long look at the darkening sky. Then, posture erect with purpose, he ventured out into the steady drizzle at last, unconcerned about the worsening weather. Even as water sprayed his face and clothes, he felt nothing but a cold dampness deep inside, a foreboding unlike anything he'd ever experienced before.

The final act in their sordid play was about to begin.

* * *

She despised doing nothing. How could she do *nothing* while she waited to become dinner for a fox? In little more than an hour she would need to enter a public pub that no doubt smelled of day-old sweat, spilled ale, and sour meat. She'd only been in such a vile place like that once before, looking for her husband and finding him in an upstairs, closet-sized, windowless room with a half-dressed whore, who was smoking his opium with him. He'd gone in search of a life Vivian couldn't provide him, and now she was here, nearly full circle, trying to save hers. If it weren't so absurd, it would likely be entertaining.

After several minutes of wringing her hands in contemplation of the grossly despicable things she was about to endure, Vivian began to pace the floor of her parlor, listening to the rain patter against the roof, feeling restless as she lingered alone, enclosed in her tiny, suddenly stuffy home. Remembering the envelope with the forgery, she glanced down to the tea table and felt an instant desire to see the craftsmanship inside.

Quickly, she reached for it, lifted the flap, and with great care, pulled out the aged document just far enough to note the signature near the bottom.

Marvelous, she thought in awe, gazing down at a remarkable copy. She almost smiled as she pondered the contacts the Duke of Trent must have to know someone with such talent he could create a work like this. True, she'd only seen the original once, but from her recollection, this one was a nearly flawless duplicate.

"Forgive the intrusion, Mrs. Rael-Lamont, but a gentleman is here to see you."

Vivian whirled around to face her housekeeper, clutching the envelope and manuscript against her bosom instinctively.

Harriet stood in the doorway, looking rather sheepish and pink-cheeked. "I'm sorry. Didn't mean to startle you, but he said it was important that he see you today."

Recovering herself, Vivian straightened and gingerly returned the forged document to the envelope. "Who is *he*?" she asked matter-of-factly.

"A gentleman from Truro," Harriet answered without hesitation. "He wants to purchase some orchids to give to his wife on their wedding anniversary. Lucky woman. Handsome, too, he is. I invited him in but he was dripping from rain and didn't want to muddy up the floors. Kind of him, actually."

Vivian felt a supreme annoyance set in. Her housekeeper was all business, as if there were nothing else going on in her life worth a moment of worry. She closed her eyes briefly and rubbed her palm across her forehead. "Why today . . ."

"I know it's sudden," Harriet said, her voice lowered a fraction as she became a trifle disconcerted, "but it is orchids he's after, and he came all the way here just to look at yours."

Her prized orchids. She could use the sale and her housekeeper well knew it. If she refused to see him, Harriet would become suspicious, even troubled. She had no choice but to show the man her wares and get rid of him quickly.

Sighing, she set the envelope back on the tea table and smoothed a few loose strands of hair off her cheeks with her palms. "Of course I'll see him. Did he leave a card?"

"Yes, ma'am." Harriet reached out, a small silver tray in her hand.

Vivian glanced at the fine print: *Mr. G. Herman, Esquire.*

She had never heard of him. Then again, he'd said he was from Truro.

"If anyone else calls, I am not at home, Harriet."

"Yes, ma'am."

Shoulders straight, Vivian lifted her skirts, side-stepped her housekeeper, and left the parlor for the nursery.

She didn't see him immediately as she walked out the back door and into her plush work area. The eaves and overgrown ivy protected the tables of greenery in the small enclosure from direct hit by rain, yet a sprinkling remained and the noise from splattering on the roof was nearly deafening.

"Such an ugly day, isn't it Mrs. Rael-Lamont?"

She froze on the spot, her back to him as he apparently stood behind the archway to her left, unseen from the house.

"I thought perhaps this would be a more . . . comfortable place to meet," he added lightly.

Garnering strength even as fear gripped and then encased her, she turned to look at Gilbert Montague, her mouth opening in surprise at his gentlemanly appearance. Now clean shaven, hair cut short, he wore a suit of deep gray and a stylish great coat to match—clothes of impeccable quality. No wonder Harriet hadn't recognized him.

"Wh—What are you doing here?" she managed to mumble, her voice low and trembling.

He smiled. "I've come for you."

She instinctively took a step away from him, venturing out into the rain where droplets struck her face and hair.

"Get out," she seethed, "before I scream."

Slowly, and with an icy coldness, he replied, "You scream and I'll break your creamy, delicate neck."

Bile rose in her throat; her legs began to shake, making her suddenly fear she might fall. "What about the manuscript?" It was all she could think of to say.

He chuckled, though his eyes remained steely hard as they stayed locked with hers. "Come, Vivian, are you so naive that you have no idea what this scheme is really about?"

Confused, and feeling more frightened by the second, she backed up even more, her body growing chilled as rainwater started to saturate her gown.

He began to walk toward her, so slowly she almost didn't notice his encroachment.

Trying to feign composure, to react with defiance, she raised her chin a fraction and said, "I have no idea what you *think* this is about, Mr. Montague, but I have done my best to comply with your wishes. I simply want the copy of my separation agreement that you have in your possession returned to me. After that, I hope never to lay eyes on you again."

This time he laughed with pleasure, as if he found her words truly amusing.

"In point of fact, the name is Herman, and although it hardly matters, you're not much of an actress."

She blinked; his expression went flat and cold again.

"We're going for a ride, Vivian. We're going to walk out of here together, get into my carriage, and ride."

Her world started to reel. She retreated another foot and this time her hip struck the edge of a short wooden table, jarring her.

He smirked. Then with a quickness she'd never anticipated, he latched onto her upper arm and leaned toward her. "You'll come with me now, Mrs. Rael-Lamont," he enunciated in a thick whisper she read on his lips more than heard.

The fog of fear within began to take a solid form as she fought the urge to simply run and chance escape. He must have read her thoughts, for at that moment he yanked her toward him, against him, and she couldn't mistake the sharpness of a blade at her waist.

She had never anticipated this, and neither had Will.

Will . . . How I need you now.

As Gilbert grabbed her around the shoulders to usher her through the nursery and toward the side gate, she glanced around furiously, trying to think of something. Anything—

He tightened his grip. "You scream, Vivian, you try to escape, and you die, right here among all your pretty little plants. I am in charge now. Remember that."

"My staff—"

"Won't even realize you're gone for at least an-

239

other thirty minutes or so," he cut in quite casually. "That'll give us plenty of time to leave the city."

Shivering, she gazed up at his smooth, deceptively handsome face. "Bastard," she spat between clenched teeth.

He grinned again, proudly, and in some very odd gentlemanly manner, lifted his free hand and wrapped his coat around her, hugging her against him, to protect her from the pelting rain.

"Yes, true," he replied as he led her through the tall wooden gate and out to his waiting carriage. "And I don't even need to act."

Reluctantly she stepped inside the dark enclosure, hoping for rescue, unsure if she could fight him or if the knife he carried would wound her mortally. One thing she didn't doubt anymore was that he would use it.

As they rode west out of town, without interruption or cause for concern by any onlookers, it became apparent to her that she was now very much on her own.

Chapter 18

❧❧❧

Darkness of night had arrived in brutal slowness. After the heavy rain of late afternoon, the sun had peeked out from behind a low cloud line on the horizon just as it began to set over the ocean. Will stared at it, unmoved, standing at the tall French doors of his corner music room that faced the western sky, noting with interest how the streak of brilliant gold gave way to the seldom seen flash of green as the blazing orb dipped at last into oblivion.

This room had been Elizabeth's. She had played the piano, and beautifully, too, and on several occasions these last few years he'd thought he'd heard the faint, melodic tones of a Bach minuet drift along the dark and ever-silent corridors of Morning House. Sometimes the euphony would seem so real it would catch him off guard, making him close his eyes and wish again for the time when a woman's laughter and songs of joy encircled him, enriched his life. But always the music faded. As the day did now.

Will finally lowered his gaze to the turbulent ocean, then closed his eyes and leaned his forehead against the glass of the beveled French doors. It felt icy cold to the touch, hard and hindering should he want to escape the empty confines of a home that had become the center of his life.

A home with no warmth, no laughter.

No love.

"Pardon the interruption, your grace, but I have urgent news."

Hastings. God, he didn't need this now.

Will felt his entire body tense, his fingertips clutch the thin, wooden panes between the squares of glass so tightly his nails whitened. In all of his thirty-five years of life, he'd never regretted his station more than at this moment.

But as in all things, duty called, the nature of the title with which he'd been born and raised prevailed.

Standing tall, eyes opened, he pivoted so that he looked at his investigator directly.

"Yes, Hastings, what is it?"

For a moment the older man seemed perplexed, glancing around suddenly as if just realizing he'd been brought to an entirely different room, and one rarely used.

"I— May I sit, your grace? I'm a bit winded."

Will gestured toward the yellow brocade sofa in the center of the room. "Please." He didn't bother to

move away from the French doors, instead spreading his feet a bit wider apart, crossing his arms over
his chest.

Hastings lowered his form onto the cushion, sitting uncomfortably, his spine perfectly straight to
contort to his usually tight waistcoat, though for a
change his choice of color was a rather subdued
brown. What Will noticed as most unusual, however,
was that for the first time, his agent of inquiry didn't
reach for notes.

"Your grace, I'm sure you realize now that Gilbert
Herman evaded us at the pub," Hastings began
gravely.

Will could swear he felt an invisible hand rip a
slice through his chest with a dagger. "I assumed as
much," he said coolly.

Hastings squirmed a little, his pudgy forehead
creasing in a slight frown. "There's a bit of important
news about which I need to inform you."

"Go on," he insisted without pause.

"Yes, sir, well—" he cleared his throat, "I probably
should have found this information before, and quite
honestly, if you feel the need to withhold any payment for my services I completely understand—"

"Hastings, please get to the point," Will said with
only a vague attempt to keep exasperation from
coating his words.

"Of course."

The investigator reached into a breast pocket and
pulled out his notes. Will almost smiled. Some
things were simply predictable without question.

"In all the checking I did with regard to Gilbert

243

Herman's past, I never thought, until just recently, to check into his father's business dealings as a financier," he continued, his voice slowly changing into one of excitement as he consulted the writing on the paper. "Then last week I assigned two men to do just that and they found something rather startling, sir."

Will waited, watching, absorbing the news without movement on his part.

Hastings loosened his neckcloth with two stubby fingers. "David Herman, it seems, was a shrewd banker, and being in the city, was able to easily obtain a certain list of clients, many of them noblemen. As we looked into *that* aspect of our investigation we found one name in particular we thought you might find interesting."

"What was the name?" he asked, feeling only negligible curiosity.

The investigator grinned wryly. "Chester."

It felt to Will as if the French doors suddenly flew open and a frigid winter wind slapped his face with clarity.

It was all starting to come together now. David Herman was Elizabeth's father's personal financier.

Oblivious to his employer's immediate unease, Hastings continued his good news.

"We found that Richard Chester kept a great deal of money in Herman's institution in exchange for small favors—erasing small gambling debts, early knowledge of changing interest rates, that kind of thing," he remarked lightly, his plump cheeks pink from a certain thrill of discovery. "They were actually quite friendly toward each other and they knew each other for years." He paused for effect, then whispered, "So did their children."

How odd that at a moment of sudden comprehension like this, Will stopped to consider the fact that Hastings hadn't checked or looked at his notes even once.

Moments ticked by in deathly silence. Then, "Your grace?"

Devoid of perturbation, Will drew in a heavy breath and clarified, if just for himself. "So, as I understand it, the children knew each other well, and the blond woman who met Gilbert in the pub was none other than Elinor Chester, my late wife's sister."

"That's correct, sir." Hastings frowned minutely, apparently confused, as if he expected more reaction than simple acknowledgment. He continued undaunted with a scratch to the back of his thick neck. "Gilbert Herman and Steven Chester were fairly good friends growing up, and I believe it could have been either Chester or Herman who initially thought of the blackmail. It's my opinion, sir, that once considered, they both concocted the intricate plan, perhaps as far back as the untimely death of your wife." Hastings paused again, then said, "What I'm not certain of, however, is how they gained knowledge of the manuscript. Could your wife have told her sister that you possessed such a document?"

Will actually smirked. "They all knew I owned it. The manuscript was Elizabeth's. It was her wedding present to me."

And it had been a marvelous one, he remembered.

She'd told him it was a family treasure before they were even betrothed, but the gift itself had been a complete surprise. That was when she had loved him.

"I see," Hastings said quietly.

"Evidently Elinor Chester and her brother Steven want it back."

"It would seem so, sir." He folded his notes and stuffed them back into his pocket. "Wouldn't it have been easier just to ask you for it, or offer to buy it back from you themselves? Seems more reasonable than blackmail."

Will did smile then, a fraction. "Yes, but I would never give it to either of them. I detest my wife's family."

He knew the investigator wouldn't ask him to clarify that point. Such a question would be unseemly, and beyond his need to know to complete his assignment.

Will rubbed his face harshly with his palm. "So this was a very well-organized and intricate plan. And since I know for a fact that the Chesters are nearly destitute, by their standards, of course, obtaining such a priceless treasure would be a sure access to wealth, assuming they could find a buyer who would keep his mouth shut."

"I suppose so, yes, sir," Hastings agreed.

He knew he was rambling, expressing thoughts aloud as they came to him. At this point, he decided, it hardly mattered.

With an anxiousness he could no longer contain, he shoved his hands into the pockets of his jacket and began to pace around the covered grand piano in a slow circle.

It all made perfect sense at last. Who else would know him so well, know his weaknesses? Elinor Chester was cunning, and he nearly kicked himself for not seeing the connection sooner. When he had known him, Steven Chester would never have lowered himself to speak with, much less associate himself with, a common actor, but then he hadn't spoken to Steven since the humiliation of his trial. What absolutely enraged him was that even after the man had accused him of murder, despite the family knowledge of Elizabeth's very unstable nature, he *still* sought to use him for his own selfish means. What hurt the most, what made him want to break things of unspeakable value, was that they had all gone through his heart to achieve their goals. His hatred had never been so focused as it was now.

At last he stopped pacing and turned to look at his agent of inquiry over the flat piano top.

"Hastings, thank you for the information. I need to consider all that I've learned tonight, so that will be it for now," he informed the investigator with a tip of his head. "I'll send my final payment."

"What of Mrs. Rael-Lamont?"

Just the sound of her name hit him hard. He swallowed, remembering the hurt he'd felt slice through his body at the discovery of her deceit, at the final realization that after all they'd shared, after all he'd given her, he couldn't control this outcome.

He was alone.

With a tightened jaw and a tone of stone, he replied, "I'm sure the Lady Vivian can take care of herself at this point. Good night, Hastings."

It was the most formal, curt dismissal he'd given in a long, long time. But he couldn't help the bitterness he felt at that precise moment from flowing through his words.

Hastings took the cue without resentment and immediately stood, offering a low bow. "Good night, your grace. I shall send word if I learn anything new that would be of interest to you."

Will nodded negligibly then turned to stare out the French doors once more, into the quickening darkness beyond, seeing nothing.

Chapter 19

"What the devil happened to the light?"

Will jolted at the shockingly loud voice of Colin Ramsey, one of his closest friends in the world, as the man spoke to him from the doorway.

"What time is it?" he asked gruffly to the shadowy figure that moved into the piano room in search of a lamp.

"Nearly midnight."

God, how long had he been standing here? "Oh."

Colin chuckled. "Oh? That's all you have to say?"

Irritated by his friend's jovial mood under such strained circumstances, Will fairly snorted. "Wilson just let you in here?"

"Why wouldn't he?" Colin replied at once. "I

woke him, I'm assuming, as he was none too pleased with the interruption."

"No doubt."

Colin nearly knocked over an empty ceramic vase as his hand searched for the lamp on the end table. "Dammit." He found the switch and turned it on, then righted the vase beside it.

The sudden bright light made him squint, his head begin to pound. He needed a drink.

"Want a brandy?" Will asked, his manner brusque as he turned toward a sidebar.

"Of course— God, you look a mess."

Will said nothing to that as he watched his friend sit comfortably on the sofa, in the same spot where Hastings had been roughly an hour ago, or perhaps it had been two? He couldn't remember.

"So answer my questions," Colin maintained. "Why are you standing here in the dark and what happened to the elusive woman you're after?"

The woman I'm after. Jesus.

Colin removed his frock coat, tossed it over the back of the sofa, then rolled up the sleeves of his linen shirt. "And where's Sam? I thought he would be here with you."

Will turned the unnecessary lock in the oakwood door of the sidebar and cracked it open, reaching for a decanter of dark amber liquid and two crystal snifters. After blowing out what little dust might be inside, he poured for two, filling Colin's glass to a respectable half, his nearly to the brim. He needed more than anyone tonight.

"Sam's chasing her down, no doubt," he replied

wryly as he set the decanter on top of an embroidered doily. "Probably lost."

"Chasing her down?" Colin took the snifter he was offered, though his eyes remained keenly on his friend. "What happened?"

Will shrugged and took a long swallow of expensive whiskey. "It's not brandy. Sorry."

"What happened?" Colin repeated, his tone sobering as he began to realize something was very likely wrong.

Will raked his fingers through his hair, sitting hard in the padded yellow rocker that faced the sofa. "I discovered how stupid I've been, that's what happened. And how every woman I've grown . . . fond of, shall we say, has tricked me with her lies of undying affection."

Colin's eyes narrowed as he took a sip from his glass. "Women tend to do that, which of course is why I don't enjoy the danger of becoming personally . . . involved with any. On a general basis, that is."

Will began to rock without thought, staring into his drink as he swirled the contents around in the snifter. "It was all a setup, you know," he said very quietly.

After a second or two, Colin asked, "What was a setup?"

He shook his head fractionally. "Everything. From the day she walked into my life."

Exasperated, Colin placed his whiskey on the tea table before him. "I don't follow. What the devil are you talking about?"

Will raised his glass and quickly took two large

swallows, downing half of what remained. It burned his mouth and throat terribly, which felt oddly comforting at the moment. "The good Mrs. Rael-Lamont, or as she's secretly known, the beautiful Lady Vivian, married but willing."

"That's rather crass, don't you think?" Colin remarked dryly. "I thought you cared for her."

Her eyes, her sensuality, her laughter, her thoughts . . .

"She certainly had a way with flowers," he returned nonchalantly, hoping that clipped answer would satisfy.

Colin placed his elbows on his knees and tented his fingers and thumbs together in front of him. "We've been friends for years, Will, and I've never seen you like this, so—shaken. Or something. You're not giving me an explanation as to why you asked me to watch her covertly, *for her safety*, and now that I arrive here, you've taken a sudden dislike to the woman. Does this have anything to do with the fact that she wasn't at the pub tonight where I waited for her?"

Unsure where to start in explanation, and suddenly feeling quite embarrassed about involving both of his friends in a scheme that had completely duped him, Will practically jumped from the rocker and stretched his neck in both directions before walking again to the French doors, his hands crossed over his chest.

"It's all about money," he said after a moment or two, staring out the doors, feet spread wide.

Colin groaned. "Isn't it always, where women are concerned?"

252

He snickered at that, but didn't add anything in disagreement.

Seconds ticked by in silence, then Colin said, "Uh . . . are you going to explain all of this to me or are we waiting for a late supper to be served?"

Will found no humor in his friend's attempt at lightening the tone of this most serious conversation. He closed his eyes and bit down hard before expounding, "I have to decide if I want to have her charged with a crime."

Colin let out a slow breath through his teeth.

It took a long time, it seemed, for that notion to sink in and penetrate the corners of his mind, and yet he'd been the one to say it. It just seemed a more realistic possibility when verbally posed, and he felt his hands fist beneath his arms of their own accord, a cringing inside that left him numb.

The latch clicked on the door before Colin could form a reply. Will didn't turn around. He knew who it was.

"Your grace—"

"What the blazes is going on?" came the unsettled and exasperated voice of Samson Carlisle as he brushed by the butler. "I've been sitting on an iron fence railing, staring at a dark building, for three bloody hours."

"Will that be *all* tonight, your grace?" Wilson asked succinctly.

"Yes, thank you, Wilson," he replied matter-of-factly, as if it were a common occurrence to have three of the wealthiest noblemen in all of Britain in deep discussion in his seldom-used music room at midnight.

Will turned to face his friends just as Wilson closed the door on them with a loud thud.

"Well, how marvelous," he said wryly. "Something like a party, isn't it?"

Sam stared hard at him. He'd already removed his coat, loosened the neckcloth that hung low around his collar, and now confronted him with a none-too-pleasant attitude conveyed in his solid stance, hands on hips. "What kind of ridiculous errand was this? The only action I saw all evening was a streetwalker who offered me a match."

"Probably the best proposal you've received all week," Colin cut in. "And here you don't even use tobacco. Pity."

Sam completely ignored that remark and continued to look grimly at Will. "Now you send for me, and for what? It's bloody midnight."

His voice had a certain deep sharpness to it that the other men recognized, and understood. Sam remained a serious man, in all his affairs, due to a past to which even his closest friends weren't privy. Seldom did he have the patience for joviality, or sitting still, especially at a time like this, when Will had asked for his help in friendship and had forced him to endure several hours of absolute boredom.

"I suppose you didn't take her up on the offer then?" Will asked dryly, moving back to the tea table where he'd left his nearly finished drink. "Not a very exciting end to an evening."

Sam's dark brows crinkled in puzzlement. "Her offer?"

"The match."

"What the devil is going on?" Sam demanded again, this time a little more insistently.

"I wonder how many times that question has popped up in the last ten minutes," Colin interjected from the sofa before finishing off his whiskey. "I, for one, am getting tired of asking it."

"Care for a drink, Sam?" Will offered.

"No." Sam continued to stare at him, then asked bluntly, "Who in hell is Vivian Rael-Lamont, and why did you ask me to watch a darkened theater in the now apparently unlikely event that she might appear?"

Will carried his empty glass back to the sideboard and lifted the decanter to pour another.

"You're drinking whiskey from a snifter?"

He glanced over his shoulder. "How do you know it's whiskey?"

Sam finally took a stride or two farther inside the room. "By the color. Why am I here?"

Will frowned and lifted the decanter to examine the liquid in the light.

"Yes, do tell," Colin interjected with a casual lift of his hand, sitting back comfortably on the cushion and raising an ankle to rest on the opposite knee.

Will poured. "Looks like brandy to me—"

"Goddamnit, Will, my *ass* is sore from sitting on metal, I'm tired, starved, and I still have no idea why I'm standing in your—" He took in his surroundings for the first time. "Is this the music room?"

"Did the large piano give it away?" Colin asked,

reaching for his drink again before realizing he'd finished it.

Sam looked down at him as if seeing him for the first time. "Funny."

Colin smiled. "This conversation is going nowhere. I was just getting ready to start playing—"

"Oh, for Christ's sake, sit down," Will ordered, lifting his half-filled snifter with one hand while he unbuttoned the top of his shirt with the other. "I'm still trying to figure out how that woman took me for everything. When I've discovered the answer to that enormous question, you two will be the first to know."

Instead of sitting on the sofa next to Colin, Sam looked to his left, then walked three feet to the piano where he proceeded to pull out the padded bench and straddle it, facing the other two men. He placed his palms on his knees and waited.

"Cozy," Colin said through a yawn. "Now why don't you start at the beginning."

A jumble of thoughts ran through his mind, from their first meeting in his library, when she came to him offering to buy a manuscript she knew would never be for sale, to their first touch, first kiss, first intimate encounter. To imagine it all to be an act on her part left him cold with rage even as he continued to feel the heated lust that raced through his veins when he thought of her.

Once more, Will sat down fast and hard in the rocker, forcing the wooden legs to creak as they moved on the marble floor.

"Mrs. Rael-Lamont came to me several weeks ago with a proposition. She wanted to buy my sonnet."

"Good God," Colin blurted as his head jerked back, his features contorted in disbelief. "This is why you needed the copy?"

"Yes, exactly."

"Why would she want it?" Sam asked through something that sounded like a snort. "She can't very well sell it."

"You know," he replied with a shake of his head, "even after asking her that very question, I never received an answer that made much sense. At the time I'd found her so . . . intriguing it didn't much matter to me."

"Ah."

That from Colin. Will ignored it.

"And?" Sam urged.

"And I told her that for me to consider such an idea, she had to agree to be my companion—"

"Oh, my God," Sam muttered very slowly.

Colin burst out laughing, standing quickly, his empty snifter in hand. "I'm going to try that one some day, I really am," he said between chuckles, walking around the sofa toward the sideboard. "You're a goddamn genius."

Will cursed under his breath and sat forward with feet flat on the floor, leaning over so that his forehead rested in his palms. "It wasn't like that."

"Of course not," Sam said sarcastically. "Knowing your taste in the female sex, I'm sure she's quite ugly—"

"I assumed as much myself," Colin cut in with a raising of his refilled snifter. "And if she wanted *my* sonnet, I'd simply require her to read it while she sat—"

"I wanted her *companionship*," he stressed again, raising his head and looking at one after the other. "And in point of fact, she's lovely, though that's irrelevant."

Sam almost smiled. "Of course it is."

"Yes, indeed," Colin agreed flatly. "I'm thoroughly stunned." Sipping his whiskey, he returned to the sofa, relaxing into the cushions, legs spread wide under the tea table, one arm splayed across the generously padded back. "So why don't you tell us *exactly* what happened."

Will wanted to punch the knowing grin right off his face.

"Mrs. Rael-Lamont is also the Lady Vivian, eldest daughter of the Earl of Werrick, a fact she's kept from the community for the ten years she's lived here."

Colin let out a low whistle. "Fascinating, though I was hoping for something a little bawdier."

Sam brushed over that as he immediately asked, "Why is she living alone in a tiny house in Penzance?"

Will felt that certain tenseness returning. "Her husband was an opium addict. Their marriage was never consummated and he refused to agree to an annulment in the fear that someone would learn of his . . . affliction, shall we say. It was her word against his, I suppose, and so she sought a separation agreement as the best that she could do under the circumstances. He returned to France, the place of his birth, while she decided to begin a new life here, away from family thereby saving them disgrace."

For the first time since they arrived at his home, both men stared at him with completely blank expressions.

"You seem quite certain of these facts," Sam asserted at last. "Yet how do you know she didn't lie about everything?"

"Because I took her virginity."

Mouths dropped open in unison. For a lengthy moment, nobody managed to reply, and it occurred to Will that it had been a long time since he'd rendered Colin speechless.

He sat back once more against the yellow cushion and began to rock.

Sam recovered first, bewilderment now played out across his typically stoic features as he rubbed his palms along his thighs. "So," he extrapolated aloud, "the daughter of an earl is passing herself off as a common but comfortable widow, when in actuality she's a . . . what? A married but legally separated lady . . . maiden?"

"That's an adequate assessment, I suppose," Will agreed, taking another full swallow of his whiskey.

"Well, no," Colin corrected. "Technically she's no longer a maiden, but I don't think that's illegal."

Will shot from the chair again, suddenly agitated. Head down, he walked behind the sofa and began to pace, arms behind his back. "This is all beside the bloody point."

Sam drew in a long breath and exhaled loudly, leaning over to rest his elbows on his knees, clasping his hands together in front of him. Quietly, pensively, he charged, "Then what *is* the point? Tell us why you sent for us and what's got you drinking whiskey like cold tea in July?"

Will began to feel his heart hammering away in his chest as the memory of how betrayed he had felt when he'd seen her leaving her home earlier this evening came flooding back in waves of additional shock and acute anger. How could he put that feeling of disillusionment into words? Neither Colin nor Sam had ever cared for a woman as he had cared for Vivian. Of that he was positive.

Masking his complex and confusing emotions as well as he could, he stopped pacing when he reached the end of the sofa, staring straight ahead at the intricate daffodil-and-ivy-patterned wallpaper.

Softly, he explained, "After Vivian and I became . . ."

"Companionable?"

"Get over it, Colin," Sam ordered irritably.

"*Intimate,*" he enunciated as he shot them a quick glance, "she told me she needed the manuscript because she was being blackmailed into acquiring it by a man called Gilbert Montague, a rather famous Shakespearean actor."

Sam chuckled for the first time that night. "I beg your pardon?"

"A famous *actor*?" Colin repeated, incredulous.

Will rubbed his eyes with the fingers of one hand and pivoted once more to face them. "I know. It sounds unbelievable."

"Rather like a very bad play," Colin amended, taking another sip from his snifter.

"So, go on," Sam urged with a fast lift of his arm. "What could an actor possibly use to coerce her into blackmail of all things?"

Agitated, Will began to pace again, moving behind and around the sofa toward the rocking chair. After reaching for his snifter and what drops remained of his drink, he continued to walk to the closed French doors, rubbing the knots in his neck with the fingers of one hand as he noticed how the night had faded to a solid, eerie black, made worse by a low, haunting fog.

He looked down at the fine crystal in his hand, desperate for another shot, then deciding suddenly that he'd had enough. In what seemed to him a childish act he felt compelled to commit, he turned away from the darkness of night and set his glass on top of the piano, knowing that if Elizabeth were still alive, she would haughtily scold him with the worst words imaginable for such a simple act of carelessness. He did it deliberately now, enjoying the fact that this was his home, his piano, his drink, and, at this second in time, his greatest desire.

"I said Vivian is separated from her husband," he finally managed to answer, eyeing his friends over the top of the piano. "She had it legally done, through a London solicitor and on paper. According to her, this actor somehow managed to obtain a copy of her signed separation decree, then threatened to expose her socially should she not do as he asked."

"Copies, copies everywhere," Colin interjected, pressing his fingertips against his brows. "Who did the work?"

"How the devil should I know?"

"Did you ever see this copy?" Sam asked thoughtfully.

He shook his head. "No, but I believed her."

"Why?"

That made him squirm in his shoes a little. "Because it made no sense for her to have devised such a scheme all by herself. She would have had nothing to gain by lying about her marriage, and besides, she's lived in Penzance for ten years. She has a life here, social acquaintances, a business—"

"A *business*?" Sam cut in.

He leaned over and placed his forearms atop the cold wooden surface of the piano, palms together. "She's a florist, supplies plants and flowers to the community."

Colin grinned widely. "A noblewoman posing as a flower girl? Incredible."

"I didn't say she sold carnations on the street for a few measly coins," he shot back testily. "She runs a business and is thoroughly respected by everyone in town; she has some of the best cultured orchids in Cornwall, though it's my opinion she sells them at a ridiculously high price."

"Did—did you say *orchids*?" Sam asked, deadpan.

"Yes, from the common varieties to the rare. Some of them are *quite* rare." He felt his face flush suddenly, and he thinned his lips with his building aggravation. "I buy arrangements from her frequently and have done so for nearly a year now. She's very good at what she does."

They both stared at him as if he'd said he planned to have his stables painted pink.

Now highly uncomfortable, Will shifted from one foot to the other, finally accepting the inevitable of having to admit what they probably already knew. "So I don't give a damn about the flowers. I never did. I'd seen her twice before, at a distance, and admired her. Buying her merchandise was . . . practical." He sighed. "And as it happens, it was the only way I could think of to get to meet her without raising suspicion."

"Good God," Colin spouted. "He's in love."

Will shot him a look of heated fury, which only made Sam snort forcefully as he attempted to conceal a crooked smile.

Nodding very slowly, Will maintained, "Of course it's all very amusing now, isn't it, gentlemen?"

"A regular comedy of errors," Colin agreed, trying in vain to subdue his mirth for the sake of a friend.

Will slammed his fist on the piano top. "I cared for her and she *used* me!"

That outburst sobered them at once.

"Sorry," Colin said meekly, lifting his snifter to finish off his whiskey.

Silence droned. Sam tapped his fingers together for a moment, then sat up straight and rubbed the heel of his shoe into the Oriental rug beneath his feet.

Will closed his eyes and placed his face in his hands. They didn't understand, and for some reason the easiness with which he should be able to explain the events of the last few hours evaded him. He decided to swallow his pride completely and tell them everything forthrightly.

Quietly, he revealed, "I'd arranged to have Sam wait for her at the theater, in the unlikely event she was taken there against her will, and you, Colin, to keep watch for her as she arrived at the pub. She didn't know who the two of you were, and neither would anyone else from Penzance, at least not from a distance and in common surroundings. Neither of you looks like a policeman or an agent of inquiry, either, so you'd blend in better than Hastings's men."

Lifting his head, he eyed them frankly again. "I arranged this not because I didn't trust her, but because I thought she might . . . I don't know . . . give herself away when she handed over the forged manuscript, might need the added protection. It just seemed a good idea, and I knew the two of you would help without questions, which I wasn't prepared to answer. Of course that point is now moot."

Standing tall, he started to walk very slowly around the perimeter of the piano, arms crossed over his chest.

"Approximately two hours before her scheduled meeting with Gilbert Montague at the pub, I was at her home, handing over the copy of the sonnet. Everything seemed fine, except she was quite forthcoming about her identity, which she finally confessed to me after a bit of nudging. I guess I was taken aback by her very well-kept secrets. I didn't see or sense any of this betrayal coming when I left there before she was supposed to depart for their rendezvous. In fact, she seemed rather nervous about meeting the man."

"The actor," Colin clarified.

"Yes," Will continued, his thoughts beginning to take coherent form for the first time all night as he pieced together the details for his friends. "My intention was to watch her house and then follow her when she left for the pub. I didn't tell her I'd be so close because I didn't want her to give my presence away by looking over her shoulder for me, or seeming too confident at the exchange. She *had* to be nervous, even scared, to pull this off. I knew she needed me, but I didn't want to lose the opportunity to arrest the man."

His stomach churned when he said it, causing a burning in his chest. He never should have had a second drink.

"That was noble of you," Sam asserted, his tone suggesting he remained quite serious, not at all mocking.

Will continued to pace stiffly, shoulders tense, throat tight. "Yes, well, as it happens she didn't need me."

"Ah," Colin broke in. "We've finally reached the juncture in the conversation where you inform us what actually *transpired* tonight and got you wound so tightly."

He ignored that. Inhaling a slow, purposeful breath, Will stopped moving as he neared Sam, who continued to sit on the bench at the front of the closed keyboard.

"God, I'm such an idiot," he whispered hoarsely, squeezing his eyes tightly shut in an attempt to ward off the vision of the two of them stepping into that nondescript carriage, so close together she snuggled under his great coat, the sound of his genuine laughter at something she said as she looked into his eyes.

"I waited as I'd planned," he went on, his jaw so taut from outrage he could hardly move it. "But I quickly discovered she never had any intention of leaving for a rendezvous at the pub at seven. No sooner had I wedged my rain-soaked body between a stone well and a hedge across the street, than she and one of the great *actors* in this despicable play walked from her nursery, his arm around her waist, his coat protectively covering her shoulders." He swallowed. "That's when I finally understood. They'd worked out a scheme to acquire the manuscript, and when that didn't work, when they discovered I'd be giving them nothing more than a forged copy, they changed the plan."

"Changed the plan to what?" Colin asked, utterly confounded.

Will suddenly felt like smashing something. With clenched teeth, he replied, "To kidnapping."

"What?"

Gruffly, Sam argued, "This is getting far too complicated for my understanding."

Irritably, Will exhaled a fast breath through his nostrils, then reached into his breast pocket to remove a small, lavender invitation card. Handwritten on one side, he read it aloud.

"We have Lady Vivian. In three days you will be contacted with instruction on payment for her safe return. Tell nobody or I will slice her throat and do it with pleasure."

Sam reached up and grabbed it out of his hands.

Colin's mouth dropped open an inch. "What is that all about?"

Will slapped his palm on the piano top so hard the strings inside rattled. "It's about a well-planned attempt to extort money from me!"

The fierceness in his voice was unmistakable, the tension within coiled and ready to explode. Colin and Sam stared at him, astounded. He had never before exhibited such raw fury in front of them. In front of anyone.

A minute or two ticked by in strained silence. Then Sam murmured, "When did you get this?"

His friend's concern flowed through his words unmistakably, and Will felt a brief second of regret for his uncalled-for outburst. "I'm sorry—"

"Don't apologize, for Christ's sake. Just answer the damn question," Colin interrupted, exasperated.

He rubbed his eyebrows roughly with his palm. "It was here, waiting for me, when I returned from town."

"Who delivered it?"

"It came by post."

"So somebody knew you'd see the two of them," Colin speculated, "and knew with enough time to send this."

"Not necessarily," he countered, though he could think of nothing more deductive to add. He hadn't thought of it rationally like that, not with his feelings so tangled.

Sam tapped the invitation against his fingertips, staring at it. "Did they see *you*?"

He couldn't stand still any longer, and so began to pace again, rounding the rocker, gazing up to the enormous portrait of his grandmother—tight-lipped, determined, and dressed in yellow silk—hanging on the far north wall.

"I don't know," he replied. "I sincerely doubt it. It was raining steadily by then and I never gave her any indication beforehand that I'd be waiting close by."

"But when you noticed the two of them leaving her home," Colin maintained, "she didn't look in your direction, or signal to you in any way?"

Will snickered bitterly. "No. She looked around briefly, then straight up to his face."

"Ah. She glanced around . . . searching?"

"Or perhaps just to see if I was watching," he rebutted.

"But you said you didn't think she could see you, and she had no idea you'd be there," Colin repeated as if trying to stress a point.

Will frowned, pivoting to face the men again.

Colin's cool and cautious surmising surprised him. Always the one to joke, to lift the moment between the three of them by interjecting some bit of dry humor, they expected nothing less from him. He was ever the reprieve from the gravest of situations; Sam the thinker; Will the one with the problems—or so it had seemed in recent years. Colin, though, had been Will's greatest strength when he'd been on trial for murder, simply because his friend's keen wit had kept him from sinking into a depression to rival Elizabeth's before her death.

But now, in a manner unlike him, Colin grew pensive, sitting forward once more on the edge of the sofa and staring at the tea table, tapping the top of it softly with his two index fingers.

"What are you thinking?" Will asked him very slowly.

"I was wondering the same thing," Sam remarked, shifting his body so that he no longer straddled the piano bench, but sat facing the two of them, leaning back to rest his elbows on the wooden keyboard cover.

Colin remained quiet for a moment, then said, "I was thinking that all of this seems too clever, too . . . contrived. Too well-acted."

"I don't follow," Sam admitted, crossing one leg over the other.

Colin glanced to the French doors, then stood abruptly, scratching his temple before clasping his hands behind his back and striding to the sideboard. He didn't fix another drink, just stared down at it.

"First, she didn't know you'd be there. She couldn't have, not for certain," he began, laying out his thoughts as if piecing together a puzzle.

"She had to know I'd be nearby. I told her as much," Will maintained, resting his hip on the back of the sofa, arms crossed over his chest.

"But not when and in what manner—dashing nobleman to her rescue, or clandestinely, to observe from the shadows." Colin jerked his head around

269

and looked at him directly. "And she couldn't have known what you'd do when you saw the two of them together."

That, Will had to admit, was a fact he hadn't thought of logically until now.

"But they *looked* like lovers," he said almost defensively.

Sam cocked his head to one side to assert wryly, "You just said you took her virginity. In all her years of marriage and separation, you're her first lover, and suddenly, in a matter of what—weeks? days?— you think she's taken a second? That's not even plausible."

For the first time in hours, Will felt a quick thrust of uncertainty course through him. "So maybe they aren't lovers, but . . . co-conspirators. You just said you thought her actions, their actions, were too contrived."

"*His* actions, Will, not hers," Colin charged, brows furrowed. "She sells flowers and has lived in Penzance for years, your words. *He's* the one who's suddenly entered her life."

For half the night, after seeing her and until his friends arrived less than thirty minutes earlier, he'd stood in this dark music room, feeling rejected beyond belief, consumed by a form of jealousy unlike anything he'd ever experienced in his life. He could think of nothing but the two of them together, his arm wrapped around her, his grin and her . . . what? He'd thought it looked like cheerful intimacy at the time, but now that they were analyzing it, he just couldn't be that positive.

"She certainly didn't appear very frightened," he said cautiously.

"Well then, let's define *exactly* what you did and did not see." Sam cleared his throat. "It sounds to me as if you saw Vivian snuggled up to the man under the partial cover of his overcoat. Correct?"

Will's stomach gnawed at him; he couldn't move, focused so intently as he was on his friend. "Yes."

Sam rubbed his jaw with his palm, staring at the floor as he continued with his line of thought. "He held her closely against him, and then the two of them got into his carriage. You didn't find them in bed together, you didn't see them embracing, or kissing, or hear them sharing words of love. You saw them, from a distance, walk from the rear of her house and get into a carriage. That's it." He glanced up. "And let's not forget it was raining and you were across the street. How clearly could you see them anyway?"

How clearly could you see . . .

A dark, foreboding coldness began to descend upon him, blanketing him, pressing into his chest as each second ticked by. The uneasiness that had engulfed him only moments ago now began to feel like panic—deep and terrifying and making his legs weak. With a tremor of unsteadiness, Will slowly grabbed on to the back of the rocker, gripping the wood tightly with both hands.

"Just tell me this," Colin said a minute later, his baritone voice slicing the stillness. "Why would a well-bred lady, who takes a romantic and sexual interest in you, a duke of your wealth and means, be even remotely interested in an actor? What would she have to gain from such a relationship? Where would they have met to plan a blackmail? And why, above all else, would she wait all these years to give *you* her virginity if she didn't truly care about you?" Colin shook his head and faced him with a candid gaze. "I'm not in any way dismissing what you witnessed, but frankly, these questions alone make nefarious involvement on her part seem preposterous."

Without pause or argument, Sam interjected, "I agree."

Will stood absolutely still, barely able to breathe. His heart thumped rapidly in his chest as the only sound to disrupt the quiet of the night. For a long moment he closed his eyes and tried to envision Vivian as he knew her. Really *knew* her. Either she was honest with him from the beginning, contacted him initially solely because she needed his help to keep the secrets of her past hidden and intact, and then nestled inside the coat of an attractive man as she got into his carriage because she was frightened, or even threatened, into doing as he wanted, or for weeks now she had lied and schemed so well that he did not detect one shred of pretense on her part. His mind immediately filled with the vivid vision of her sitting so beautifully on the grassy coastline, alone with him, letting him make love to her, hearing her whisper, "I like touching you . . . I like the way you look at me . . ." And that first perfect night they were together. "This will only end if you want it to . . ."

That was not an act. Suddenly it all became very clear and Will started to shake.

272

"You don't understand the whole situation," he said at once through a ragged exhale, opening his eyes again and rubbing his face with one of his palms to try and keep himself calm. "My investigator informed me this evening that Gilbert Montague, whose real name is Gilbert Herman, was a childhood friend of Elizabeth's."

"Jesus," Sam blurted. "Why didn't you tell us that before now?"

Will felt like jumping out of his skin. "Because I didn't see the connection before now!"

His outburst didn't faze them this time.

Colin leaned on the sideboard, both palms flat on the top surface. "Well what *is* the bloody connection?"

"Oh, God," Will breathed as he became grossly aware of the incredible danger he had ignored.

"Will," Sam repeated intently, slowly walking toward him, "what's the connection?"

His blood turned to ice; his shaking became pronounced as he gazed from one friend to the other. In a tone a shade above a whisper, he replied, "Vivian got into that carriage with Steven Chester."

The shock inside the music room grew to a tangible thing. For ages, it seemed, nobody moved a muscle, nobody uttered a sound.

Then at last, Sam stammered a simple, "What?"

Colin said nothing, transfixed.

Will's legs gave out at last and he slid down into the rocker again. "I saw them together and I couldn't believe it," he gruffly explained, staring at the floor in a daze, clutching his hands in front of him as the fog in his mind gradually began to clear.

"The second I laid eyes on the two of them I just assumed I'd been manipulated for money. Aside from Elizabeth's manuscript, that's all Steven and Elinor have ever wanted from me. So as I stood in the rain and watched Vivian step from the back of her house and into her front garden, held so protectively in the arms of Elizabeth's handsome, titled brother, I just assumed they were lovers because then everything seemed to fall into place and make perfect sense, all arranged from the very beginning."

Freezing inside, Will brushed beads of sweat from his upper lip with the back of his hand. "But Steven, Elinor, and Gilbert Herman used Vivian to get to me, which now seems much more logical. She was always just an innocent pawn." He paused and looked back at his friends. "They set her up to coerce me but when we became lovers and she told me everything, it spoiled their plan to get the manuscript returned to them. That's when they realized how very much *she's* worth to me and decided to alter their well-thought-out conspiracy. And I've been sitting here doing nothing for nearly six hours—" Suddenly he was so choked with fear for her he could not continue.

"Jesus Christ," Sam said almost inaudibly.

Colin started walking toward him, his tone grave as he stated with conviction, "You cannot wait for them to contact you."

"No," he whispered in a sweeping, fierce determination, abruptly standing again and turning to face them both, rage replacing his fear in an instant of decision. "I don't think Elinor is dangerous, but Steven will kill Vivian if he thinks he needs to. I've never been more certain of anything."

"Which means—"

"Alone, she has no options. I must take her back."

Deafening silence reigned once more. Standing in a semicircle, they stared at each other. Then Sam said, "*We* will take her back. You can't do this alone."

Colin groaned and stretched his neck to the ceiling. "I knew you were going to say that."

Will's nostrils flared, his lips thinned. Fisting his hands at his sides, he tried not to think about how desperately she needed him, how he had nearly betrayed her trust in him. How scared she had to be right now. He swallowed hard to keep from breaking down.

In a shaky voice, he said, "We're wasting time. Let's get out of here."

"Where to?" Colin asked as they all began to move toward the door.

Over his shoulder, Will replied, "We're riding to Truro tonight."

Chapter 20

~~~⌒◯◯⌒~~~

He banged on the tall front door at the main house on the Chester estate well before the dawn. Colin and Sam stood behind him and to his left, beneath a broken, hanging trellis and atop overgrown weeds that snaked their way onto the stone steps leading up to the landing. He had known the Chesters were in need of money, but upon riding onto the property, it became very apparent why they were so desperate for his manuscript, and when they couldn't acquire it, why such a once decent family had sunk to the depths of kidnapping for ransom.

Impatiently, Will glanced out to the still-dark eastern sky. They'd ridden northwest from Penzance at full pace, but the dense fog had slowed them down in spots where they should have been able to make better time. The roads had been relatively empty, though, and they didn't speak to anyone on the journey.

But the time in silence did afford Will the opportunity to reflect on the last few passionate weeks, to worry about the future, and the closer he got to Elinor and the haunting of his past, the more infuriated he became at the indignity she and her family had caused him and those he cared about for so many years. Now they had sweet, beautiful Vivian, the one innocent person in all of this, stolen as they might steal a diamond necklace, held for a price somewhere in the south of England, desperately needing him as she'd never needed anyone in her life.

Will banged the door again, this time using the pad of his fist instead of the knocker. If he could, he'd break it down, but two things held him back: The door was heavy and thick, and, as he rationally considered it, with so much at stake during the day and night to come, he couldn't afford to break an ankle right now.

Fortunately, he didn't need to try. Seconds later the latch clicked and almost instantaneously he shoved his body on the door and forced his way inside to stand in the dimly lit foyer, staring into the sleepy eyes of the Chesters' night-dressed butler, Stockard.

"Wake the Lady Elinor," he demanded, his tone low and cool and utterly menacing.

The older man took a step back and blinked in surprise. "Your grace—"

"Now," he insisted, "or I will walk upstairs and yank her out of bed myself."

Colin and Sam had followed him inside and now stood behind him, Sam closing the door softly, making it clear that this was no social call, and they would not be slighted into leaving anytime soon.

The butler eyed each of them quickly, tight-lipped with annoyance, then nodded once. "I will see if she is at home."

Will almost laughed. Even in the middle of the wretched night, protocol reigned. "I would do so at once," he pressed with obvious restlessness.

They didn't have to wait. As soon as Stockard turned toward the bottom landing of the formal staircase that descended from the private quarters above, Elinor appeared at the top step, dressed in a frilly pink robe, buttoned from neck to ankles. She gazed down at the three of them, a tiny, snide smile curling her upper lip.

"My goodness, you're here so early, your grace," she purred with false sweetness. "You're looking . . . as well as could be expected."

Just the sound of her shrill, little voice after all these years made his flesh crawl and his heart start to hammer away in his chest from unresolved anger and intense animosity. He hadn't seen or spoken with Elinor since the end of his trial, and yet the disgust he'd felt all those years ago suddenly flooded back through him in tumultuous waves.

"Where is she?" he asked in deadly softness, his stance forward and intimidating, hands fisted at his sides.

Elinor slowly glided down the steps, one hand on the railing, her expression lit with a disdain one might associate with a corrupt and regal queen regarding her worthless subjects.

"I see you also brought your friends," she remarked casually, ignoring his question and mood altogether. "How quaint. But you are a bit early for breakfast, don't you think?"

Will remained unmoved by her sarcastic facade. "Where is Mrs. Rael-Lamont?" he asked again, his voice chilling the musty air surrounding them. "Tell me now or I will force your filthy secrets from your lying lips."

The butler gasped, indignant, glancing from one to the other, unsure what to do.

Sam pointed a steady finger at him. "Do not interfere."

Stockard said nothing to that warning, stunned into silence.

Elinor hesitated in her stride as she reached the foyer floor, though her chin remained high. "My, my, your grace," she fairly snorted. "You've now resorted to threatening me and my staff? It's no wonder your former good name has been tarnished far and wide. I suppose you'd like to murder *me*, too—"

Will was upon her in two strides, one hand grabbing her braided hair and wrapping it around his fist, yanking her head back so that her face met his, his other palm laid firmly against her throat, poised to add pressure.

"The only woman I've ever *wanted* to kill was you, Elinor," he admitted in a dangerous whisper. "For every calculated lie, for every wicked deceit that cost me part of my life. And yet here you are, still alive for the moment." He paused, his upper lip curling snidely. "But for the first time you are at my mercy, in my very strong grip."

Her eyes widened in absolute shock at a demeanor she had never expected from him. Will relished in it.

She attempted to recover her composure, spitting at his face; he ignored it, securing his fingers around the smooth hollows of her neck, forcing her lower back firmly against the staircase railing so that she couldn't move unless he allowed it.

"Tell me where she is," he demanded, his tone ominous.

"You killed Elizabeth," she hissed, pushing her palms into his chest to no avail.

He shook his head, tightening his grip ever so slightly. "This is not about Elizabeth."

"Murderer," she choked out, her face reddening from rage and an ever growing fear she could no longer hide.

Calmly, beyond pity, Will said, "It is only murder to you because you could never face the shame and scandal of her suicide. What I've found *sickening* is that you and your brother would rather lie to the court, your peers, and to God to see an innocent man die in prison, than admit the truth of Elizabeth's illness." He leaned very close to her. "But it's over, and I am through with you."

The disgust in his voice was unmistakable. Suddenly Elinor's eyes flickered over the men standing off in the distance, and she began to claw at the hand that clung ever more forcefully to her throat.

"Help me," she managed to plead. "He's insane."

They simply watched from a distance; Colin crossed his arms over his chest nonchalantly.

Will gripped her tighter, pulled harder on her hair, his face now only inches from hers. "Where is she?" he whispered.

Elinor began to panic. She gasped for air, tried to swallow and gagged instead. Water welled up in her eyes while she fought him bitterly, scratching the skin on his fingers. "Stockard—"

Innate barbarity and base terror outdid him. He squeezed, shoved her body hard into the railing, and shouted into her face. *Tell me where she is!*

His outburst was of such magnitude it echoed across the great walls, stunning everybody, including himself. But he did not release his grip, or look away.

She began to tremble. Tears streamed down her cheeks. Then in a soft raspy wisp of defeat, she said, "Wh—with Steven."

"Where?" he charged, shaking her again.

"In Li—Lizard."

He loosened his hold of her just enough so she could draw a deep breath, though he didn't let her go.

Seconds later she added, "He has a cottage—" she gasped, then swallowed, "out—to the west—of the peninsula."

Will released her at once. Elinor's knees buckled and she shrank to the floor, coughing, gripping her neck, moving away from him and panting for breath as she tried to raise herself up on one unsteady hand.

"Bastard," she sputtered without looking at him.

Fiercely, in a voice a shade above a whisper, he stared down at her and replied, "If she is harmed in any way, you will rot in prison for the remainder of your despicable life."

With that, he turned and headed for the door.

After clearing his throat, Colin spoke for the first time to the butler, who remained rooted to the floor, his face pale as he gaped in bewilderment.

"I'm sure you won't remember anything that happened here this morning," he stated in a fashion almost cheerful.

Will saw the butler give a rather wobbly nod. It had been a warning well taken.

In silence, the three of them walked quickly out into the cool and misty dawn air, mounted their steeds, and headed south.

Chapter 21

_____⌒∞⌒_____

Vivian lay on her side on top of the tiny cot and stared at what she could see of the wall in front of her. There were no windows so the only light available came from one short, narrow crack below the door that led to the main room of the cottage where the continuous quiet remained almost unbearable.

She'd been here for many hours now, although she couldn't keep track of time enclosed as she was in relative darkness. They were close to the ocean, though it had been nighttime when they'd arrived the day before, so she also wasn't certain of their distance from the Lizard Peninsula. But he'd told her that's where they were going, and she didn't think he had reason to lie to her about their destination.

Gilbert, or Steven if one could believe he spoke

the truth now regarding his real name and identity, had talked freely to her on their journey. She had been tense, extremely frightened and physically uncomfortable—cold and nauseated; he'd been relaxed and rather content under the circumstances, expecting her complete submission. And she had given it. She continually reminded herself not to act without thought in an attempted escape, since she knew that at least for now he wouldn't randomly kill her unless she gave him reason to. That she would not do, not only because she valued her person, but because she refused to hand him the satisfaction of exercising his power over her demise.

She'd been at first surprised and confused to learn that Gilbert Montague was really Steven Chester, Will's brother-in-law, and that the man and his sister had been planning this conspiracy against him for more than two years. Steven had been quite revealing on their journey south, relating how he and his sister, Elinor, had accused the Duke of Trent of the murder of their sister, Elizabeth, after the duke had refused to help them financially beyond what was required and expected at his wife's death. At Will's subsequent acquittal, due in part to the testimony of his noble and well-respected friends, Elinor had become enraged at what she felt was a complete lack of justice. Gradually, she put her thoughts, talents, and efforts into at the very least acquiring the one piece of property that had belonged to Elizabeth, property that had physical, emotional, and financial value to all of them. Since that idea had apparently failed, it had been Steven's notion to kidnap Vivian for ransom.

Since their arrival at the cottage the night before, he'd fed her a small meal of cold potato soup with bacon. It had tasted like melted lard to Vivian, but she had eaten it, knowing that keeping her strength would be paramount to keeping her senses sharp and her body alive. She'd been left alone in the small room since their arrival, with an old and sagging cot in one corner and a chamber pot in the other as the only items at her disposal. But what bothered her most was the lack of light. Vivian thought she could truly go insane not knowing what time of day it was and having nobody to talk to, hearing nothing but the sea wind bluster against the stone walls as hour after hour ticked slowly by.

She'd tried screaming when they'd first arrived, but Steven had only snickered at her willfulness, which forced her to accept the fact that they were isolated on the coast and there would be nobody nearby to hear her cries and attempt a rescue. From that point on, she'd admonished herself to conserve her efforts. Time was all she had, and only God knew if it would be on her side.

Will remained constantly in her thoughts. Keeping him there allowed her to concentrate on all that was good in her life, and the man who would surely be her savior. At least that was her greatest hope. She had no one else. Steven seemed fairly confident that the Duke of Trent would pay his ransom demand, and he was apparently awaiting word of that fact. So far he hadn't touched her in any injurious or illicit manner, but she could never trust that he wouldn't. So, until there was communication of some kind from Will, she was at

Steven's mercy; more than anything she prayed he would just drink himself into a stupor and forget she waited, restless beyond belief but painfully quiet, just a few feet away, locked in blackness and counting the minutes as best she could.

Suddenly, through the minuscule crack in the floor, she noticed a shadow shift, heard the muffled sound of a chair being shoved a few inches across the floor. Vivian sat up abruptly, her senses attuned to every faint whistle of the wind, every creak in the floor timber. Then she realized Steven was coming for her, and her body froze in an icy twist of fear.

It took only seconds for him to unlock the door, and then it swung open and he stood beside her, grabbing her by the wrist as he yanked her off the cot. He twisted the arm he held behind her back and pushed the sharp, cutting edge of a knife blade against her throat.

"Keep your mouth shut, Vivian, and you might live through this," he whispered as he pushed her toward the door. "Your duke has arrived."

Will braced his boot against the thick wooden door of the cottage. The small light he saw in the window as he rode in had abruptly gone out, telling him with no uncertainty that they knew he was there. It didn't matter. He'd seen his share of stone cottages and could guess the layout of this one well enough, so by placing Colin, with his quicker, nimbler stature, at the back door, he knew no one could escape without confrontation. He was fairly certain there were only the two of them inside anyway, and surprise didn't matter because he knew Steven wouldn't kill her until he had money in his filthy, greedy hands, until he knew his greatest adversary watched in horror. Will understood how the man's mind worked.

Pistol poised in his right palm, Will motioned to Sam, who stood on the other side of the entrance; then without a second thought this time, he shoved the heel of his booted foot against the latch in two fast, hard thrusts. The door gave way immediately, and just as quickly the two of them moved inside, crouching low to avoid the outside light streaming through the open door, making use of the total darkness surrounding them until their eyes became adjusted. They didn't have to wait. Almost at once, Steven lit a lamp and illuminated the room.

Standing tall and cautious, Will saw Vivian first, and with one look at her haunted eyes and terrified expression he nearly shot the man who held her without a word between them. But she stood too close to Steven, more or less in front of his rather large frame, her wide skirts shielding him as he held a twelve-inch blade horizontally against her smooth, dove-white neck. It was all Will could do to stand his ground and bide his time.

"Well, your grace, I was beginning to doubt your ability to find us," Steven remarked with feigned cheerfulness. "What took you so long?"

"Are you sweating from the sudden surprise?" Will asked in a cold, deadly whisper.

"Sweating?" Steven repeated through a chuckle. "You are still so pathetically predictable. I've been waiting for hours."

Will shook his head with purpose. "You're a very bad actor, Steven. You didn't expect us at all."

Steven's eyes narrowed. "I expect to be paid. Where that transaction occurs is unimportant."

Will's jaw tightened as he leveled his weapon with both hands. "I took time to visit your aging, malicious sister, to put an end to what power and prestige your family still holds. Rest assured that the past is finished now, and when I am through with you today, you and Elinor will be scandalously ruined." His top lip curled upward in derision. "Securing that outcome is what took me so long."

Steven's eyes flickered negligibly before he grinned snidely. "I thought surely this woman meant more to you than my family's reputation."

"She means everything to me," he replied, his tone firm despite the rapid beating of his heart in his chest. "But my rescuing her from your clutches was never in any doubt."

"And yet you left me ample time to toy with her," Steven added.

Will's mouth went dry; his anger threatened to bubble over the surface. Still, he stared the man down, undaunted. "Don't attempt to goad me with your base thoughts and useless tactics. It won't work. What you've done is irrelevant now. I've found you and I'm here. The outcome of this match is not in question."

Sam remained silent during the exchange, all the while stepping very slowly around the back wall of the cottage to stand near the small kitchenette, hands behind his back. Steven didn't look at him, kept his eyes focused on Will, but he did grasp Vivian a fraction tighter and backed the two of them up against the small stone fireplace to provide himself the safest view of the otherwise fairly bare room.

"You clearly have a flair for the dramatic, your grace," Steven said, his voice taking on a raw edge as his expression turned black. "You should have been the actor."

Without lowering his gaze to look directly at her, Will took note of the fact that Vivian trembled as she was forced to stand against the man, blocking him from direct assault as he firmly gripped her arm behind her back, held the knife at her neck. One false move on her part and it would surely slice her skin. But her eyes remained open and alert, no doubt beseeching him to help her. He didn't dare glance into them, though. If he did he would falter and lose control, and she would most certainly die.

"Speaking of actors," he asked as evenly as he could, "what happened to the real Gilbert Herman?"

"You murdered him, your grace."

Will's eyes narrowed as he hid his confusion. "I've never murdered anyone before you, Steven."

Steven chucked again. "You really are stupid," he replied. "Of course it wasn't a direct kill on your part. All these years you've been living in seclusion and self-pity, ignoring all that was going on around you, absorbed by the death of your wife." His countenance instantly sparked with a hatred he no longer chose to hide. "But if you had just paid me what you should have, what we deserved, his death, Elizabeth's death, *none of this* would have happened."

"What you *deserved*?" Will asked, incredulous.

Steven's face reddened. *"Elizabeth married you for your goddamned money!"*

His booming voice shook the lone window at the panes. Will remained motionless, pulse racing, thoughts, memories spinning in his head as he tried to understand. And then the light suddenly struck him.

Steven had been the one to arrange his and Elizabeth's marriage. It was true that a union between their families had been discussed, even expected, since Elizabeth was a child, but it had been Steven who took the initiative of setting up the courtship after their father's death. Steven had pushed, and Will had relented, only when he knew it was time to settle down and provide an heir. Elizabeth was a logical, practical choice, in many ways, and it was true they liked each other well enough. But the motive, he now understood, was a fabrication from the beginning.

"I see you didn't know," Steven said, his smooth, casual demeanor returning in a flash. "How pitiful that someone of your power, your wealth, could be so blind. How utterly unfortunate your longtime greediness has been for you."

Will continued to subdue the rage burning inside of him the best he could. He refused to act until he had received all the answers he sought.

"Greediness was never the issue. You may have used me, Steven, but I was never blind," he murmured, jaw tight, his gaze formidable as he stared directly at the man. "If I had been so ignorant of your deceit and intentions, you and your sister would be living in luxury to this day. As it is, you're practically penniless."

For the first time, Steven hinted at a lack of assurance, as if such a thought had not occurred to him. He shifted ever so slightly from one foot to the other; perspiration broke out on his forehead.

"So what did you do with Herman?" Will asked softly, although the pieces of the puzzle were already beginning to take form in his mind.

Steven grinned wryly. "I sliced his throat and buried him. I'm very good with a knife."

He jerked Vivian back against his body once more, and she whimpered either in pain or in a sudden sense of panic. Will clutched his weapon tighter, tried to breathe deeply.

"Why?" he whispered, a certain dread enveloping him.

Steven cocked his head a fraction. "Because he and Elizabeth were in love and had been for years. But I could never allow her to marry a working man with no title, a Jew and an *actor* no less. The gossip would be appalling. I'd never be able to show my face in society again."

Those words were a physical pain that sliced hard through his chest, wounding him on many levels. Without any doubt, he knew that Elizabeth had cared for him, had tried to make him a good wife, and in general, she had succeeded. But hearing of her love for another, a love she carried through their short time together, was not only reasonable, it actually put many of his memories of her and her actions in perspective. As he considered it now, she was never truly happy with him, even during their best times together. Something was always missing in their relationship, in social gatherings and in bed. He'd rationalized at the time that it was her extreme turns of mood that kept her from enjoying married life to its fullest. Now, with such a shocking revelation, he realized that along with her particular affliction, her depression flowed from the knowledge that she could never be with the man she loved. Her own brother had seen to it.

Indeed, he believed Steven, and although it hurt to know that his wife loved another man while she'd been with him, he had to respect her deeply to this day for her ability never to mention it. To her good credit, Elizabeth never used her affection for Gilbert Herman as a weapon.

"She must have hated you for denying her that one bit of happiness," Will said in a tone of disgust.

Steven feigned an exaggerated sigh. "Alas, so did he." With a focused calculation, his eyes black and intense, his expression hardening, he added, "Elizabeth took her own life because she couldn't have one with him. Did you know that, your grace? I did. And so did Herman."

So did Herman . . .

"What was the point of killing Gilbert Herman after she died?" he asked in a grave, low timbre, the fog in his head beginning to clear.

Steven's eye twitched, his lips thinned. "He wanted to testify at your trial that he knew my dear, departed sister actually committed suicide because she loved him and couldn't bear to live a life without him." He chuckled. "Ridiculous female rationality, but I could

292

not, you understand, allow that to happen. Not only would your death be convenient for all concerned, I could not ever allow her suicide to be mentioned in good Christian circles. Murder yes, accident yes. But never suicide. You know what society would think."

Will swallowed, shaking his head minutely in a feeling of disbelief and hatred never more keen and focused than it was right now.

"You are a sick son of a bitch," Sam said from the corner of the room.

Steven seemed less startled by that interruption than Will was. But he remained steady in his stance, poised to strike, noting that it would have to be soon. Vivian visibly shook now; she'd shut her eyes. His heart ached to grab on to her and never let go; his body yearned to strike the man who had so altered the course of both of their well-ordered lives. Still, one question remained.

"Why bother to change identities?"

"Why not?" Steven replied immediately. "It afforded me the opportunity to leave for the Continent after your rather unjustified acquittal. Gilbert Herman and I sort of . . . evolved into one man while I traveled there, eventually becoming the great Shakespearean actor Gilbert Montague, a new identity that wouldn't be associated with either of us. Since I turned out to be a much better actor than he ever was, I had no trouble going abroad for a while then resuming my performing here in England, after the business of your trial had died down and there was no hope of the authorities recovering Herman's body, or at the very least, identifying it." He smiled arrogantly. "And of course Steven Chester was simply traveling abroad. One only had to ask his sister."

Will's blood felt like ice.

With an audacity that surely shocked them all, Steven leaned over and gently kissed Vivian's cheek. She winced, and it was all Will could do not to take the shot.

"Years later," Steven continued, eyeing him again, "as I started to consider all the ramifications of my actions, I one day realized it was surely the most brilliant thing I had ever done. It occurred to me that I could use Montague's identity to become a rich man by getting the manuscript from you and selling it on the Continent, or the Middle East or America, where it could be authenticated and easily traded for a hefty sum. Then Gilbert would disappear and Steven would come home at last to settle down comfortably in society. Unfortunately, I will have to leave the country to settle down now. You have seen to that. But no matter, the Mediterranean is lovely any time of year." He lowered his voice and very somberly asked, "Now where is my money?"

Will took careful note of his sudden change in mood. "So, you and your sister took some time to plan," he maintained as his tone became darker as well, "then you moved ever so subtly into my life again by using an innocent woman to get to me."

Steven glared at him with blackened eyes. "And she was good, your grace, in so many different ways." He dropped his voice to a deadly whisper. "Now where is my money?"

Will's heart pounded, his head ached, his body

broke out in a cold sweat that drenched him with a fear he had never felt in his life. He clenched his teeth together to control himself, for he could not lose it now. If he did, she would die.

With an odd sense of satisfaction, he replied, "What would make you think that I would pay for something that belongs to me?"

It took seconds for Steven to grasp the intent behind his words. Then his face immediately turned a brilliant red as his eyes opened wide. His body shook with a fury so harsh the edge of the blade that still rested at her neck began to nick it, forming drops of blood at the surface.

"You will never know what your stupidity has cost you," Steven said in a thick, raspy voice.

Will's gaze never wavered from Steven's. The muscle in his cheek twitched slightly as he countered in whisper, "And you, Steven, will never know what hit you. Suddenly he shouted, *"Let her go!"*

Almost instantaneously the back door crashed open as Colin rushed inside then dropped to the floor and rolled. The unexpected noise and movement from his left startled Steven so that his grip on Vivian loosened enough for her to react. With amazing strength and determination to escape his clutches, she shoved her foot back into his kneecap. Roaring in rage, Steven grabbed her by her hair and threw her, headfirst, into the stone wall. At just that moment, Will fired his weapon, hitting the man squarely in the temple. For a split second Steven seemed stunned, then his knife fell from his lifeless fingers and he dropped to the floor.

Chapter 22

Vivian had yet to regain consciousness, and it terrified him to think she might be dying. He held her on his lap as best he could as the four of them rode quickly back toward Penzance, cold and wet from a light, lingering rain, all of them silent but for clipped, necessary conversation. For Will, it proved to be the longest ride of his life.

He had reached her side instantly after disposing of Steven, noticing at once how her head bled profusely from a deep puncture at the hairline on her forehead where she'd struck the sharp edge of the rock wall. Will had swiftly ripped off a section of Steven's shirt, tying it securely around her head before lifting her in his arms to rush her back to safety. They had stopped briefly on the road, as she'd moaned once then vomited across his stomach, seconds later sinking back into darkness as they moved on even faster. He held her tightly, securely, trying with every bit of strength he possessed not to think of anything at all save the desire to get home and attend to this brave woman who had done nothing to warrant such evil retribution.

At last they turned into the front drive of Morning House, where Will thought she'd get the best care. As soon as he'd stopped near the front steps, Colin and Sam were off their horses to help him as he lowered her into their arms. After dismounting, he quickly took her back from them and carried her up the front steps, glancing curtly to a stunned Wilson who held the front door open wide for their entrance.

"Send for my surgeon at once; tell him it's an emergency," he ordered as he moved into the foyer and toward the grand staircase. "And I want a bath prepared in my bed chamber now."

"Of course, your grace," Wilson responded decisively. "Right away."

Will was breathing hard and fast when he reached the top of the landing and headed for his bedroom at the end of the hall. He carried Vivian into it and gently laid her down on the plush coverlet, resting her injured head on his pillow with great care.

Subduing emotion as much as he could considering the potential seriousness of her condition, he tried to think only of the practical for the moment, getting her clean, having her looked at by his doctor, making her comfortable and helping her to get better in any way he could.

Yet she looked like death, like a fallen angel, filthy and weak as she rested in perfect peace, taking slow, deep breaths, the rise and fall of her chest the only movement she made.

Although it seemed an eternity, he could have only stood by her side staring down at her for moments before there was a knock at the door followed by four servants entering—two carrying a brass tub, one holding two big buckets of steaming water, and another carrying towels and soap.

With a short curtsy, one of the young girls said, "More water will be here momentarily, your grace. Is there anything else?"

"No. I'll send for you when I'm through," he replied, his voice commanding even under the circumstances, uncaring what they thought of him bathing the Lady Vivian alone in his bedroom. He knew this situation had already gone well beyond, and was far more important than, a matter of protocol.

Another two chambermaids entered seconds later with water buckets, and within moments the tub was filled nearly three quarters full.

"Leave us," he fairly barked. "And I want no interruptions until the doctor arrives."

"Yes, your grace." After curtsies of acknowledgment, the room was emptied once more save for the two of them.

He removed his soiled shirt first, then, bare-chested, he slowly went to work on Vivian. First, he untied and removed her shoes, then turning her on her side, he unbuttoned her gown from neck to waist, carefully removing it and her petticoats which he tossed on the floor beside the bed. Next he rolled her stockings down her legs until they were bare, then tipped her on her side again to unhook her corset. With great care and trembling hands, he tugged and loosened it until he could easily lift it from her body.

Will stared down at her naked form, knowing that this beautiful vision of her would forever be embedded in his mind. But it was the bloodied makeshift bandage still wrapped around her head, marring his first-ever look at her unique and luscious femininity, that brought tears to his eyes and a lump to his throat for the first time in years.

He squeezed his lids shut to recapture control, then rubbed his eyes with his fingertips, breathing deeply, feeling a sudden, inescapable physical exhaustion and emotional weariness envelop him. If he could, he would gladly collapse right here, beside her, cuddled into her peaceful form, and sleep for days with only her for warmth and strength. But such thoughts weren't practical. He needed to regain his perspective. He had to make her better.

After a few seconds of steadying himself and his thoughts, Will wiped his palms harshly down his face and over his still-wet hair, then went to work, placing one arm under her knees, the other behind her neck, lifting her once more. He carried her to the tub, then tenderly lowered her body inside after a quick test of the water temperature with his fingers.

He eased her down, still cradling her neck as he reached for a washcloth. He wet it and first wiped her face, removing grime and blood that had run down her cheek, now pale and cool to the touch. He ran warm water across her neck, cleaning the nick she'd received from the knife, though thankfully it wasn't more than a scratch. As her arms dangled freely in the water, he added soap to the cloth and began to wash her body, her breasts and legs, feet and hands, only barely brushing the delicate skin between her thighs. At last, with one hand, he carefully untied the material wrapped around her head and loosened it just enough to make sure the wound had stopped bleeding. After assuring himself that it had, he removed the bandage, dropping it to the floor.

Not wanting to affect her healing, he decided not to wash her hair, though he did squeeze the water out of the cloth then lightly tapped her hairline to better view the injury.

He noticed only the one sharp puncture that had already closed over, but beneath it was a large knot about half an inch high and the width of a woman's fist. She had been flung hard, with fatal intent, and suddenly Will felt the overpowering urge to murder Steven all over again.

But he couldn't consider his rage and the indignity borne him and those he loved now. His late wife's family didn't deserve any more of his time or contemplation. If he allowed his thoughts, his anger and resentment, to linger on the injustices they had done to him over the years, they would ultimately win in their desire for his life's destruction. He refused to let them win. It was all truly over.

Vivian still hadn't made a sound, hadn't moved at

all since he'd brought her inside his home. She rested her neck and head against his arm, but he felt he had cleaned her body as much as he could. There was nothing more he could do for her now. They could only await his doctor.

He reached for a towel with his free hand and fanned it out over his shoulder. Then bracing his legs on the floor beside the tub, he lifted her once more, resting her wet body against him as he returned her to his bed.

Placing her gently upon the coverlet for a second time, he proceeded quickly but softly to dry her off. Once finished, he pulled the coverlet out from beneath her and covered her body to the neck, brushing her hair back from her face with his fingertips.

Will sat on the edge of the bed near her covered feet, dangling the towel from his hand, looking at her as she rested, so quiet and lifeless.

"I'm sorry," he breathed, his voice barely audible. "I'm so sorry."

For a long time he sat there, motionless, his bedroom deathly silent except for the steady, relentless tapping of the rain on the windows.

At last his exhaustion overcame him. Will stood, walked to his wardrobe and found a clean, casual shirt and dry pants. He donned the fresh clothing, then pulled his favorite cushioned rocker from next to the fireplace to Vivian's side, where he sat heavily and leaned forward, resting his weary head on his crossed arms, next to her covered breasts.

Her steady breathing sustained him, relaxed him, and after a time, he slept.

* * *

A resounding knock at the door startled him awake. Will sat up abruptly, momentarily confused by his surroundings, the time. Then the knock again.

He glanced down at Vivian's still, sleeping form and a flood of memory came rushing back, haunting and hurting.

Running his fingers through his hair, he said, "Come." He stood up from the rocker, his body feeling tense and tight, his muscles sore. Before he could take a step, Wilson entered, glancing only briefly at Vivian lying in the bed, then looking at Will, no expression on his face whatsoever. It occurred to Will, oddly enough at such a moment, that Wilson was a marvelous servant. Loyal and nonjudgmental.

"Your grace, Doctor Braithwaite has arrived," Wilson stated, standing tall, hands behind his back.

Will wiped a palm down his face. "Send him up here immediately."

"Yes sir."

"And I want a fire started and the bath removed," he added, becoming aware for the first time of the damp chilliness in the air and the steady, continuing rainfall that made the room look gray and gloomy.

"Right away, your grace," Wilson replied. "Will there be anything else?"

Suddenly he remembered he hadn't come home alone. Hands on hips, he asked, "Where are Colin and Sam?"

Although Will had spoken of his friends informally for years, Wilson answered his question with strict decorum.

"His Grace, the Duke of Newark has retired to the blue room, and His Grace, the Duke of Durham has retired to the green salon. Both have eaten hearty meals and are now presumably resting."

He nodded once. "I see. What time is it?"

"Nearly half past eleven, your grace."

God, how long had he been sleeping? "Thank you, Wilson, that will be all."

Wilson bowed, then quit the room.

Will glanced down at Vivian again, who lay in the same position he'd placed her in after her bath. But, in a flicker of hope, he noted that she was still breathing steadily and strongly, and that her color looked a trifle better. At least he thought so.

Moments later, another knock sounded at the door.

"Come in," he ordered again.

Wilson entered first and announced the surgeon, then went to the grate to light a fire.

Doctor Gilmore Braithwaite followed immediately, his corpulent form barely fitting through the doorway. He wore a perpetual smile on his nearly fifty-year-old face, though most people rarely took note of this once they placed their attention on his long and curled, waxed mustache.

Today he wore casual clothing, though that said very little of the individual who spent most of his days relaxing with his wife and seven children in Penzance. The man had a rather mundane business, an ordinary home life, but he was considered by all to be the best surgeon in Cornwall.

"Good day, your grace," Braithwaite said jovially

as soon as Wilson retreated and closed the door behind him. "I hear you're in need of assistance."

"Indeed, doctor, I have a patient for you. Mrs. Vivian Rael-Lamont. A head injury. She—" He stumbled over the words as his chest tightened. "She had an accident—"

"How long has she been unconscious?" the doctor cut in, his tone growing serious, frowning so much his mustache drooped as he walked directly to the bed, clutching his brown leather bag of medical sundries.

Will backed up from her side a little as the man moved in to peer down at her. "About . . . I'm not sure. Maybe eighteen hours."

The doctor placed his bag on the coverlet. "Any vomiting?" he asked as he touched her face with the back of his hand.

Shaken by the grave inflection in Braithwaite's voice, Will crossed his arms in front of him and tried to remain composed. "Yes, once."

The doctor leaned over her and lifted one of her eyelids. "How old is she?"

For a second or two, that question confused him. Then he mumbled, "Five years and thirty or thereabouts."

"Mmm-hmph."

Silence ensued for several minutes while the doctor examined his patient, opening his bag to utilize one contraption or another. Agitated, Will couldn't watch, so he instead turned his back to them and walked to the grate, staring down at the beginnings of a good, warm fire. The room still felt altogether chilly, but the heat on his face as he gazed absentmindedly into the blue-red coals felt somewhat soothing.

Finally, he heard the rustle of the doctor's things as the man finished his examination. Turning, he watched Braithwaite place his items back in his leather bag and close it with an annoyingly loud click.

Will clasped his hands behind him, standing as tall and stately as possible.

"She cannot die," he fairly charged, though his voice sounded weak and verging on hopelessness to his ears.

The doctor drew in a long breath and pulled down on the sleeves of his linen shirt. "You grace, if I may be direct?"

He felt like roaring to the rafters and tearing the room apart with his bare hands. Instead, he replied as evenly as possible, "I would expect nothing less, doctor."

Braithwaite cleared his throat, then reached for his bag which he held with both hands in front of him. "Sir, this woman has a nasty injury that may include damage to her brain. These things . . ." He shook his head. "These things are unpredictable."

Will felt his jaw tighten, his eyes burn in tired irritation. "You're saying that as a surgeon you can do nothing for her?"

"I'm saying," the doctor answered without any defensiveness or annoyance on his part, "that any healing must be done by her own body. Physically she is strong and healthy otherwise. That is in her favor. But I would suggest this: She will either wake up or she will not, and there is nothing you or I can do to change whatever outcome it will be. If she's to awaken at all, it will likely be in the next few hours. If not, she will slowly starve to death in the next few days. In that event, there is nothing you can do but attend to her comfort and keep her warm."

Will swallowed, feeling a slow tearing of his heart at the seams. "I see," he whispered.

Braithwaite cocked his head to one side, eyeing him cautiously. "Your grace, I'm sorry I can't do more, but the healing of the brain is delicate and not, I'm afraid, understood. If there is positive news, it's that she has a good-size lump. That means there's swelling on the outside, less pressure on the inside. If she awakens, I would give her only broth, tea, and toast for the first two days. She may not want that, but it will help with her strength. She will most probably be in pain for several days as well. I will suggest laudanum for the discomfort, but do not give her too much or it could force her into unconsciousness again. She must sleep on her own to recover, but not so deep that she cannot be awakened."

"As she is sleeping now," he maintained.

"Yes."

After a few seconds of steady silence, Will inhaled sharply and nodded once to the man. "Thank you for being candid, doctor."

Braithwaite almost smiled. He lifted one hand and rubbed the oiled edge of his mustache. "I will be at home should you need me."

"Thank you."

The doctor clicked his heels and bowed once,

then, with leather bag in hand, strode to the door. As he opened it, he glanced back over his shoulder.

"I wish you all the best, your grace."

Without waiting for response, the doctor took his leave, closing the door softly behind him.

For hours, it seemed, Will stared at the Oriental carpet beneath his feet and didn't move from his spot in front of the fire. He felt nothing emotionally—no hope, no happiness, no sense of good. It was all too much, too much. Everything had happened too fast.

And then as his eyes drifted upward and focused on Vivian, lying helpless in his bed, at his mercy yet healing only by God's good grace, Will sensed a vulnerability surrounding them that he'd never experienced before. It squeezed his chest tight, and sent his head reeling.

Gasping for air of a sudden, he went back to her, sitting awkwardly in the rocker. He could hear her slow, rhythmic breathing just above the lingering rain and the gentle crackle of the fire. All else remained silent, and it felt to Will as if there was no one else on earth. No reality but this one. Nobody but them.

His throat constricted as he inhaled shakily. He reached forward and pulled one of her hands out from beneath the coverlet. Tenderly he ran his thumb across her soft knuckles, marveling at the beauty of her pale, smooth skin. Then he folded both of his hands around it, enclosing its small form in his larger palms. Leaning forward, he rested his forehead on the bed and closed his eyes.

"Don't die, Vivian," he whispered, shaking his head. "Please don't die. I need you. I need you . . ."

After a time, he turned his head to the side and rested again, though he never let go of her hand. Sleep must have overcome him once more, for sometime later, he awoke sharply.

Night had fallen and the rain had stopped. Will sat up abruptly, feeling a marked foreboding that wasn't there before. He shivered as he glanced first to the grate, noting that the fire still burned adequately and had now sufficiently warmed the room. Then, still holding her hand, he looked down at Vivian.

The site of her watching him with open, glazed eyes startled him almost physically. For a few seconds of sheer panic he thought she had died. And then he saw her blink and a rush of raw emotion overwhelmed him.

Shaking, he faintly squeezed her hand. "Forgive me for doubting you, my darling Vivian," he murmured to her motionless form. "Please forgive me, forgive me . . ."

In a raspy voice barely heard, she breathed, "I love you, Will . . ."

He could not handle the warmth and joy that instantly sealed his heart. He wanted to laugh and cry at the same time, but as she closed her eyes once more, a single tear reflected the fire behind him as it slid to her temple.

Reaching over, he kissed her lashes, lingering there, feeling the sweet wetness on his lips as he whispered against her, "I love you, too . . ."

Chapter 23

Vivian felt as if she were living in a daze. One moment she would awaken to find Will leaning over her, speaking softly to her in words she couldn't quite understand, the next minute he would be there attempting to spoon something into her mouth. She'd gagged, but swallowed, tasting very little, though she thought it might be beef broth. Some times she heard voices, others in the room, speaking in low tones, once in a while one of them giving her laudanum, which she took wholeheartedly for the splitting pain in her head. Then she would sleep again, only to awaken to find it dark and silent save for a fire always lit in the grate. But Will never left her side, which even in her confused state of mind, she realized to be the most comforting and safe feeling she'd ever experienced in her life.

She was fairly certain she remembered most everything that had happened to her after Steven took her from her home—being held captive at the cottage, Will and two other men coming to her rescue, Steven holding the knife against her neck, and then his slamming her head against the stone wall. After that things had become fuzzy in her mind. She didn't remember their ride back to Morning House at all, or how she ended up nude in Will's large bed. But she did, absolutely and with a melting heart of elation and pure contentment, remember when she had seen him for the first time after waking from her deep slumber, his tired features drawn with grief and worry, him kissing her tear as he said he loved her. She would never forget that moment, the moment when she realized that the tribulation that had brought them together had truly ended. Since then she'd slept on and off, sipping tea as she was told, trying not to move too much or too fast because it made her head ache. Twice, a young servant girl had entered and helped her use the chamber pot that had been placed under the bed. Finally, gradually, the disorientation cleared as the pain slowly dissipated, and the times she stayed awake began to grow longer.

Now Vivian lay on her back in his bed, wearing one of her own cotton nightgowns. Today had been the first time she'd felt able to ask for a bath, to clean her teeth, and just a short while ago, another servant, an older woman this time, granted her request at once and returned with three young girls carrying a brass tub, buckets of water, soap, towels and a toothbrush and powder. It took them nearly forty-five minutes to help her bathe and don her night-gown again, and in the end the ordeal had exhausted her, but she felt marvelous when they finished and left her once more, in bed, with the warmth of the burning coals in the grate to dry her washed hair and a fresh dose of laudanum to help ease the pain during the night to come. Alone for the first time, it seemed, noting that the shutters were drawn signifying nightfall, and that the room had grown dark save for the glow of the low-burning fire, she found herself able to study Will's personal bed chamber for the first time.

Accented with old mahogany wood of intricate carvings, the room favored him uniquely. The area seemed spacious to her, from the rather large bed with footboard and sideboards padded in burgundy velvet, to the high chiseled ceiling painted in squares of contrasting woodsy green and brown. The papered walls were covered with a foliage design that more or less matched the coverlet, and a pale green carpeting enhanced the dark, wooden floor, over which he'd laid two or three small oriental rugs for contrast. He had little furniture aside from the worn, padded rocker sitting next to the bed, a dressing table and wardrobe that stood very near his dressing room, and one full length mirror in a frame of carved mahogany placed in the corner next to the grate. His fireplace mantel, although made of the same dark wood, was entirely bare, as was the wall over it, around which, she noticed with some puzzlement, the paper had faded as if a large painting or portrait had once hung there, not replaced.

Vivian supposed the chamber was cozy enough, and certainly masculine, but it did seem to her as if it missed a certain . . . personal touch. In fact, as she thought about it now, the entire house seemed to be decorated with an unusually impersonal flair. Except for the library. She had known from the moment she'd entered that room, with its connecting conservatory, that it was the only place in Morning House where Will enjoyed spending his time and making it his own.

Before she could begin to contemplate such an interesting conjecture, the door from the hallway creaked open and Will entered at last, drawing her gaze immediately with his formidable stature. Half-smiling, she sighed. She had truly fallen in love with a remarkable man.

He grinned slightly when he noticed her watching him.

"How do you feel?" he asked, closing the door behind him.

"Better. My head still hurts," she replied, her voice somewhat weak.

Slowly, he walked toward her and sat at the foot of the bed, rubbing his hands over the coverlet, beneath which her legs were stretched. "Can I get you anything?"

She smiled broadly at that. "You're like a nanny already."

He shrugged good-naturedly. "Anything to help you recover, my dear Lady Vivian."

Watching him closely, she took note of the fire reflecting off his clean, smooth skin, the way his hair fell over his forehead and brushed against his brow.

"How long have I been here?" she asked softly.

"Nearly five days."

She paused, then scolded, "You shouldn't have brought me to your personal chamber. I should not be in your bed, your grace."

Never dropping her gaze, he drew in a long breath, then leaned back on the bed, resting on his elbows. "Frankly, there's no other place more appropriate than my bed."

That unnerved her a little. "People will talk, and the longer I am here—"

"Nobody knows you're staying in my bed chamber save for the doctor and my staff, and I fully trust they'll tell no one. I pay them well enough. As far as anyone else is concerned, they'll all simply think you're staying in my care in a guest room, as your housekeeper does who brought your clothes two days ago at my summoning."

Unable to counter his argument for the time being, Vivian stretched a little and pushed her hands up under her pillow, cradling her head. "As usual, you've thought of everything."

Turning on his side, he laid his cheek in his palm, tracing his fingertips along the coverlet, eyeing her with soft speculation. "When you are well—completely well—we'll discuss where we go from here."

Where we go from here . . .

Her stomach churned suddenly, and she wasn't altogether sure it was from hunger. She was married, would always be married to a selfish, indulgent man, and scandal would ruin her. But she wanted to avoid any serious discussion until she could really think with clear and focused considerations. Changing the subject, she asked hesitantly, "Were you the one to dress me?"

He grinned wryly and murmured, "No, but I was the one to *un*dress you."

Vivian felt her face flush with keen embarrassment. Although it was perfectly true that they'd been lovers, he'd never seen her naked; no man had, in fact, for years. "Well?" she asked a bit defensively.

He chuckled. "You're still here; I'm still here. I couldn't have been too shocked or disappointed."

She pulled her arms from beneath the pillow and folded her hands together on her stomach as she stared at the ceiling. "So I suppose you liked what you saw," she said rather flippantly.

Unexpectedly, he crawled up beside her on top of the covers, wrapped one leg over hers, one arm over her chest, and snuggled his face into her neck. With his lips, he pulled teasingly at the strings of her nightgown.

"I liked it plenty," he whispered against her jaw, tickling her with his nose.

She giggled, then immediately touched her forehead with her fingers. "It still hurts when I move too much."

He scooted into her as close as he could without covering her body completely. "Sleep," he ordered

314

tenderly. "I want you to recover so I can see you naked again. The wait is driving me mad."

Vivian cuddled against him, placing a palm on his rib cage, running her fingers along the lines of his fine silk shirt. He made no effort to move away from her, and so she closed her eyes to the peacefulness and comfort of him, listening to his steady breathing until she drifted off once more.

Chapter 24

❝**I** need you . . .❞

Through a misty haze he could hear her voice, see her beautiful face, even smell the trace scent of roses as his mind worked furiously to distinguish the reality from the vision. Then he felt her warm lips on his mouth and he slowly opened his eyes.

"Vivian?"

She smiled down at him from above, her long hair softly brushing against his neck and cheeks.

"You were expecting someone else?" she asked in a husky whisper.

Will blinked, confused for a second or two, and then she kissed him again, a bit more persuasively this time, lingering at his lips.

He had fallen asleep beside her, he suddenly realized, though now he remembered that he'd removed his shirt first and pushed his way under the covers where he could be next to her. It still had to be the dead of night; the room remained very dark, though the fire still burned enough for him to see her lying next to him.

"I didn't think you were real," he whispered against her mouth, bringing his hands forward to cup her head gently.

"I didn't think you were really here when I woke up either," she replied as she placed her warm palms on his bare chest. After a moment of staring into his eyes, she said timidly, "I never did thank you properly for saving my life."

He felt the onslaught of his guilt again for leaving her with a madman, for distrusting her intentions. "Vivian, don't thank me. I'm so sorry—"

"Shh . . ." She pressed two fingers against his lips to silence him. "You were marvelous," she whispered. "I needed you and you were there for me. Never fear that you will always be the greatest man I have ever known, my darling, Will."

He gazed into her tempting eyes, his throat closing with emotion as he embraced her fully, wrapping his arms around her waist and pulling her against him.

"Did he—touch you?" he asked, his breath catching.

She sighed a little, though she didn't look away. "Would it matter to you if he had?"

He thought about how to answer her as she watched him, her slight frown conveying a hint of

317

trepidation. With conviction, threading his fingers through her hair to hold her steady, he maintained, "Nothing that happened to you in the cottage would ever change my feelings for you, Vivian. You're a brave woman beyond compare. But I don't want to hurt you physically if he—"

She kissed him again, cutting him off. "He didn't," she said against his mouth, her tone low and assuring as she began to rub her fingertips over his chest.

His relief, her nearness, tender caress, and inviting warmth were all starting to melt his resolve. "Vivian, you need to rest."

She chuckled very softly, pulling up to look into his eyes again. "I've been resting for five days. What I need more right now is you."

He groaned. "And your head?"

"It throbs a little," she answered honestly. "But my feminine desire aches more at the moment."

He couldn't believe she said that aloud, and suddenly he was hard and aching as well. "I suppose I can't deny you," he admitted wryly.

She sat up a little, grinning as she began to untie her nightgown at the neck. "Would you like to see me naked again?"

Growing serious once more, he replied, "I want to *feel* you naked, my love."

Her eyes flashed a bit in surprise at his candor, the intensity of his inflection. Then she drew in a shaky breath and whispered huskily, "And I want to feel you deep inside of me."

Will stared at her lovely face so sincere of expression as it reflected a trace of remaining firelight. He ran his thumb over her cheek, her mouth, before he faintly touched what remained of the bump on her forehead. Then in softness, he pulled her head down to meet his.

He kissed her delicately at first, their bodies remaining motionless as they held each other in a simple embrace. She slowly responded to his touch, her palms sliding from his chest to his neck, her fingers playing lightly through his silky hair as she parted her lips for him to deepen their kiss.

Will gently forced his tongue into her warm, sweet mouth, playing with and teasing hers as she followed his lead in kind. With rising abandon, she scooted closer into him, nearly covering him, her breasts against his chest, one of her legs crossed over his hips, surely feeling his erection restrained tightly in his pants. It was time to get undressed.

Will placed his palms on her waist and gently lifted her, turning her over on her back as his tongue continued to dart in and out of her mouth, lightly flicking over her lips, first the top, then the bottom, then going deep again to grasp hers and suck. She placed her hands on his shoulders while he went to work on the ties of her nightgown, unlacing them quickly so that her bare breasts nearly came free. Finally, he sat up a little as he pulled the cotton fabric up from her legs, past her hips and stomach while she helped lift it over her head and off.

Holding her gaze with his own, he quickly went to work on the buttons of his pants, releasing each one then lowering the remainder of his clothes over his hips and pushing them down his legs until he kicked them off and they dropped to the floor.

Both naked at last, Vivian whimpered when he leaned over and practically scalded her lips with more of the same, arousing her without yet touching her body, making her ache for the joining yet to come. At last, at her body's silent yearning, he allowed his lips to break from hers as he sat up to gaze with purpose at her beautiful form bathed in dim firelight.

Her hair spread out along the pillows, flowing in thick waves of rich, clean color, framing her remarkable eyes that shone up to him with a lazy, sensuous hunger in their depths. Her silky legs were long and graceful as they led to the soft triangle of dark hair between her legs. Her stomach remained flat as a woman's who had never borne a child, and her breasts nicely formed and gently rounded, their rosy nipples already peaked from arousal.

"God, you're beautiful," he whispered thickly, his fingers slowly gliding up and down her thigh.

Vivian offered him a crooked grin. "The most beautiful woman you've ever seen?"

He leaned over and kissed her nipple once, making her gasp in surprise. "I don't remember any other women," he said huskily as he looked back into her eyes. "Were there other women?"

She laughed very softly until he covered her nipple again, this time taking it into his mouth to suck. She arched her back in response. "You're making me tingle to my toes . . ."

After several seconds of offering such delicious

torment, he pulled up again and gazed into her eyes. "Good. You're making *me* tingle to the tip of my—" he grinned as her eyes widened "—toes, too."

Her gaze of delight and contentment locked with his for a moment or two, then her features grew serious once more. Reaching one of her hands up and brushing her fingertips along his jaw, she whispered with tenderness, "Thank you for always making me feel cherished."

He swallowed hard at her words, so simple yet filled with a keen display of gratitude and adoration. Instead of replying, he chose to show her how he felt, taking her extended hand in his, gently drawing it to his lips and slowly, deliberately, kissing the delicate skin inside her wrist. She inhaled a shaky breath at the sensations he created with his tongue as it moved across her palm to one of her fingers, placing the small tip of it inside his mouth to suck gently.

She moaned with abandonment, closing her eyes, and as her passion began to rise to match his, he placed her palm on his chest and murmured, "My heart beats only for you, Vivian . . ."

Before she could respond, he took her mouth with his once more for a long, lingering kiss as he turned his body to lie beside her at last, stroking the top of her hair with his free hand, rocking his hips forward slightly to hold her down, his thigh crossing over hers.

He began to trace her skin with his fingertips. Teasing her waist and the underside of her arm, he felt gooseflesh rise. His breathing grew increasingly uneven, shallow, as his tongue played with hers again, plunging in, out, around, his palm finally finding her breast and covering it completely as he began to knead gently.

Vivian drew in a sharp breath as his thumb and finger stroked her nipple, the exquisite torture forcing a low moan to escape her throat. He ached to be inside her but he wanted the moment, their first time truly together, to last until he could bear it no longer. She arched her back, beckoning him for more, and he complied, pulling his lips from hers to look briefly into her passion-filled eyes, and then beginning a slow path downward with his mouth. He kissed her jawline, her neck, her pulse point where he felt the frantic beating of her heart. With wondrous satisfaction, he moved lower to kiss her chest, and when he thought she could stand the wait no more, he closed his mouth over her breast and began to tease, to suck, to flick her nipple quickly with his tongue.

Vivian moaned deeply, her breaths coming in rasps as she clutched his shoulders with tight fingers. He lowered his left hand from her hair to give equal attention to her other breast, marveling at the feminine sounds she made as he pleasured her nearer to the fulfillment he knew she desperately needed.

Will could not get enough of her, she tasted so good, felt so smooth and sweet against him as he suddenly felt the dire need to enter her hot, wet softness and let himself go. His hands lightly rubbed her satiny skin, up and down her stomach in small, feathery strokes, then quite suddenly he pulled his mouth from her breast, circling the rosy tip with his tongue as he placed his hands underneath her and pulled her with him onto their sides.

His face was even with hers now, side by side, both of them breathing raspily. Will kept one hand beneath her as his fingers played with her long satiny hair, his other hand running slowly up her hip to once again find her waiting breast, his palm teasing her nipple as it stood out tautly against his gentle caress. He kissed her face this time, all of her face, with smooth, tiny brushes of his lips against her flushed cheeks and warm, soft lips. She held to him as her hands slowly stroked the skin up and down his back, and then as he claimed her mouth for a long, deep kiss, he felt her bring one hand forward to caress his chest.

Gently, she rubbed the curls between his nipples, her fingers like velvet against his tougher skin, and then he brazenly moved his hand to her smooth bottom and pulled her hips firmly against his rigid erection.

He watched her for reaction, wanting her to feel comfortable in his bed but burning with desire. Then she sucked in a breath through her teeth and whimpered, "Yes . . ." and he nearly lost himself.

Will tried to remain still, to regain a bit of control before moving on, but she crossed her leg over his and rocked into him, running her wet cleft along his tip.

He grabbed her hip and stopped her movement. "You'll make me come if you do that," he whispered, his voice strained.

She opened her eyes to his once more, firelight reflecting the passion within. For a second, he thought she might have smiled with satisfaction, and then she lowered her lashes again and simply lay there, waiting.

"I'm glad to know I'm doing it right," she breathed, her voice barely audible.

He kissed her nose, then said shakily, "You're doing it perfectly. You just can't know how erotic it feels when you rub your sweet juices over me like that."

Without looking at him, she fairly purred, "And you, my love, cannot possibly know how intensely marvelous it is to feel how hard you are for me. It makes me want to lose myself in you."

Will swallowed with effort, watching her flushed face, listening to her quick breathing, knowing at once how hurt she must have been never to feel this desire from her husband.

In a husky timbre, he replied, "I've never wanted a woman more than I want you right now, Vivian."

Her lashes flickered open, and as tears filled her eyes, an expression of pure love crossed her face. Will knew he would cherish this moment, remember that look, for as long as he lived.

There were no more words to say.

Tenderly, he pressed her back to lie flat on the bed once again as he began a trail of fine kisses down her body. He kissed then teased each nipple with his lips, his tongue flicking across then tracing a pattern around each rosy tip. Ever gradually he moved downward and Vivian started to moan softly once more. She closed her eyes as her hands began to knead the tops of his shoulders, her fingers moving to glide through his hair as her head began to sway from side to side against the pillows. He kissed her flat stomach, her navel, his free hand roaming up and down her legs as it slowly worked its way toward the curls between them.

Will leaned over to kiss her thigh, hoping she wouldn't close up to him. Her honeyed, musky scent assaulted him with an urgent need to taste, to experience her dewy softness on his lips. He moved his body so that he knelt between her legs, then gently pried her thighs open.

He traced his lips along the sensitive skin of her inner leg, stopping twice to kiss her there, and then he reached out with his tongue and drew it very slowly up her cleft.

Vivian gasped and lifted her hips to meet him. Will grew bolder, tasting her with abandon, wishing he could plant his face right here at the juncture to paradise every night for the rest of his life. The flavor of her, the smell of her, was nothing short of ecstasy, and he reveled in it.

Her whimpering grew; she clung to his head with rigid fingers. She moaned, rocking against him, his name escaping her lips in a whisper barely heard.

And then she cried out. He wrapped his arms around her thighs, clinging tightly to her as he moaned through her orgasm, feeling every rhythmic movement she made, with every gentle contraction of her muscles.

Quickly, before she recovered, he raised himself

above her, bracing his body with his palms on the pillow, staring down to her flushed face, her tightly closed lashes, listening to her rushed breathing.

"Beautiful," he whispered.

She opened eyes drugged with desire, gazing at him as she licked and then bit her bottom lip with surprising sensuality. Her chest rose and fell rapidly, her hands massaged his shoulders, then her thumbs rubbed his nipples and he thought he might explode.

He inhaled sharply through his teeth, then lifting her legs a bit at the knees, he centered himself against her cleft, and watching her closely, began to push himself inside her.

A deep groan welled up in his throat as he eased into her soft, feminine walls, as he tried to experience every nuance of her body, feel every plush angle that belonged only to her. Her tightness encased him, her wetness soothed him, and seconds later he noticed her relax as she took him in as far as he could go, completely, his hips joined with hers at last.

She moaned faintly, closing her eyes once more. "You feel—so good . . ."

Will attempted to get his pounding heart to still. He breathed deeply and squeezed his eyes shut, refusing to pull back or kiss her until he had control again. "Don't move," he said, his tone uneven and tense. "God, this is heaven."

Suddenly he felt her fingertips brush his temples, his cheeks, with tenderness. But he didn't want tender, not yet. He wanted her to come again, to remember this night as the best it could ever be.

With resolve, he leaned over to capture her warm,

sweet mouth once more as he lifted his hips minutely to fit his fingers between them, resting them at the springy curls between their bodies. He kissed her long and slowly, his tongue caressing hers, his chest just barely brushing her nipples that instantly grew hard to the touch.

"Vivian . . ." he whispered against her lips.

She wrapped her palms around his neck, holding him close as he began to stroke the tiny nub of her pleasure, finding a rhythm she liked. She whimpered and began to match the action with the easy lifting of her hips to meet his fingers.

Will quickly felt himself drawing closer to the point of no return. But desire drove him to first see her satisfied, to feel her climax around him, the ultimate urging that would send him over the edge. He concentrated on her flushed face, pulling out of her just a fraction and keeping his body still as he stroked her faster.

Instinctively, she lowered one of her hands and pushed his fingers down a little.

"Yes," he coaxed in a soft murmur. "Show me where . . ."

She turned his fingers a bit and whimpered again, gasping, squeezing her eyes shut, arching her head back as he changed the pace.

He shifted his hips to accommodate her as she grabbed his wrist to guide him. The pain of an intense lust swelled in him, making his legs shake, his body break out in perspiration. He embraced the delicious heat, the marvelous tension now coiled within his belly, ready to ignite.

"Oh yes . . ." she breathed.

"Come for me, love," he whispered. "I can't hold back—"

Suddenly she jerked against him, her legs tightly clutching his as a quiet sob escaped her throat.

Will felt it all as it happened, relished the sensations—that divine feeling of her wet, heated muscles pulsating rhythmically around his rigid erection as she reached her crest and climaxed for a second time. As he knew it would, the feeling of it carried him across the brink of sanity.

With a shudder, he thrust into her once, twice; she grasped his head with both hands and leaned up to meet his mouth with hers. And then he exploded deep inside her, feeling each exquisite pulse as he spilled himself within. He clung to her lips as long as he could, then gasped for air, groaned, and finally collapsed on top of her, lingering where he found himself, breathing hard and fast, joined with her in blissful surrender.

Lazily, Vivian wrapped her arms and legs securely around the man lying peacefully beside her. She was truly amazed at what had taken place between them only a few short hours ago, and in fact had found herself thinking about it over and over, unable to sleep. Unlike him, it seemed. She'd been fitful; he hadn't moved at all since he'd dozed off while still inside her. It made her smile to think of how different men and women were in so many ways. Different, but at the same time remarkably complementary.

But it was true, she supposed, that she'd never thought lovemaking could be so . . . powerful, so intimate. She smiled to herself as she considered how rare it must be to have a man like Will entice her into reacting in ways she'd never thought possible.

"What are you thinking?"

Vivian glanced up into his lovely eyes, still groggy and half-closed from slumber.

"I was thinking about my sheltered childhood," she replied, running her fingers down his bare back.

He drew a long breath and snuggled down farther into the feather pillow. "Childhood?" He grunted. "I was expecting something else."

She grinned. "I was remembering, my lord duke, that when I was young, one of my lady's maids told me that coupling in marriage was a repulsive act that must be endured, that it consisted of ten full minutes of my sweating husband pounding away on top of me every night. For years, I never wanted to marry because I was deathly afraid of having someone 'pound away' inside my body." She lightly kissed his nose. "I was just considering how glad I am that I took the risk."

He gazed at her, his expression nothing short of incredulous. Then he chuckled and turned over onto his back, rubbing his eyes with his thumb and forefinger. "God, it's amazing what ladies are told."

"I suppose your wife thought much the same thing?" she asked without hesitation.

He nodded. "It took me two hours to coax her into bed on our wedding night. She kept clutching her blasted sewing scissors and threatening to cut off my—" he quickly tossed her a glance. "You know."

She laughed softly, eyes wide with amazement. "You're joking."

"I am not."

Shaking her head, she confessed, "I am so, so thankful she spared you your . . . parts, your grace."

He watched her, then suddenly leaned over her and embraced her fully. "I am, too, for obvious reasons." He paused, then asked in murmur, "What did you think of last night?"

Her heart warmed from a concern that radiated through his casual words. "I think," she replied as she wrapped her arms around his neck, "that you are very, very talented, your grace."

He grinned soundly, and she nearly rolled her eyes at his obvious pride. So like a man.

"What did you think of me?" she asked coyly.

He groaned and leaned over to kiss her fully on the mouth. "Matchless," he whispered.

She giggled beneath him. "If nothing else, I certainly hope I satisfied you."

"Satisfied me?" he breathed against her lips. "I'm besotted."

"Goodness, besotted, your grace?"

He snuggled his face into her neck. "Besotted, enamored, and finding myself overcome with an addiction to your smell."

She stretched her head a little to the side to accommodate him. "Mmm . . . my smell? What do I *smell* like?"

"Like you," he whispered. "All uniquely woman. Roses. Sunshine. Lovemaking."

In some very odd manner, his words sounded beautiful to her. She sighed audibly. "I never want to leave this bed."

He stopped teasing her neck for a moment, then pulled himself up again to look into her eyes. "Then don't," he said, his tone sparked with a hint of gravity.

She ran her fingers through his hair. Oh, how she wished it were possible to stay with him, to be with him. To marry him.

Vivian swallowed with an emotion she had trouble containing, then raised up enough to kiss his lips, thoroughly, showing him what words could not convey.

He responded in kind, as she knew he would, kissing her back, first tenderly, then with a growing fervor. Suddenly, he wrapped his arms around her waist, and in one quick movement, pulled her up on top of him as he leaned back against the pillows.

She smiled down at him, her hair flying about his shoulders, her breasts flattened against his chest. She would gladly give up everything she possessed if she could stay here just like this. Laughing with him, loving him . . .

She gave him a sly smile. "Now what are *you* thinking?"

Grinning, he began to trace his fingertips down her back. "I'm thinking of making love to you again."

Her eyes widened with a feigned gasp. "Now? You're so terribly insatiable."

He lowered his palms to her bottom, gently massaging her.

"True. But I promise there will be no pounding," he added as he reached up to plant a small kiss on her chin.

She could suddenly feel him getting hard beneath her, and it occurred to her that just the feel of his reaction to her made her weak, both inside and out.

"You make me want you so badly," she murmured as she lowered her head to rest it beside his on the pillow.

"Jesus, Vivian, do you have any idea at all how saying something like that makes me feel?"

He'd spoken lightheartedly, but contrasting his inflection with his words confused her. "Good?"

He chuckled again. "Yes, good. And aroused."

"I can feel that," she admitted in a teasing voice, rubbing her hips against his. Suddenly she wanted to see all of him. The room was darker than when they had made love before, as the fire had now nearly died out with the coming dawn. Still, it was an opportunity she couldn't refuse, even as she admitted to herself that curiosity had overcome her.

She nuzzled her nose against his earlobe, then without further discussion, she gradually sat upright, beside him, pushing the covers back to get a full view of his strong, hard body.

"Do you like what you see?" he asked in wry drawl.

She offered him an exaggerated sigh in response, then giving him a wicked grin, she leaned over and kissed his thigh. "I'm still here; you're still here. I can't be too disappointed . . ."

He snorted.

She laughed. With what she hoped felt like agonizing slowness to him, she started to drag her nails upward from his knees, stopping just before she reached his rigid erection. "Can I kiss you here?" she asked huskily.

"Not if you don't want me to ravish you in appreciation," he said at once, his arousal very apparent in his instantly hoarse voice.

She didn't reply. Instead, she leaned over and touched the satiny skin of his erection with a brush of her lips, moving back and forth over the length of him, top to base. He sucked in a quick breath and quickly threaded his fingers through her hair as it fell over his stomach and thighs.

"You make me crazy," he whispered.

His reaction to her words and the simple touch of her lips to his soft skin gratified her immensely. In sheer boldness, she stuck the tip of her tongue out and glided it once over the very tip of him. Immediately, he grabbed her arm and pulled her up, her body lengthening out on top of him as he claimed her mouth for a long, hungry kiss, his hands cupping her breasts as they lay nearly flat once more on his chest.

Vivian felt desire quickly infuse her as he gently played with her nipples, rolling his thumbs and forefingers over each one in slow form, the heat of his body searing her flesh, the musky scent of him invading her senses.

"Climb on me, Vivian . . ." he whispered against her mouth.

She moaned in response, needing no more encouragement.

Sitting up a little, she straddled his hips with her own, keeping her balance on her knees so that she didn't actually sit on him. She leaned forward to kiss him once more as he reached down with one hand and closed it over the curls between her legs, his fingers starting a slow stroking rhythm against the slick heat of her, bringing her near climax almost at once.

He kissed her deeply now, his tongue playing with hers, his breathing uneven and mingling with every one of her shallow exhalations. She whimpered, moving her hips instinctively against his fingers, trying to hold back her impending release but finding the wait almost unbearable. At last, sensing that she was almost there, he placed his hands on her hips and guided her down on top of him.

Vivian tensed momentarily as she enveloped him tightly, her eyes closing to the feel of him beneath her, inside her, but she wasted no time as she began to move up and down to stroke the length of him.

Will grunted softly with each quick thrust she made. He covered her breasts with his palms again, teased her nipples. She braced herself with her hands on his shoulders, gazing down to his strained face, looking into his eyes.

Suddenly she was there. Pushing all the way down on him, she rotated her body in tiny circles until she could feel her climax begin.

"Will—"

"Yes," he breathed, urging her on.

Her eyes widened, her moaning grew louder. "Oh, God . . ."

His face grew tight. "I'm coming, Vivian," he said gruffly. "Make me come."

She cried out, exploding inside, rocking against his hips, squeezing her eyes shut as her head dropped back. He continued to push himself into her for a few more seconds, then sat up and grabbed her around the waist, tightly holding her against him as he climaxed, as he moaned and shuddered and spilled himself within her.

They sat clutching each other for a moment or two, both breathing hard, both perspiring, Vivian so closely attuned to his fast heartbeat, his strength, his marvelous, masculine scent and the warmth of his skin. He placed his face in her neck, nuzzling her, dropping small kisses on her shoulder. She clung to him, her arms wrapped around him, the fingers of one hand threaded through his hair as she kissed him back along his temple.

"I'm spent," he said through a quick exhale.

"Me, too," she replied, breathing deeply to help her racing heart to still.

He chuckled, and she felt the vibrations ring through her entire body. It was a feeling she would cherish always.

"You're laughing at a time like this?" she scolded teasingly, smiling as her nose skimmed his cheek.

He drew in a long, slow breath and backed away from her so that he could look into her eyes. As he touched the pad of his thumb to her lips, he whispered, "Where there is laughter, there is joy. Where there is joy, there is love, my darling, Vivian."

His beautiful words were edged with a sweetness and longing that struck her profoundly. For the first time she truly realized that he didn't understand, or refused to acknowledge, that they wouldn't be able to be together like this anymore. The thought choked her, affecting her emotions in numerous ways she couldn't even begin to identify. But she refused to let him see her cry.

Instead, she lowered her lips to his and kissed him softly, slowly, embracing him until at last she felt him slide out of her. Then with gentle guidance, and not another word between them, she pulled him down to lay beside her again, snuggling her backside into his warm body, staring at the dark red coals as they died in the grate.

Chapter 25

Vivian stood in front of his full-length mirror and examined herself, now fully dressed in a morning gown of pale rose, ready to face Will in the conservatory where she'd been told he awaited her for breakfast at nine o'clock. She looked good, she supposed, considering her injury, now six days old, was still somewhat visible as a healing scratch and small bump at her hairline.

Only an hour ago, she'd been awakened by a lady's maid who brought hot tea and the necessary items for her toilette. She'd noted that Will's side of the bed felt cold to the touch, which meant he'd been gone for some time, presumably leaving her at dawn to avoid unnecessary speculation by his staff. He'd obviously had a guest room prepared for his use during her stay, although he hadn't told her any such thing. But last night had been the only night he'd slept with her that she could remember. And what a night it had been.

Sighing with warm contentment, Vivian thanked the lady's maid at her side for attending her dressing and coiling her hair on top of her head in two tight braids, then followed the woman out of the bed chamber and down to the library.

She walked the length of the hallway, then entered on her own. The library itself was empty, though Will had opened the windows to the conservatory. He was no doubt waiting for her at the table where they'd shared their first meal together.

With steadfast resolve, Vivian made her way toward the back of the room and walked out into the makeshift garden area. A hint of a morning breeze off the ocean ruffled the plant leaves, lifting the intoxicating scent to swirl around her, boosting her spirits and enticing her to smile regardless of the fact that she was soon to have a most important and heart-wrenching conversation, and one she dreaded more than any other of her life.

She noticed him at once as she turned the corner toward the west end of the conservatory. As always, he looked magnificent, dressed casually and leaning against a windowsill, his side to her, the breeze blowing strands of hair off his forehead as he stared out to the southern ocean.

As if sensing her presence, he glanced in her direction, a slight smile curving his lips as his gaze brushed over her figure, head to toe and back.

"Good morning," he fairly drawled, turning to face her directly and resting his hip on the sill as he crossed his arms over his chest.

"Good morning to you, your grace," she replied with a gentle nod.

"You look radiant," he added, his lowered tone just hinting at a bit of mischief.

Vivian felt heat suffusing her cheeks as she moved toward him, hands clasped behind her back. "You look excellent as well."

He chuckled softly as he watched her saunter to his side. "I could feel nothing *but* excellent this day, Lady Vivian."

"Indeed, I'm flattered," she whispered in wry humor, tapping his arm teasingly with her elbow.

His eyes crinkled in amusement, then he shifted his gaze to her forehead and his smile faded. "Your injury is still noticeable, but it does look better. That's good."

She lifted her fingers to her head and touched the scar faintly. "There's almost no pain left, though. It really only aches now when I touch it."

He smiled down at her again. "Then don't touch it."

She batted her lashes. "Thank you for such sound advice, my lord duke."

Grasping her chin with his fingers, he said in whisper, "I adore you when you flirt with me."

She grinned outright. "I thought perhaps you adored me anyway."

He ran his thumb across her lips very slowly, sensually. "I adore you in every way possible, always."

A sudden seriousness enveloped them, a slow

building awareness of the complexities and hardships to come. Vivian looked into his eyes, noting the stark emotions of caring and worry and even desperation that she felt as well, brimming just below the surface. But no regrets. Never that.

With abiding tenderness she kissed his thumb without ever looking away.

"We need to talk," he said softly, his tone reflecting the enormity of the conversation to come.

Vivian breathed in deeply, revitalized by the scent of sea air, greenery and flowers, and a trace of his spicy cologne. "Why don't we walk outside. It would give us more privacy."

His brows pinched in a negligible frown. "As you wish. Would you like to eat first?"

She shook her head. "I don't think so. I'm not hungry." And she wouldn't be for a while, she didn't think. Not after the discussion they were about to have.

Nerves on edge, Vivian took the arm he offered, and together they walked to the stairway that led to the garden below. He followed her down each step, his palm resting lightly at the middle of her back, and just such a simple, protective gesture made her wish she could turn and let him embrace her totally, hold her forever in his arms.

Alas, it wasn't to be, and it would be her job to convince him of that.

"I know things between us will be difficult," he started, walking beside her as they took the path away from the house. "But not . . . unmanageable."

She smiled and locked her arm around his, lifting

her face to the comforting sunshine. "Unmanageable?"

He inhaled deeply and pulled her close. "I realize I can't marry you," he acknowledged, his manner and choice of words conveying the opinion that he had considered this carefully. "But that doesn't mean—"

She stopped abruptly, effectively cutting him off as she turned to face him. "Doesn't mean what?"

He gazed into her eyes, his expression now troubled, as if he were waiting for *her* to jump in and explain how they were to work out the circumstances between them that he somehow thought would be manageable.

"It doesn't mean we can't be together," he stated as no explanation whatsoever.

Vivian let go of his arm and stepped a pace away from him to stand under a palm tree, its unusual leaves shading her eyes from the brightness of the sun. He didn't move, though he clasped his hands behind his back in a posture of defense.

She could feel the prickling in her nose from tears hidden just below the surface, waiting to unleash themselves and gush down her face. But she held them off bravely, for now. There would be time enough for crying later.

Lowering her voice to a whisper in the wind, she said, "We can't be together, Will, under any condition, and I think you know it."

For seconds he just watched her, no movement at all save for a slight twitch of his upper lip. Then his eyes narrowed and he bit down hard, his jaw tightening. "I love you, and I want you with me. What I *know* is that we *should* be together and to hell with the rest of the world."

For the first time in her life Vivian grasped the truest feeling of hopelessness in her conviction. She suddenly felt weak beyond words, trembling in her skin from an inner ice in spite of the warm morning weather, and she swallowed tightly in an attempt to stay focused, to keep rationality the cornerstone of their exchange.

Crossing her arms over her chest in a measure of self-protection, she replied in a tenor of pure regret, "And you know I want what you want, but reality must be faced. Life is not so simple."

"Not so simple?" He stepped forward and grabbed her upper arms. "Life is never simple, Vivian, but we have a chance to actually be content, to make something of our lives with each other, to gain some years of happiness, together. We only need to find a way, and I believe we can."

"How?" She glared at him, tears filling her eyes as she hissed. "I am married. And that, my lord duke, is the only factor that matters in any relationship between us."

"You are *not* married, you are separated legally, granted by the Church of England," Will stressed, undaunted. "You aren't doing anything illegal by being with me."

"This isn't about legalities," she argued, waving her hand through the air. "This is about *living*. Day to day, year to year. We have situations in our environment that affect us both, friends and people around us who—"

"Who what? Gossip? To hell with them," he grumbled irritably.

Why couldn't he understand? With a palm to her forehead, she closed her eyes briefly and scolded, "Stop being naive, Will, and start looking at our situation practically."

"Practically," he repeated.

"Yes, practically." She placed her hands on her hips and looked at him directly. "I won't leave my work, my home, my reputation that I've built for myself, and I can see no other way to be together. Divorce would ruin me, and frankly speaking, it might be as bad for your position as if you *had* murdered your wife."

He considered that for a moment or two, his intense anger at her willfulness threading through his large, rigid body, his tight jaw, his dark and fiercely probing eyes.

She remained steadfast, never moving her gaze from his.

"What we do together is not unseemly," he countered after a moment, voice low and commanding. "I am the Duke of Trent—"

"Yes, you are, aren't you," she cut in, "and as one of your powerful station, you always get what you want. Well, I am the lowly Mrs. Vivian Rael-Lamont, regardless of my birth and so-called widowhood. I live in a small community with many friends and acquaintances. I am an average woman who grows

343

costly flowers that are displayed each week at church, at weddings, in homes. I live a modest but exceptionally proper life—"

"I want you to live that life with me," he said softly, slumping minutely and tilting his head to the side.

His change in demeanor startled her. Somehow it was so much easier to admonish him when he was mad.

Sniffling, she wiped a palm down her cheek. "You say that but you have no answers as to how. How would that be possible? As your mistress here? In secret, save for your staff and all the whispers below stairs? Or are you going to visit me for nighttime love trysts, your grace?"

She could see that logic had an effect on him. He looked stricken—his face pale, his eyes wide and hurting to their dark depths. It was all she could do not to throw herself into his arms and bury all her doubts in his goodness, no matter its irrationality.

"We can be discreet," he said, grasping for ideas. "Society won't know."

She shook her head, amazed at his stubbornness. "Won't know what? That I visit you for lovemaking rather than simply delivering orchids to adorn your great hall? Or that you visit me at my home at night, for a quick rendevous on the bench in my nursery?" Heart racing, her belly in knots, she maintained, "They would most certainly know if I got myself with child. And after all we've been through, Will, rumors would be everywhere and I would be ostracized. Everybody in Penzance would know it's yours."

Such detailed thoughts had clearly not occurred to him. His mouth opened a little even as his gaze fell on her waist, now trim and tightly corseted. Vivian kept her hands resting on her hips and ignored the blush heating her cheeks.

Abruptly, he walked to her, backing her up against the palm tree, standing so close his legs pressed against her gown. Peering down at her, he grabbed her chin with rigid fingers and forced her to look into his eyes.

"What if you're carrying my child now?" he asked in a seething whisper. "What will you do in three months' time, Mrs. Rael-Lamont? Run to avoid scandal as you did before? Move to Bath or Brighton and explain your widowhood in another less controversial way? Would you dare, madam, to raise my child in a lie?"

His questions, asked with such bold assertion, shocked her immensely. She wanted desperately to slap him for his audacity, for presuming to strike her back with her own contentions, and yet she couldn't because with nearly every word from his lips he spoke the truth. She hadn't considered pregnancy before now, as she had thought herself too old. But in attempting to force him to accept the inevitable, she'd hit a very delicate issue, for both of them, and as she considered it now, one not entirely impossible.

"If I remained here," she answered, her voice shaking with powerful emotion, "regardless of the circumstance, I would be forced to raise a bastard. Would you want that for your child, your grace?

Unlike you, I don't have the benefit of being beyond reproach."

She watched him, refusing, in defiance, to lower her gaze, now fisting her hands at her sides and trying very hard not to break down into uncontrollable sobs.

For a moment she thought he might shove her away from him and dismiss her with a formal good riddance, never to speak to her again. His nostrils flared and his eyes flashed with an odd blend of his returned deep-seated anger, confusion, and despair, as the reality of their inability to be legitimately together finally seemed to hit him. As awful as she felt about forcing him to see reason, to consider everything from her point of view, she also felt a dash of relief that although he might not completely understand, at least it was her wish that he'd started to see the hopelessness of their situation from her perspective.

Her expression softening, she whispered, "I'm sorry, Will. I'm sorry."

Without warning, he yanked her against him, enveloping her with his body, his warmth and strength, his arms wrapped around her, one hand holding the back of her head as he lightly stroked her hair with his thumb. Vivian squeezed her eyes shut, resting her cheek on his chest.

"We'll find a way, do something," he insisted, his tone comforting even as it pulsed with intense feeling. "I won't give up on you now."

"Don't you think I've tried to consider every possibility? There's nothing we can do," she whispered.

After a moment, he asked, "But you *would* marry me if I asked you and it were legally possible."

He'd said it as a statement, with profound conviction. Her heart ached from resolve—and the loneliness to come. "Don't think about that, Will. What could or might have been no longer matters."

He said nothing to that, and with frustration, she couldn't decide if she was glad or not. Silently, they stood together for a long time, embraced by sorrow, comforted by each other, afraid to let go. Vivian closed her eyes, drawing in his scent with each breath, listening to his heart beating steadily against her temple. He gently massaged her neck, laid small kisses on top of her head, ran his thumb along her cheek.

At last she pulled away. Grasping one of his hands in hers, she lifted it to her lips. "I have to leave."

He squeezed her fingers. "Stay for breakfast."

Closing her eyes briefly, she shook her head and replied, "I can't."

He exhaled loudly. "What else do you have to do that's so pressing?"

With a forlorn smile gracing her lips, she glanced back up into his beautiful eyes. "I have to see to my house, your grace, water my plants that I haven't tended to in a week, answer correspondence that is surely piling up on my desk—"

He cut her off with a tender, unexpected kiss. She responded in kind, allowing his mouth to linger on hers for minutes, it seemed, expressing all the passion, frustration, and longing in his touch that he couldn't otherwise convey but that he so desperately needed to show her. Finally she pulled back, begging an end to the torment.

Resting his forehead on hers, he murmured, "I won't let you go."

Shakily, she replied, "You have no choice."

Vivian couldn't look at him as she stepped aside. Then in one last press of her lips to his fingers, she breathed against them, "I will always cherish our time together. And I will never love anyone more than you, Will."

"This isn't over," he said, his admonition almost convincing.

Afraid to peer once more into the depths of his eyes for fear of acknowledging his hope as fact, she released him without comment. Then lifting her skirts, holding her chin high, she walked with dignity back toward the conservatory, leaving him to stand alone in the windswept quiet of his magnificent garden.

Chapter 26

The day so far had been irritating. After waking with a nagging headache, Vivian met with the obnoxious and difficult Ida Bledsoe regarding flower arrangements for her daughter's wedding. Of course to Mrs. Bledsoe nothing she suggested would be quite appropriate for her daughter. Vivian should have expected such opposition from someone well known in the community as enormously difficult to please.

At noon she spilled tea down the front of her best silk day gown, which annoyed her because she'd intended to change after her meeting with Mrs. Bledsoe and had been too piqued to bother. As her head began to ache again, she'd decided to do some work in her nursery and had changed into a brown work

349

gown that subsequently ripped at the hemline. With all the frustrations this day, it was any wonder that she felt like potting. At least she could take out her aggressions on the soil.

Now she stood with her back to the warm, mid-afternoon sun, working with controlled thoughts as she planted tulip bulbs. Spring had finally arrived in Penzance, the winter being unnaturally cold and dreary. Of course it had been unbearably long for her, being alone again and back to her daily routine after the excitement of the previous late summer.

She hadn't seen Will in almost five months, and every day her heart longed tremendously for him, for the comfort he gave, for his wisdom and superb good humor. She missed his smile, his lovemaking, his care for her, body and soul. Her only consolation, she supposed, was knowing very well that he had to be hurting as much as she over the loss of their relationship, however they each might have classified or described it. One thing she did realize, though, was that their love had been built on mutual respect. Vivian had never admired anyone more than William Raleigh, Duke of Trent, and it frustrated and infuriated her when others spoke of him as the reclusive Duke of Sin, continued to discuss him as some vague mystery, and left her no opportunity to correct such coarse and frankly wrong assumptions.

But there had been more talk of late. Steven Chester's death had created quite a bit of scandal. But there had been no proof of motive or intent by anyone. Elinor Chester didn't dare put herself at any fault by telling the police that she had been aware of attempted blackmail and kidnapping, and nobody save Will's friends had seen him near the cottage at the Lizard Peninsula or had known of her rescue. To Elinor's credit she had played the ignorant bystander, admitting no clue whatever into the strange and unexplained death of her brother. In the end the death of Steven Chester had been ruled hopelessly unsolved, and Vivian's name never mentioned at all. To everybody in Penzance, she still remained the Widow Rael-Lamont, free of scandal, and Will, because of his relation by marriage to the man, the one enigmatic individual on whom everyone focused the latest rumors. Even after the ordeal in which she came out relatively unscathed, nothing in her community had changed—except for the matter of her heart, and she couldn't discuss that with anybody.

Vivian's head hurt again when she thought about it. She dug deeper into the soil at her fingertips, turning it, then placing one of the delicate bulbs at the center and covering it. The direct sunlight, though not exactly hot, nevertheless made her perspire uncomfortably and she rubbed her forehead with the back of her hand before returning to her flowers. Finally, as she finished the last pot of six, she picked it up to begin moving them all to the wooden shelf near the back fence where they would get the best sun and could be easily watered in the coming days. After this chore, she would take a long, tepid bath, eat a small supper, and go to bed early. This day couldn't end fast enough.

Then suddenly she saw him. The flowerpot fell from her hands and shattered into a thousand bits of clay and a pile of dirt that spilled down her skirts and covered her expensive bulb. She stared, open-mouthed, at the vision of him.

He stood near the side gate, dressed down in casual clothing, his hair wind-tossed as if he'd ridden in alone. He watched her with one hand at his mouth and his eyes lit with humor.

She blinked, stunned, and then as her eyes filled with tears of joy at simply seeing him again, she began to giggle.

Puzzled, his brows rose with his curiosity. "You're laughing, madam?"

She covered her mouth with her palm for a moment, then said, "I dropped this flowerpot as I caught sight of you and the first thought that came to my mind was that it's been such a bad day."

"You are a mess," he returned wryly.

Slowly she lowered her hand as her laughter faded. "And you're really here."

"I really am, yes."

Her pulse began to race as he started to stride toward her. "Why?" she asked softly.

He clasped his hands behind his back, his gaze on the ground. "An issue of some importance has arisen and I wanted you to be the first to know about it."

She swallowed as an enormous lump of panic and sorrow lodged in her throat. "You—you're leaving Penzance?"

Cocking his head a bit to the side, he repeated, "Leaving Penzance? No, I have no intention of leaving Cornwall, Vivian."

Just her name on his lips, spoken so formally yet sounding so intimate, made her legs feel weak. She still hadn't moved but as he neared, she reached behind her, grabbing on to the workbench to steady herself.

He rubbed his chin with his fingers and thumb, brows furrowed in thought as he came to stand a foot or two in front of her. She caught a trace of his cologne, urging her to reach out and touch him, and it took all that was in her not to let herself go and melt into his arms.

"Actually, I came here with a . . . consideration for you," he revealed quietly, watching her intently for reaction. "But before I get to that, I have to ask. Have you missed me?"

Her head tilted to one side as her shoulders fell. "Will . . ."

"Answer the question."

She'd never lied to him about her feelings before, and refused to do it now, even if it meant allowing those feelings so well hidden to bubble to the surface again. "I miss you every day," she breathed.

His gaze softened in understanding. He stood very close to her now, taking in all of her as he scrutinized her face, her hair, her filthy, torn gown. She looked positively frightful and it made her uncomfortable, sensing that he assessed her with a critical eye.

He noticed her discomfiture. Smiling again, he reached out and ran his thumb slowly down her cheek. "You look beautiful."

His low husky voice and that small touch of his

flesh to hers made her tingle, made her—just for that moment in time—forget what they'd lost.

If only . . .

Closing her eyes, she inhaled deeply, then stopped breathing altogether when he traced the outline of her lips. She couldn't help herself. Tenderly, she kissed him on the pad of his thumb.

"You have been in my dreams, my thoughts, my life in everything I've done these last few months, Vivian," he murmured. "I didn't realize not having you by my side would be so hard."

She nodded minutely, then lifted her lashes once more, her gaze finding his. "I didn't either. I just wish . . ."

"Wish what?" he urged.

She glanced down for a second or two, rubbing her toe into the dirt at her feet. "I wish things could have been different. I wish I could have met you fifteen years ago. I wish I could have married you, come to your bed first and carried your children." Looking back into his eyes, she added, "But we can't change our pasts, and thinking about what could have been just isn't worth the heartache. I'm trying so hard not to dream of a future with you when we are both very aware that it can never happen."

She'd said that boldly, in some vain attempt at stifling any conversation about hope for them as a couple in love before he delved into it with vigor. Assuming that he was here to do just that.

He grasped her chin gently and forced her to look into his eyes.

"Do you still love me?" he asked huskily.

Sighing inwardly, she shook her head. "Why are you doing this?"

"Answer the question," he insisted, his tone a trifle rougher.

She could no longer hold back her feelings. Tearfully, she whispered, "Of course I do."

The faintest smile crossed his lips, and for seconds, she thought he might kiss her, and that terrified her because she knew if he did, she'd lose herself in him all over again. She simply couldn't take the pain.

But he didn't kiss her. He studied her for a long moment, as if waiting for something, some reaction or a deeper response on her part, or perhaps simply to consider his decision to come here today. Then surprising her, he backed up a little and turned, his hands behind his back again as he dropped his focus to her potted plants on the workbench.

To say she felt disappointed would be a lavish understatement.

"Have you been working diligently?" he asked.

His change in topic confused her a little. "Yes. I prefer to keep busy."

He nodded. "I suppose you heard the results of the inquiry into Steven Chester's death."

His statement warmed her, and replacing the subject with one less intimate made it easier for her to talk to him.

"Yes, I did," she replied, finally feeling relaxed enough to let go of the workbench behind her. "I wanted to thank you for being so discreet where I was concerned."

He looked back into her eyes. "I hope you would have expected no less from me where you are concerned, madam."

She so badly wanted to touch his face. "I don't think there's anyone on earth I trust more, your grace," she returned, clasping her hands in front of her.

An awkward moment passed between them, and Vivian could positively feel the tension, the desire, the need they shared to be together physically at that moment.

"I'm so glad you were never mentioned in relation to the man's death," she said. "Please know how truly sorry I am that I put you in such a position—"

"Shhh," he breathed, placing all the fingers of one hand on her mouth to silence her. "It's over. That family will never bother either one of us again, and your secret will remain undisclosed. That's all that matters now." Reaching down, he took both of her clasped hands in his, so strong and caring. "I want to talk about something else."

She marveled at the feel of his skin against hers. It would be so lovely never to let go. "Something else?" she repeated faintly.

With gentle urging, he pulled her away from the plants and led her toward the bench where they'd first made love. Another memory he was certain to be considering at that moment. At least she wanted so much to think so.

"There's been a major undertaking this year at Parliament," he began, his tone reversed to dry formality as he sat beside her.

She had no idea how to respond to that, so startled

was she by his abrupt turn to practical matters on the nature of politics. "I see," was all she could think of to say.

"Later this year," he continued very slowly, as if every word were held by a captive audience, "there will be a reformation to the divorce laws now in effect."

Vivian felt a jolt of something unusual slice through her, something marvelous though as yet undefined. Her mouth went dry and her pulse began to race.

"A reformation?" she repeated sluggishly. "I don't understand."

"I have good word that this new reformation will pass as law," he expounded after tossing her a sideways glance, "allowing a London court to grant civil divorces without bringing them before the public, before Parliament, and with little scandal aside from a bit of town gossip and perhaps a mention in local newspapers."

Vivian began to shake inside and she tightly held onto his powerful hands for support. Her mind started swimming with a mix of uncertain relief, paralyzing fear, and an overflow of joyous possibilities.

He turned his body on the bench a little so he could face her directly, sitting tall and rather stately regardless of his casual dress, his eyes narrowed now as he peered down at her stunned face.

"How do you feel about that?" he asked in a low whisper.

She blinked quickly, shaking her head negligibly as she teetered in the midst of stupefaction. In a choked voice, she replied, "I—I don't know. I'm not sure I understand all of what you're telling me, of what—of what this means."

He nodded gravely, his lips thinning as he considered her words. After a few long moments of thoughtful silence, he got to the point of clarification.

"I am positive, in my soul, that at one time you wanted to marry me." He paused, watching her intently for reaction, then asked, "Do you still feel that way?"

"Will . . ."

"Do you?" he asked forcefully, squeezing her hands once.

Through a shaky exhale, she maintained, "Such thought is but a dream, not reality."

He reflected on that for a moment, tilting his head to one side. Then he offered her a crooked grin. "I like to think dreams can become real if we desire them badly enough."

His smooth articulation and words of affirmation caught her completely off guard—and heated her insides like butter at a flame.

"This move by Parliament, my darling Vivian," he continued in a low voice as he began to caress her fingers with his thumb, "will be called The Divorce and Matrimonial Causes Act, and it will, in effect, free you to marry with only the slightest bit of local scandal that will surely be nothing like you or I have already experienced. And I think, in your case, nobody in Penzance will need to know because everybody already assumes you're a widow and free to marry at any time." He pulled her hands up to his lips and kissed them once. "Quite a benefit, I should think."

She said nothing, truly unable to speak a coherent word, noting how the sunlight reflected beautifully off his clean dark hair, how his skin looked so vitally fresh, how the trace of afternoon stubble on his chin and jaw made her want to rub her cheek against him and feel the roughness. And from such odd thoughts at a time like this, she felt like giggling.

Suddenly he let go of her hands and stood abruptly. "I thought you'd like to learn of it, my sweet Lady Vivian."

After a moment, she whispered, "I cannot ask for a divorce. Think about it. Of all that it would mean."

He grinned fully. "I must leave. If I'm caught here it could be a bit unseemly."

Her brows furrowed in frown. "Unseemly?" Raising her body gracefully to stand beside him, she admitted boldly, "I'm positively dying for you to kiss me."

His smile faded and he sighed. Then he raked his fingers through his hair as he dropped his voice to a deep whisper. "And I am dying to make love to you again, right here on this bench. But even a kiss unchecked right now could be noticed by someone, bringing even more gossip upon us." He reached out and caressed her cheek with his palm. "We must be careful, and have patience. And above all you must trust me."

She didn't think he could say anything else that could make her feel more comforted, more wonderful, and at the same time more bewildered by his attitude, his pronouncements. But before she could tell him so, ask him to clarify, he withdrew his hand and graced her with a slight bow.

"Until next we meet, Lady Vivian."

And then he turned and walked from the nursery, through the side gate, the same way he'd silently entered only a few minutes before.

Chapter 27

It was a glorious day for a wedding.

Dressed in a day gown of violet silk with pale yellow lace trim, Vivian climbed the steps of St. Mary's Church to attend the noontime nuptials of Grace Tildair's daughter, Matilda, and Mr. Roland Parker, a man twenty years her senior who had lost his first wife to childbirth three years ago. Of course the entire town would be present since the Tildairs were well-respected exporters and Mr. Parker the wealthy son of a knighted medical surgeon. Vivian had been asked to supply the floral arrangements, which she'd done for a decent price, and naturally she wouldn't turn down the invitation to attend. In general she adored weddings, and as someone

361

highly visible in their small community, she would be expected to be seen at such a function.

She stopped once or twice on her walk to the church to acknowledge those she knew, mostly men and women of prestige, even one or two members of the lower peerage who had settled in Cornwall, to whom she smiled formally and curtsied as she should. The bells of the chapel rang continuously to announce the blessed event and soon they would all take their places inside.

At once she noticed Evelyn Stevens, her unmarried, twenty-three-year-old daughter Edwina, and the frail-thin figure of Patrice Boseley walking toward her with grim determination planted on her thin lips, her expression tight with a look of exasperation, as usual.

Vivian sighed. Of course it would have been hoping for too much to be able to avoid them.

"Mrs. Rael-Lamont, how lovely to see you this bright June morning," Evelyn piped in before she'd even reached her.

Vivian tried to keep her acknowledging smile from appearing too forced. "Indeed, it is a lovely day," she replied, holding her parasol so that it shielded the sun from the side of her face.

Winded, Patrice Boseley stepped around Mrs. Stevens and her daughter, and suddenly Vivian felt caged by a flock of chirping birds.

"I imagine the flowers on the altar today will be from your collection," Mrs. Boseley said easily, with only a trace of impertinence slipping through her tone.

362

Vivian nodded once. "They are—an array of spring and summer blooms."

"How nice."

Edwina, a rather round woman dressed in a frilly pink gown that made her peaches and cream skin look almost deathly yellow, stiffened beside her. "How is your . . . business, Mrs. Rael-Lamont?"

She knew that was a question meant to insult in small fashion, or perhaps just to remind her of her class. Either way, she ignored the rather rude intent, looking Edwina directly in the eye. "Business is excellent, especially this time of year, Miss Stevens. Thank you for asking."

"I suppose your experience with weddings is why someone of your station is invited to the nuptials today," Patrice Boseley offered with a penetrating gaze. "After all, Grace Tildair's lovely daughter is marrying into the peerage."

Vivian restrained herself from rolling her eyes. The son of a knighted surgeon didn't exactly rank with nobility, but she supposed to these women it was close. And she, of course, ranked with the working class, a bit beneath them all. At times like this, Vivian wished above all things that she could reveal her background, her own station as the daughter of an earl, and most of all the reason she remained so gracefully composed when goaded by those who thought themselves superior, a trait of character brought on by her elegant upbringing. If nothing else, it would give her immense satisfaction to see them all fan themselves with supreme embarrassment.

But with her usual tact, she continued smiling congenially, though she did clasp her parasol tighter with her gloved hand. "How very fortunate for Miss Tildair. I'm sure the family is no doubt very proud that one of their own made such a successful match. We should all be so blessed."

Each of the women squirmed a little from that remark, not at all certain if such a comment, stated so pleasantly, was meant to be cutting since not one of them had married above the middle class. Vivian had to admit it did feel good to mystify them into silence, though Mrs. Boseley did manage to mumble, "Yes, of course, naturally," which to Vivian's ears meant absolutely nothing.

For an awkward moment the five of them stood on the church steps in silence, glancing around with interest and acknowledging one or two wedding attendees as they passed them by and entered the chapel.

Edwina began to fan herself with her fingers. "My goodness, it is hot," she said sullenly. "I suppose that means it will be unbearable inside."

"Stop fidgeting," her mother half scolded, reaching for her daughter's arm to still it. "Everyone worth seeing is here."

Meaning, Vivian supposed, that husband material would be present, and if the nearly-on-the-shelf Edwina was to find one at all she would need to be noticed for something besides her dour, complaining behavior and perspiring, moderately corpulent form.

With Edwina's loud gasp and her expression suddenly changed to one of pure shock, Vivian thought for a second that she might have been overly appalled by her mother's blunt chastisement of her actions in front of others. Then it caught her attention that all the ladies in their particular semicircle were staring with open mouths and wide eyes past her to the street below the steps.

Vivian glanced back over her shoulder to the cause of the commotion—and nearly fainted.

In the brilliant morning sun, the Duke of Trent's formal carriage turned the corner of New Market Street as it made its way in their direction. It was a monstrous private coach, likely worth more than she made in a decade, freshly painted in deep forest green, the duke's crest blazoned on the side in brilliant red, gold, and black. Two footmen dressed in scarlet livery sat atop the front seat, urging the easy, forward motion of four black stallions dressed in full regalia that pranced along in a natural harmony borne of the best breeding stock and years of high-priced training. There was never any doubt as to who occupied the plush interior, and within seconds every person on the front steps of St. Mary's Church had grown silent, had turned to stare, to witness the magnificent, official arrival of Cornwall's most discussed, powerful, mysterious, and feared nobleman of the realm.

Vivian couldn't decide if she should laugh with glee, rush into his arms when he alighted, or make her escape now and hide under a pew. He couldn't *possibly* be coming to the wedding . . . could he?

"Good heaven, you don't suppose he plans to at-

365

tend the wedding!" Elizabeth Carter blurted in a rush.

How odd that they were all thinking the very same thing. Vivian had to actually catch herself from giggling. What an extraordinary turn of events. What marvelous fun.

"The nerve," Patrice Boseley huffed, pulling at her gloves for something to do. "Hides from the public, causes scandal here and there, and then expects to attend a blessed event? Does he hope to remain inconspicuous with this kind of pomp?"

Vivian tossed her a quick look of annoyance. "Clearly he doesn't, Mrs. Boseley. But then really, when he's attending a formal affair, you should expect no less from your duke, a person far above your humble station."

Patrice blinked quickly from such unexpected audacity, then pulled a face of indignation, her lips scrunching into a bow of tiny lines, the sagging skin at her neck wiggling unbecomingly as she shook her head. To her credit, though, she didn't comment in return, probably because there was nothing she could think of to say to counter such a truth.

Vivian once more centered her attention on the coach as it finally pulled up alongside the steps. Various individuals instinctively backed away, staring in amazement, the air quiet around them except for the ringing of the church bells and the snorting and clomping from the horses.

Without delay, the footmen stepped down from

the top seat, and with great flair, placed a leather footstool at the side door, then opened it.

What followed was a fanfare fit for a duke attending a state function at court. Vivian stood in as much awe as everyone, not six feet away from the opened coach doorway, when he stuck his head through and then stood up tall and stately as he stepped from his carriage. In an all-encompassing joy that burst through her heart, he looked directly at her and took her breath away.

He wore formal dress in rich black, his white silk shirt and diagonally striped cravat in charcoal and white perfectly accenting the sharp, masculine lines of his handsome, deeply tanned face. His hair had been cut shorter than usual, and his piercing eyes bore into hers in a manner that touched her intimately as a secret shared between two in love. The picture was simply stunning, and for a moment, the Duke of Trent held a street full of people positively speechless.

He began to climb the steps toward her, never looking away, and after only a few seconds, the murmurs began around them.

"My lady Vivian," he drawled, his eyes lit with humor as he nodded once.

Mouth suddenly dry from seeing him again, from hearing his deep and textured voice, she clutched her parasol as she curtsied. "Your grace."

The other women followed her lead, each curtsying appropriately, apparently not as yet taking note of the fact that he called her a lady. He more or less ignored them, however, as his lips turned up in a wry, almost secretive smile meant for no one but her.

"I was told you would be attending the wedding today," he said rather casually.

Vivian could positively *feel* the attention of the masses turn instantly to her. Her skin flushed pink, no doubt, as she felt the heat rise to her cheeks and her corset dig into her ribs, making it extremely difficult of a sudden to draw a full breath.

"I am," she managed to reply, her voice sounding raspy to her ears.

His grin broadened. "Yes, I see that."

Uncomfortable, she shifted from one foot to the other. "How lovely to see you here as well, your grace. It's a perfect day for a wedding."

His brows rose fractionally at that somewhat tedious statement.

"Indeed," he agreed, "but if you'll beg my forgiveness, madam, I am here for a far more . . . selfish reason."

Evelyn Stevens coughed, breaking the spell between them as Vivian realized everybody in the vicinity stood motionless around them, watching in stupefaction.

"A—um—selfish reason?" she repeated, her insides churning now with a blend of uncertainty and heightened anticipation.

After several long seconds of consideration, his expression softened and he took a step closer to her so that he now blocked the sun with his large form as he peered down into her eyes.

"Selfish, yes," he continued, hands behind his back.

"It's occurred to me over the last several months that I enjoy your company immensely, my lady. Your talents overwhelm me, your beauty staggers me, and with each passing day, I find myself wishing I could walk in your presence and be charmed by your elegance with every waking moment."

Murmurs grew around them; Edwina began to fan herself again and her mother batted her hand; Mrs. Boseley fairly grunted in disapproval, though she maintained her dignity by not saying anything. Even acknowledging these trivial things around them, Vivian just stared at him dumfounded even as her body began to tremble and her heart swell with hope.

He reached for her hand and held it boldly, causing a whisper or two from someone behind her. Yet she didn't dare move.

"My darling Vivian," he said after a long exhale, "wife to the late Leopold Rael-Lamont, eldest daughter of the Earl of Werrick—"

Audible gasps from several of the women, low grumbles from the men, cut him off, but he didn't falter. Instead, he steadied his gaze and caressed her fingers through her gloves.

"Every breath I have ever taken," he maintained softly, "every trying season of my life, has been merely a bridge that has led me to this moment with you." He raised her fingers to his lips and gently kissed them. "I love you, and would beg you, in front of the good people of Penzance, before the church of our Lord, to accept my humble proposal of marriage, to become my duchess in name, in rank, and in my heart. Do me this honor, and I will cherish you always."

It took her seconds to comprehend what he asked her, but it wasn't until he pulled a ring of fine, glittering emeralds from his pocket and slipped it over her gloved finger that the emotion of the moment overcame her at last and it struck her fully that he had just asked her to marry him— on this beautiful June morning, all dressed in finery, in front of Evelyn Stevens, in front of Patrice Boseley and Elizabeth Carter, and possibly two dozen other people who now stood around them in stunned silence.

Never could a moment have been more magical.

She trembled, inside and out, her throat closing tightly as tears of happiness and pride and love spilled onto her cheeks.

"Vivian?" she heard him ask in whisper, though he smiled knowingly and with complete assurance of her acceptance.

She grinned, raising his hand to her mouth, kissing his knuckles in return. "I would most gladly accept your gracious proposal, your grace, for indeed, I love you, too."

For a slice of a second nobody did anything. Time ceased. Then a cheer broke out from behind her, followed by waves of well wishes and a host of steady congratulations. Good blessings abounded as the church bells rang in celebration of the commitment of love. Then the Duke of Trent offered her his arm and together they entered St. Mary's for an inkling of the joyful day to come that would be their own marvelous beginning of a lifetime shared.

Epilogue

They sat together on a gorgeous fall day, side by side on the shoreline, gazing quietly at the water, watching boats enter the harbor as the sun began to make its downward pitch toward dusk.

They'd eaten a late luncheon of cold chicken, cheese, and wine, and now the two of them simply relaxed in the quiet of each other's company, content.

It had been more than four months since Will's magnificent proposal of marriage, and in that time, they'd enjoyed each other, posing as a betrothed couple awaiting their time to marry, which by all accounts would be next summer. They were usually chaperoned in some manner, or at least in the company of servants, so their intimate time with each other had been practically nonexistent. Although somewhat frustrating, both she and Will knew that in only a matter of months they would be together privately, as husband and wife, and until then they cherished the hours they shared as they grew closer in their love.

And love him she did. Every day more, sometimes so much her heart ached and she found it difficult to describe her feelings to him, though she also realized without any doubts that he cared for her as much.

The Matrimonial Causes Act had passed, and they only had to wait a little more time before she would begin the application for her quiet divorce. She prayed the scandal wouldn't touch her family, and with Will's reassurance, she felt satisfied that all concerned would do their utmost to keep it hushed. Still, she wouldn't change her mind about it now. Nothing on earth would ever keep her from the man she cherished with every breath.

"I'm getting chilled," she said at last, grabbing onto his arm and rubbing her palm along his shirtsleeve.

He chuckled. "I can't believe you ever lived in Northumberland. Good God, it's beautiful out here."

She snorted forcefully. "Of course it's beautiful. That doesn't mean it's warm."

He sighed and stood, reaching down to help her to her feet. "Then I suppose it's time to see you home, my lady."

"Do not make me feel guilty, you brute. I shall see you tomorrow."

He made no comment to that, which she found odd, and after brushing off her skirts, she glanced up to notice his attention now focused on the house.

372

Vivian turned. A lone servant girl walked toward them in quick strides, note in hand.

"Your grace, an urgent note just arrived for you," she said breathlessly, handing it to him.

Will took it immediately, dismissing the girl with a nod. Lifting the flap, he removed a single sheet of white paper and began to read.

Vivian watched him, unconcerned at first, until she noticed his brows draw together negligibly.

"What is it?" she asked, hands on hips.

And then he grinned, his grin soon becoming a chuckle, then an outright laugh.

"What?" she pressed, reaching for the card.

He let her take it from him—the note that would change her world.

Your grace, through thorough investigation into the whereabouts of Leopold Rael-Lamont, it's been discovered that the man died nine years ago in a Paris brothel, the cause of death an apparent overdose of opium . . .

The paper floated from her hand like a feather in the wind.

She looked up to his face, a mix of emotions crossing hers, some she had only just begun to feel.

"It's over," he said softly, gazing intently into her eyes.

For moments she didn't know what to say, how to respond. Then he reached for her, and with no hesitation at all, she walked into his arms.

It truly was over. Her new life had begun.

373

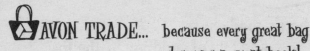